RE~~N~~ ~~DE~~

ROB SINCLAIR

BLOODHOUND
— BOOKS —

ALSO BY ROB SINCLAIR

JAMES RYKER SERIES

The Red Cobra

The Black Hornet

The Silver Wolf

The Green Viper

The White Scorpion

THE ENEMY SERIES

Dance with the Enemy

Rise of the Enemy

Hunt for the Enemy

THE SLEEPER 13 SERIES

Sleeper 13

Fugitive 13

Imposter 13

THE DI DANI STEPHENS SERIES

The Essence of Evil

The Rules of Murder

Echoes of Guilt

STANDALONE THRILLERS

Dark Fragments

1

At nearly midday, Ryker's seat at the edge of the café's terrace was in full fierce range of the summer sun's rays. The blinding light was one very good reason why he slipped on his sunglasses. The other reason was so he could continue spying.

The café, at the north eastern end of a modern square in central London, a stone's throw from Tower Bridge, was flanked on all four sides by ultra-modern and sleek office blocks of varying sizes and shapes. There were a total of five cafés and bars clustered around, each with generous outdoor seating areas that were already brimming with punters dressed in office garb and munching on trendy titbits. A constant flow of people crossed the middle of the square, heading in all directions. Although a little public for Ryker's liking, this was a perfect spot for blending in. Which perhaps explained why the targets had chosen this as a location.

Ryker had nothing but a sparkling water in front of him on the bistro table. Kaspovich, in his tailored blue suit and sitting next to Ryker, had the same. Behind their shades, both had their eyes on the grand canopy entrance of the office building directly across the way from them at the other end of the open space.

'He's late.' Kaspovich glanced at his watch.

Ryker took a sip of his water.

'Anything?' he asked.

Not to Kaspovich. He was talking into the mic on his lapel.

'Nothing,' came the series of three responses from the other eyes in the area immediately beyond the square.

Kaspovich let out a big sigh. Ryker ignored him. He kept his eyes busy, as subtly as he could, his gaze never leaving the entrance of the office building for more than a couple of beats.

Finally...

'Here's Parker,' Ryker announced.

A man strode out from the revolving doors of the office, walking tall, if that was possible for someone several inches away from six foot. Parker's grey suit fitted him like a glove, and showed off his slender and athletic figure. His tanned face and neatly coifed salt-and-pepper hair topped off the immaculate image of a fifty-year-old man as successful in life as he was confident about his appearance.

Yet as he looked around him, and then walked off to his left, Ryker thought there was a slight nervousness in the man's step.

'Where's he going?' Kaspovich said.

'Just relax,' Ryker responded.

Kaspovich shot him a look. At least Ryker thought he did, though the sunglasses shielded the glare.

Parker walked into the small Waitrose store at the corner of the office building and moments later was out of sight.

'Shit,' Kaspovich exclaimed.

'He's just buying time. He's late. But Yedlin is even later.'

'Or he's running out of the back entrance as we speak.'

'No. I'm seeing nothing at this side,' came the response to

that in Ryker's ear – presumably in Kaspovich's ear, too, given he stopped whinging.

'I have something here.' A different voice this time. 'Two Range Rovers travelling in tandem along Merchant Street. Just approaching the traffic lights on the corner of George Street.'

Two vehicles.

'Yedlin was supposed to be alone,' Kaspovich uttered.

'You didn't really believe that, did you?' Ryker said.

'They've passed the traffic lights. Pulling over into the loading bay just after the Starbucks.'

'Registrations?' Ryker asked.

'Can't see from this angle. I'll only be able to see them after they've pulled away again.'

Ryker held his tongue. He'd suggested they needed more eyes high up. Instead, Kaspovich had opted for a tactical team on the ground. Backup. But due to late planning and pure geographical logistics that team were a couple of hundred yards away right now, and had no eyes on anything except the inside of the back of a panel van.

Ryker's senses worked overtime as he scanned the square, searching for anything untoward. Given the word in his ear just now, the two vehicles were all of twenty yards from where Ryker was sitting, around the corner at the other side of the café.

'Doors opening.' That same voice in his ear. 'Two men. No, three men out now.'

'ID?'

'Give me a minute. But I'm pretty sure it's not Yedlin.'

'It's probably just some arsehole stopping for a coffee,' grumbled Kaspovich.

No. Ryker didn't think so. And if Yedlin wasn't there, in those two cars, he didn't think that was a coincidence, or a positive development.

'Both drivers still in the vehicles. The three on foot are

moving toward the square now from the south-west side. You should see them any moment.'

The south-west side. The opposite side of the square to where Ryker was.

He got to his feet.

'Where are you–'

'Wait there,' Ryker said.

Kaspovich screwed his face up with disdain, as though hugely insulted by the basic instruction, but he didn't challenge Ryker.

Ryker slowly sauntered across the square. The three men from the cars were soon in view. They were pretty damn obvious – at least to Ryker. They were young, mid-twenties probably, yet they had a presence. Confidence, arrogance and a certain knowing. Their jeans and T-shirts were casual and trendy – too figure-hugging to conceal a firearm, Ryker noted.

'Any IDs yet?' he said. From a little more than twenty yards away, and with their sunglasses on, he didn't recognise any of the men, though hopefully facial recognition would. One of the men had a patchwork of tattoos covering both of his arms and reaching up from the neck of his T-shirt. On-trend, no doubt, though hardly subtle, and it should make him easily identifiable.

'Eyes on Parker yet?'

Kaspovich. His voice sounded even more sulky through Ryker's earpiece.

'Yeah,' confirmed Ryker. 'He's at the till.'

Two more slow steps for Ryker as the shop's doors opened and Parker emerged with a paper under his arm.

The three men were less than ten yards from him. Parker clocked them. Did a double take. The sudden questioning look on his face suggested to Ryker that he, too, was unhappy about this development. Parker stopped and the three men headed up to him. A prominent and influential banker talking to three trendy-looking guys in their twenties. The picture looked as wrong as Ryker knew it was.

Mr Tattoo stood ahead of his chums and a conversation began as Ryker cautiously closed the distance. It was clear Parker's usual confidence was already in pieces. He was trying to stand tall before the youngsters who towered over him, talking with meaning, his face showing the first signs of anger, but Ryker knew it was a front. Parker was scared.

The man to Tattoo's right turned his head in Ryker's direction. Ryker paused and grabbed his phone from his pocket and fake-swiped away.

'This isn't right,' Kaspovich said. 'We should get Red team here now. Take them all in.'

'No,' Ryker interjected. For starters Red team were too far away. Ryker knew they'd not have enough time to get to the square if this lot scarpered.

Tattoo half-turned and indicated with his hand for Parker to walk. Parker looked tentative but began to move, Tattoo by his side, the two others a step behind.

'Seriously, Ryker, what are we doing? They're heading for the cars. We can't let them take Parker.'

'Red team are to the north side,' responded one of the overseers. 'We don't have a vehicle on the south side at all.'

'Red team, it's a go!' Kaspovich said. 'Go now!'

Ryker clenched his teeth but he didn't try to pull back the order. Kaspovich wasn't his boss, far from it, but he did have direct operational command of the other team members here.

'Ryker, you need to stop those vehicles from leaving,' Kaspovich said.

Ryker had already decided this. Which was why he was now quickening his pace to catch up with Parker. And which was why he was so focused on the view ahead that he didn't see the figure off to his left until she was only three yards from him.

'Ryker, to your–'

He didn't catch the rest of Kaspovich's sentence. He abruptly turned to the left, to the woman who was striding directly for him, head down, staring at her phone.

She barged right into him. Ryker was jolted but stood firm. The woman's phone went clattering and she was sent sprawling onto the flagstones.

'What the hell!' she yelled, pure indignation.

Her angry shout caught the attention of nearly every person in the square. Several dozen heads turned to Ryker. A crowd immediately drew in. Two bystanders reached down to help the woman off the pavement. She was tearful now.

'He shoved me over,' she sobbed. 'What's wrong with you!'

There were mumblings from several other people around.

Beyond, Parker was almost at the edge of the square, he and the men with him seemingly oblivious.

Or were they? Was this woman with them?

'I'm sorry,' Ryker said, and he made to move away.

A burly man in a white shirt stepped in Ryker's way.

'What did you do?' he blasted.

Other bystanders were pulling out phones – no doubt hoping for a ruckus so they could upload footage to social media and gain popularity points with people they'd never met.

Ryker said nothing but went to push past the man who tried to grab him. Ryker was about to react when there was a panicked shout from behind.

'Bomb!'

2

The voice was Kaspovich's.

'He's got a bomb!'

Deflection, Ryker knew. But the general public didn't. Yet even in ever-alert central London, there was no sudden mass hysteria. No immediate stampede of pedestrians and office workers clearing the area. But there was a clear turn of attention away from himself at least.

That was all Ryker cared about. He barged past the man, easily avoiding a half-hearted attempt to stop him, then continued to push and shove past the bystanders until he was free from the group.

The problem was, Parker and his chaperones had apparently heard Kaspovich's shout too, and perhaps seen Ryker's altercation. Whatever had alerted them, they were now moving far more quickly.

Ryker burst into a sprint. Now the panic was steadily building. People were shouting, beginning to run. With Parker and the group with him, and Ryker all moving at speed, it took mere seconds for the cascade to amplify, and the mood to switch from curiosity and worry to full-blown panic.

It was the last thing Ryker wanted. He was closing on the edge of the square, but the crowd before him swelled and Parker moved out of sight.

'Anyone see them?' Ryker shouted into his mic as he tried to barge his way forward.

'They're nearly at the vehicles.'

'Red team, where are you?' Ryker said.

'We're... a few seconds... out,' came the out-of-breath reply.

A white-haired man inexplicably sidestepped in front of Ryker, who tried to change his course but couldn't move quickly enough. He steamrolled over the older man and sent him tumbling to the ground. Ryker groaned in frustration, but he had no time to stop and apologise as the crowd swept him up and carried him along.

Merchant Street was soon in view. Traffic was moving freely. A few more steps and Ryker spotted the vehicles. Two identical-looking Range Rovers. Black, with tinted glass.

No sign of Parker.

'Where are they?' Ryker said.

'Already in.'

As the words came through the front car pulled away, closely followed by the second vehicle.

Past the bottleneck at the exit of the square, the crowd was quickly dispersing, and Ryker had the space to burst into a sprint again. His arms and legs pumped in a blur.

'Which one is Parker in?' he asked.

'Second one.'

That Range Rover sped past Ryker a moment later. By the time he reached the pavement of Merchant Street, the car was nearly fifty yards away. The first Range Rover was out of sight altogether.

There was heightened shouting and panic behind Ryker

now. Red team had arrived, no doubt. Armed and all tooled up. Too little too late.

In front of Ryker, the drivers on Merchant Street remained oblivious, but some of the pedestrians were starting to notice the growing hubbub emerging from the square.

Then a siren cut through the city noise, and a marked police car, blue lights flashing, came rocking to a stop where the Range Rovers had been moments earlier.

The driver and his colleague shot out.

Ryker hated to do this, but had no choice.

The two policemen rushed toward him, heading for the square. When the driver was almost next to him, Ryker shimmied left and the policeman smashed into him in a scene reminiscent of how he'd felled the white-haired man just before. Except this time it was the policeman who clattered into Ryker, and Ryker who ended up on the ground. Unlike before, the policeman did attempt to stop, but Ryker quickly rose to his feet.

'It's fine,' he said. 'I'm fine.'

The officer didn't hesitate, and was soon speeding away. Speeding away minus the key fob for his car, now clutched in Ryker's hand.

Moments later he was inside the car and he fired up the engine, indicated, then swerved out into the road. The Range Rovers were nowhere to be seen.

'Anything?' Ryker said.

'They went left onto Richmond, but they're out of my sight now.'

Which meant it was all down to Ryker. He pushed a button on the dash and the siren came back to life. The effect on the cars in front was immediate, and a pathway slowly cleared as Ryker pushed his foot down further. He went past forty, then fifty, then sixty miles per hour as he raced toward the next junction – speeds that seemed impossibly fast on the tight inner-city road.

He was only a few yards from the traffic lights when he spotted a police car approaching in the opposite direction – blue lights flashing. Were they after him? No, too soon. The car sped past.

He took the left turn sharply. The two Range Rovers were in view again, stuck side by side in a queue of traffic at a red light further ahead. They hadn't yet realised they'd been followed, or else they surely wouldn't have let a red light stop them. But which one had Parker? With them now side by side, Ryker wasn't sure.

The lights turned back to green just as he approached. The drivers in the queue did the decent thing of squeezing left and right to clear the way for the fast-moving police car. All the way up to the Range Rovers. One of the drivers floored it, scraping past the car next to it to blast through a gap and through the lights. The second Range Rover was in close tow, and Ryker was soon edging past sixty again as he chased the speeding SUVs down. In close unison the Range Rovers took a sharp right, tyres screeching as the drivers battled to keep control. Both did.

They emerged onto the wider, four-lane Hilton Avenue. But on this occasion wider also meant busier. Up ahead was gridlock.

'What was the plate of the car with Parker in it?' Ryker enquired.

No response.

He tapped his mic. Asked the question again. No response.

What the hell?

Then the front Range Rover took another hard right, nearly sweeping over a mother with a pram crossing the road. Ryker was set to follow but the other Range Rover veered left instead.

'Shit.'

Ryker had only a second to make his choice.

He went right.

This street was narrow, one way only. And they were going the wrong way. Which meant that after only a few seconds the Range Rover was heading straight for another two cars which had turned into the street further along.

'Don't do it,' Ryker muttered.

The driver didn't heed his advice. The Range Rover mounted the pavement. There were screams as pedestrians dived out of the way. The Range Rover weaved left and right through them. It clattered into a wall, then veered back the other way into the side of a car.

A man walking up the street, his back turned, seemed oblivious to the whole thing, but he was directly in the Range Rover's path. The driver honked the horn. The man finally realised his predicament and darted left. The Range Rover edged to the right and it looked like it would just about squeeze past.

Then the Range Rover clipped a car on the right, and the driver must have panicked. He swerved left. The vehicle jumped up off the kerb. Three tyres left the ground and the driver had no way to adjust the direction as the vehicle flew through the air. It ploughed into the man, smashing him up against a wall. The Range Rover bounced back the other way, rocking on its suspension as the driver tried to regain control of the beast.

He couldn't, and the veering worsened until the car was perpendicular to its direction of travel. It flipped. All tyres in the air, the two-tonne hulk spun and crashed down onto its roof. Whatever anti-roll stabilisation the car had wasn't enough and the roof caved from the impact. The vehicle slid along the pavement, upside down, and came to a crashing halt against the front of a parked van.

Ryker slammed down the brake pedal and a moment later was out and racing toward the carnage.

He went right past the fallen man, whose face and clothes were torn and bloodied. He was already being attended to by a kind and luckier bystander. Ryker would have stopped, too, if he'd thought there was anything he could do to help, but it only took one glance to realise the poor man would never breathe again.

Ryker reached the battered Range Rover and slid down to his knees, next to what remained of the front passenger window. There was no one in the seat there. The driver across the way was wedged in place, head pushed back against the broken roof at a horrific angle to his neck. Blood was dripping everywhere.

He was dead, no doubt about it.

Ryker tried the door but it was wedged stuck. So, too, was the rear door, though the glass there remained strangely intact. He pulled back his elbow and clattered it into the window.

The glass shattered on the third strike. Ryker gazed inside. Two occupants in the rear seats. Just like the driver, one was clearly dead. The other was close to it, the blood around his nose bubbling softly with each faint breath.

Ryker roared in anger and frustration. Not just at the bloody trail of carnage that had been left in his wake across the city, but because it was clear, looking at the lifeless faces, that he'd chased the wrong vehicle.

And now Parker was gone.

3

Ryker made a quick exit from the scene. A scene that should never have occurred at all, and one that he should have been nowhere near. At least not officially.

How had what should have been a simple surveillance operation gone so badly wrong?

The time was edging past 5pm when Peter Winter finally arrived to meet Ryker at the bench near Southwark Bridge on the bank of the Thames. Office workers trawled across the pavements heading to the nearest Tube station, joggers were out in force taking advantage of the warm, dry weather, and bars and restaurants were filling even though it was a Monday.

Winter was as ever smartly-dressed – a pinstripe suit and jacket over a cotton shirt. In his late thirties, he was only a few years younger than Ryker, though he looked fifteen years younger. The difference between a life behind a desk and a life in the field, Ryker guessed. Though the job had taken a physical toll on Winter: he still had a noticeable limp – the most obvious reminder of a bomb blast that had nearly taken his life.

'I told you I didn't like working with that guy,' Ryker said as Winter sat down next to him.

'Kaspovich? You're hardly going to try and pin this on him, are you?'

Ryker sniffed. The set-up had been wrong all along. But it wasn't his gig. MI5 had been in charge of the operation to ensnare Parker and Yedlin. Ryker had been called in by Winter as a favour. An experienced hand, but not really one of them. Not anymore. But more often than not, Kaspovich had ignored Ryker's input, including his advice on how to plan the op that day.

'Any word on Parker?' Ryker asked.

'I was hoping you might be able to tell me something about that.'

Ryker shook his head. 'Nothing. I don't know who those men were.' Though he hoped he now had the means to find out. But he wasn't about to let on to Winter or anyone else that he'd pilfered the phones from the men in the Range Rover before he'd scarpered. 'Yedlin was nowhere to be seen. I don't think they were his crew.'

'You're sure about that? He could have been in the other car. No one had eyes on the insides of those vehicles.'

'You think he suddenly got an entire security detail we'd never before seen? Young guys with tight T-shirts and tattoos?'

'What's the alternative?'

Ryker didn't have an answer to that one. 'I made a few calls before you got here. Both vehicles were using fake registrations. ANPR picked up the second Range Rover, the one with Parker in it, but lost it again after it left the M25 heading north past Watford.'

Winter sighed. 'I heard the same. What about the dead men?'

'In the car?'

'Yes, in the car. I already found out about the pedestrian obliterated on his way to lunch. He was twenty-three years old.

A Belgium national working for a big bank. He only flew into London on Sunday night. Was due to be home this time tomorrow.'

Ryker held his tongue. Something in Winter's tone suggested that he held Ryker at least partly responsible for the death of an innocent. Ryker wasn't sure yet if he felt that was justified or not.

Was he responsible?

'Anyway, I meant the three guys in the Range Rover,' Winter said.

'So none of them survived?'

'No. One of them nearly made it to hospital still breathing but not quite. From what I understand no ID was found for any of them. A little bit of cash. No phones either. What they did carry was weapons. Three handguns in the car.'

Winter paused as though waiting for Ryker to add something.

'And fingerprints pulled up nothing,' Winter said.

'My best guess is none of them were British nationals.'

'A guess? That's the best you've got for me right now?'

Ryker said nothing.

'I'm not sure where this leaves us,' Winter said.

'Us?'

'You and me. The JIA. This op turned into carnage on the streets of London. There'll be some heads rolling in MI5 over this, but we'll stay out of their internal politics as much as we can. For now... why don't you–'

'I can help find Parker.'

'I know you *could*. But why not wait for the shit to blow over before you go wreaking any more havoc.'

Ryker glared at Winter but kept silent and the conversation took a pause.

No matter what events the two men went through together, the dynamic always came back to this. Winter still saw Ryker as his employee. Someone he could give orders to, and rebuke when those orders weren't carried out to his satisfaction.

Ryker hadn't signed up for that.

Winter had still been at school when Ryker had first joined the secretive Joint Intelligence Agency in his early twenties. Set up just a couple of years before that, in the wake of 9/11, the JIA had originally been funded jointly by the UK and US governments, and created to combat terrorism by operating even further under the radar than the CIA and MI6. Ryker had been brought into the fold by his old mentor, Mackie, and the two of them had worked closely for years. Worked closely? No, it had been more than that. Mackie had acted like a father figure in Ryker's eyes, though in reality over the years he'd moulded a troubled teenager into a machine-like black ops agent, carrying out orders regardless of what they were. Ryker wasn't that man anymore. Years later, tragedy and trauma had finally reawakened him and, after Mackie's untimely death in a Russian op gone wrong, he'd left the JIA for good.

Winter, Mackie's assistant by then, had assumed his old boss's role as Commander of the JIA, but the last few years had been tumultuous for all involved. The US government pulled out of the operation altogether when a new administration took over, and slowly funding from the UK government was being pulled too. Yet the JIA continued to operate, and despite wanting a life away from the chaos and violence that went hand in glove with his old employer, Ryker kept getting pulled back in.

Like for this operation, which he'd been brought into by Winter who was having a hard time working with MI5 to crack open what they believed to be shady dealings between Clint Parker – a senior executive at a multinational bank – and Yuri Yedlin – the outspoken frontman of an ultra-right-wing Israeli political group. Intelligence had suggested the meeting due to take place earlier in the day would formalise further significant funding for the group, but Yedlin had never shown. And now Parker was missing.

Ryker would have liked to have said he'd done his bit. Winter was asking him to stand down – or at least pause – and he should have been more than happy to go back to his private life until Winter – the world? – needed him again.

But as much as he wanted to be, Ryker wasn't that guy. He was involved now. He knew he wouldn't be able to sleep until he'd figured out who'd ambushed the meeting, and where Parker and Yedlin were.

Winter got to his feet.

'How's Moreno doing?' he asked.

'She's fine.'

Winter stood over Ryker, staring down at him expectantly as though waiting for an expanded answer. Was he really interested?

'Why don't you go and spend some time with her,' Winter added. 'Put your feet up. I'll call you when I need you again.'

'I have no doubt you will.'

Winter turned and hobbled off.

4

It took Ryker thirty minutes to reach the South Greenwich Hospital – a private clinic in an ominous-looking, blue-brick Victorian building. He'd never liked this place, and longed for the day that he'd finally be able to turn his back on it for good. While Sam Moreno remained here though, Ryker would come to visit.

It was over a year since the events in Africa which had nearly cost Moreno her life. Over a year of mental and physical toil for her. A year inside a hospital with barely a visitor except for Ryker. Ultimately those events in Africa had cost her the lower part of her left leg, and a significant amount of mental trauma that perhaps remained a bigger scar than her physical ailments.

Africa. Just another in a long line of operations that had left a devastating impact on countless lives. Moreno – an MI6 agent – and Ryker had been part of an elite close protection group sent to work alongside – and spy on – the ailing government of Chabon. The operation had ended with civil war and Moreno and Ryker nearly being blown to bits.

Because the UK government had significantly strengthened its interests in the resource-rich nation following the civil war, the operation was considered a success. Ryker wasn't so sure Moreno agreed. He also knew she hated this hospital as much as he did. If MI6 hadn't been footing the bill for her twenty-four-hour care then she would surely have left long ago. But day by day she was regaining more of her old self, and Ryker knew she'd be out of there soon, ready to pick up her life.

He found Moreno in her room on the rehabilitation wing. Although there was nothing that could be done about the clinical feel of the many corridors and wards and waiting areas within the sprawling complex, some of the modern live-in spaces were more like swanky city-centre apartments. Moreno's space was like a one-bed studio, with its own lounge area, kitchen, and private bathroom, and there were enough personal touches around the place to make it clear this was hers. She even had a decent view of the skyscrapers of central London. The only difference marking this as something other than a private dwelling was the raft of medical equipment spread about the place.

'Long time no see,' she said to him when she opened the door, a crutch held under her left armpit. She didn't have her prosthetic attached and was propped on one foot, grimacing from the effort of holding herself up.

'I was here two days ago!'

'That's a bloody long time when you're cooped up in here on your own.'

She turned and was about to struggle back to the sofa when Ryker stepped in and shut the door before grabbing her under the arms to assist her. She struggled for only a second – an obligatory show of defiance – before she let him help her back to her seat.

The widescreen on the wall was showing the BBC News channel. Not surprisingly, centre stage was the chaos in central London from earlier in the day.

'It's got James Ryker written all over it,' Moreno said with a cheeky smirk.

She'd no doubt meant it in jest, but it still riled Ryker.

'I recognised your baseball cap straight away.'

As she spoke a grainy CCTV image of Ryker jumping into the police car played on the screen. He rolled his eyes. In his line of work he was always careful not to get his face plastered all over the news. At least that was one part of the day that had gone successfully. Though it was surprising that MI5 hadn't already got the footage of the chase pulled from the news networks. They may not have been quite so secretive as the JIA, whose very existence was unknown to most, but they still wouldn't like the national news showing such detailed coverage of an operation – particularly one gone wrong.

He looked down at Moreno on the sofa. Her short, dark hair was freshly washed, her face free of make-up and she was wearing baggy joggers and a hoody. She looked good, even if Ryker knew that behind the ever-present tough exterior Moreno was still struggling with how her life had turned out. The mental impact of what agents like her went through was another of the reasons why MI6 were so keen to keep her in a facility like this. If she'd been on the NHS she would have been home eleven months ago, but the sad fact was that a horrifyingly high percentage of agents like her – and him – spiralled into self-destruction: alcoholism, drug addiction, self-harm, suicide. Their secretive lives meant agents were often isolated from friends and family, so when trauma struck, they were on their own and could sink fast without support.

Despite the sexual chemistry which had been between them in Africa, he and Moreno weren't a couple. Ryker wasn't sure that would ever happen now, though he liked to think that his presence in her life over the last year was one of the reasons she'd stayed so strong. The other reason was that she was a natural fighter.

Could Ryker have loved her under different circumstances? Possibly, but the reality was he couldn't afford to love anyone anymore. There'd only ever been one person who fit that bill: Angela Grainger. An FBI agent, he'd met her during the darkest days of his life, a few months after he'd very nearly been executed by a psychotic terrorist who he'd been trying to bring down. That moment had been Ryker's reawakening. Or Carl Logan's reawakening, as he'd been called then. For years before that he'd been the JIA's and Mackie's machine, but the trauma he'd suffered at the hands of Yousef Selim had given Ryker a new sense of life, a new outlook, a new sense of loyalty and morality.

Grainger had come into that life, in her own troubled way. They'd fallen in love. They'd killed for each other. He'd left the JIA for good for her. They'd started a new life, new names, new location far, far away. It was perfect. Until Ryker's demons had caught up with them. Grainger had been murdered by those demons. With little else left to call a life, Ryker had been drawn back into the JIA since, never officially, but always intent on putting bad guys where they belonged: in the ground. But he'd never properly moved on from Grainger, and wouldn't ever fully recover what he lost with her death.

That was why he could never be with Moreno. For her protection, and for his.

'Nice of you to show up, anyway.' She looked from the TV to him. 'I thought you'd be in the midst of a two-day debrief by now.'

'Yeah,' Ryker said.

It was quite strange actually that Winter had dismissed him so readily. Was that a good thing or a bad thing?

'You want a coffee?' he asked.

'I'd rather be taken for champagne at the Ritz.'

Ryker said nothing to that as he headed over to the kitchen and the coffee machine.

'What's with you anyway?' Moreno called over, less than impressed now. 'If you're just going to be sullen you may as well piss off somewhere else. I don't exactly need the negativity here.'

It was a fair point. And he hadn't intended to be sullen. More pensive. He couldn't stop replaying in his head what had taken place earlier. Who the hell were the men who'd taken Parker? If they weren't with Yedlin, then how had they even known about the meet?

He flipped the machine on and waited for it to warm up. After a few seconds, though, he turned it back off again.

'You're right,' he said.

'I normally am. But... what about?'

'You want to go out?'

She looked unsure now. 'I'm not really a fan of the Ritz. Not my style.'

'I wasn't offering the Ritz.'

'Pizza sounds good.' She went to pull herself up to her feet. 'I'll have to check with Mum and Dad.'

Mum and Dad. A playful reference to the workers at the hospital. Technically, she remained an in-patient, so freely heading out whenever she felt like it wasn't exactly protocol, and if she pissed the management off enough they'd simply turf her out and her all-expenses-paid recuperation would be at an end.

But Moreno wasn't a natural rule follower. Another reason why Ryker was drawn to her so much. And he wasn't surprised when she exclaimed, 'Sod them. We'll sneak out. It'll be a bit of fun to see if we make it without being spotted.'

She smiled. Ryker did too. She was probably the only person in the world who could get such a response from him whenever she wanted.

'Crutches or wheelchair?' she said. 'Or shall I go the whole hog and get the boot on?'

The boot was what she called her prosthetic. She still didn't like it, even though it seemed to Ryker that she could move almost normally with it on. He chuckled at her words. Not because it was in any way funny that she relied on those devices to keep her mobile, but because of the irreverent way in which she'd asked the question. Self-deprecation of the highest order.

'I could carry you over my shoulder.'

'Ooh, there he is. The macho man I know and love.'

That final comment made Ryker's insides stutter, and it took him a moment to regather his thoughts. He was about to fetch the wheelchair from the corner of the lounge when his phone vibrated in his pocket. He lifted it out. Winter.

Given their earlier conversation, this was unlikely to be good news.

'Yeah?'

Ryker listened. He didn't say a word until Winter had finished.

'Got it. I'm on my way.'

He pulled the phone from his ear.

Moreno's face had dropped, just like Ryker's.

'No pizza tonight?'

'Not tonight,' he said.

'So?'

'Parker's been found.' Ryker was still working the development through in his head. 'Dead.'

5

The amber summer sun had fallen beyond the horizon by the time Ryker made it to the spot off the A418, a few miles east of Oxford. In the dim dusk light, the strobes of blue drew Ryker in, and he parked up, then spent several minutes at the police cordon that was blocking the road while his credentials were verified before he was allowed to pass through.

Together with the two ambulances on the scene, there were several police cars, as well as three unmarked cars. Ryker had a good idea who at least one of those might belong to, even before he clocked Kaspovich, a moment before the MI5 agent recognised him. Kaspovich, who'd been busy talking to an older suited man Ryker didn't recognise, pulled away and strode over. He looked seriously pissed off at the new arrival.

Which was just one reason why Ryker was already prepared for what happened next.

'You stupid fucking–'

Kaspovich may as well have been frothing at the mouth. When he was a yard away, his balled fist came hurtling through the air toward Ryker's face. About as lousy and cheap a shot as he could imagine.

Ryker stooped to the left, grabbed the flying fist. He twisted the arm back, pulled and Kaspovich was soon on the ground, Ryker kneeling above him, the twisted arm prone and pushed to bursting point. Kaspovich's face screwed in pain.

'You serious?' Ryker didn't sound anywhere near as calm as his moves had suggested he was. The truth was, after so many years of physical combat, it came naturally to him, but Kaspovich's childish move had angered him and Ryker's demeanour wasn't hiding the fact.

'Let go of my arm!' Kaspovich hissed through gritted teeth.

One sharp push and the arm would snap. For plenty of reasons, Ryker really wanted to. But as he looked around and realised that every pair of eyes at the crime scene – mostly belonging to police officers – was on him, he managed to see sense. He'd had a hard enough time persuading the police to let him onto the scene. Breaking an MI5 agent's arm was hardly the wisest next move if he wanted to be driving home from here in his own car.

Ryker let go and Kaspovich uncoiled his arm before nursing it. Ryker grabbed Kaspovich's other arm and hauled the agent to his feet.

'It's fine,' Ryker shouted to the onlookers. 'Just a bit of secret service bonding.'

He slapped Kaspovich on the back.

'What are you doing here?' Kaspovich said. 'Haven't you caused enough shit for one day?'

'I was asked to come here.'

'You can see where your *help* has gotten us. We don't need you here anymore.'

'Apparently that's not up to you, is it?'

Kaspovich glared at Ryker, but the simple fact remained that Ryker was here because someone higher up in the food chain than either of them had asked for him.

'Are you going to explain to me what happened, or do I have to go find out myself?' Ryker's tone barely concealed his anger.

Kaspovich looked like he was genuinely mulling that over. As if it was going to be a massive effort for him to share whatever he knew with Ryker.

Then Kaspovich sighed. 'The police received a 999 call at seven thirty. A passing motorist had seen what she thought was a man collapsed by the side of the road. The lady parked on the verge further ahead and made the call but she was too scared to get out and check on him.'

These were the same basic details Winter had relayed to Ryker.

'Have the police followed up with her since?' Ryker asked.

'Not yet.'

'They should.'

'Thanks Sherlock.'

'Seriously. It needs to be done. Don't forget that woman who just happened to bump into me in the square earlier too. Have you found her yet?'

'Not yet. What are you saying?'

'What do you think? That woman in the square was a plant. Whoever took Parker knew we were there.'

'And you think it could be the same woman who called this in?'

'It's worth finding out, isn't it?'

Kaspovich didn't say anything. He moved off and as Ryker went forward he could now make out the white tent that had been erected at the side of the road. Parker had been a key target in an investigation by MI5 and the JIA, but in many ways this was now a straightforward police crime scene. Detectives were here. Forensics. Everything by the book and the letter of the law. Which Ryker would freely admit he had only fleeting experience of, and interest in.

'You'll need to be suited and booted to see the body,' Kaspovich said.

Ryker nodded. It took him a couple of minutes to don the white suit and hood, the blue gloves and shoe covers, before he and Kaspovich – similarly attired – stepped past the flap-opening and into the tent that was lit inside by a single bright-white spotlight. There was no one else inside. The body on the ground was twisted, arms and legs hanging awkwardly.

'He hasn't been moved yet,' Kaspovich said. 'This is exactly how he was found.'

Ryker got down on his haunches. It was definitely Parker. He was still wearing the same suit he'd come out of the office in, earlier in the day, except now it was scuffed and torn and muddied and bloodied.

'He was thrown from a car,' Ryker said.

Kaspovich raised an eyebrow. 'That's the theory we're working on. You can see even from this position that there's plenty of cuts and scrapes consistent with that, but no obvious fatal wounds. No gunshot. No stab wounds.'

'Strangled?'

'Do you see marks around his neck?'

'No. But as you and I know, a chokehold can restrict the carotid artery and wouldn't show the ligature marks of a strangling by asphyxiation. You might not see anything untoward at all.'

Kaspovich shot Ryker a glance. 'Strangulation is a possibility,' he admitted. 'So is poisoning. So is a broken neck. The pathologist will hopefully help narrow it down when he finally arrives.' He impatiently checked his watch. 'The main point is, we think he was killed somewhere else and dumped here.'

'Somewhere else.' Ryker straightened up again.

'That's what I said. The body wasn't found until seven thirty.

He got into the Range Rover a few minutes past twelve. It didn't take seven hours to drive over here.'

'We don't know exactly what time he was dumped though, do we?'

'No. But this is normally a busy road. I struggle to believe it was hours before that call came in.'

Ryker pondered it over. What Kaspovich said made sense, but Ryker was struggling to understand what it all meant.

'They hadn't originally intended to kill him,' Ryker said.

Kaspovich's eyes narrowed.

'The intention was to take him from the square. But not to kill him.'

'Take him where? Why?'

'Good questions. Judging by the fact we last saw the Range Rover leaving the M25 heading north past Watford, and we've found his body here, barely an hour from that spot...'

'Means that we've got a pretty bloody big area as to where that Range Rover went in the intervening six hours or so.'

'Does it? Logic would suggest they were somewhere between Watford and here. That's not bad for a starting point.'

'Maybe. Maybe not. But what changed? You said they, whoever *they* are, didn't want to kill him. So why is Parker now dead?'

Ryker shook his head. There was one inescapable answer that he kept coming back to.

'Ryker?'

'Parker was killed... because of us.'

Ryker made it all of five miles from the scene before the inevitable call came in.

'Are you kidding me?' Winter exclaimed.

Ryker was mildly surprised the question hadn't included any profanity.

'Am I?'

'You've gone beyond petty bickering. Now you've actually tried to knock out an MI5 agent. In public. In full view of a bunch of policemen.'

Ryker ended the call. He really didn't need Winter's crap, and couldn't be bothered to explain how whatever he'd already heard of the incident with Kaspovich was plain wrong. What Ryker needed was answers, because he kept coming back to the same unwelcome explanation. That Parker had been killed because the MI5 operation had been rumbled.

It was the only conclusion, for several reasons. It should have been a simple meet between Parker and Yedlin. Instead, Yedlin was nowhere to be seen, and Parker was taken away by a bunch of heavies, of unknown allegiance. On its own that could just have been Parker getting screwed over. Or even just Yedlin being more cautious than normal. Except none of the guys who'd taken Parker were part of Yedlin's known associates.

Then there were the plants in the square – the woman who'd bumped into Ryker, possibly the man who'd tried to start a fight with him too. They had specifically targeted Ryker as he made his way toward Parker. Which meant they had not only realised Parker was being watched, but had known that Ryker, and probably Kaspovich, were the watchers.

But were those two with the heavies or another party altogether? Yet how had anyone else known about the meet? The worst-case scenario was a leak within MI5, and Ryker couldn't rule that out. Kaspovich? It wasn't unthinkable, though it didn't make much sense. Was the guy clever enough for that kind of deceit?

The biggest missing piece of the puzzle was Yedlin. Had he taken out Parker to eliminate a threat, prevent Parker from getting into MI5's hands? Or was he in just as much trouble as Parker? Which would mean a third party existed, operating above both Parker and Yedlin. Ryker had no clue who that could be.

There was only one way to get the answers. Ryker had to find the Israeli. Before anyone else did.

6

Fists clenched, Daisy Haan stared across the room at the phone mounted onto the miniature tripod on the glass table. She didn't feel uncomfortable that this so-called 'meeting' was being recorded. What made her uncomfortable was the accusatory undertone to the whole set-up.

'Explain it to me again.' The scowl on Kathy Chester's face deepened.

Haan didn't like the way she said that. 'Which part?'

She flicked her gaze from the phone to Chester, and then to the tall windows which gave a clear view of the manicured gardens of her employer's home, still bathed in the white beams of the security lights.

'The part where you abruptly woke up and shoved a knife into the guy's groin,' Chester said. 'A moment before you gutted him.'

Haan sniffed. 'You forgot the part about him being bent over me, his stinking breath in my face.'

Chester scoffed at that, as though the point was irrelevant. She sat back from the table and folded her arms, her manner stiff and formal as always. Stiff and formal in a way that could make your skin prickle and your heart race with fear. Haan stared at her, not wanting to show any sign of weakness. Not now, or ever. It wasn't that she didn't like Chester, but she was wary of her. Wary of her at any point in time, given that she had the ear of the big boss, but particularly wary now, with her own actions under the spotlight.

'Just give it to me once more, in your own words,' Chester said, holding Haan's eye. 'Then you can go get cleaned up.'

Haan hadn't yet been given the option of changing out of her 'work' clothes. She was still covered in the now dried blood of the schmuck she'd gutted, her hair matted and unkempt. She really wanted to strip and take a long hot shower. Chester, on the other hand, looked pristine in her tight-fitting blue suit, loose blonde hair framing a face that was made up to just about cover the crow's feet around her eyes and the lines on her fore-head that would otherwise give away her age. She always looked this neat and ready. Even at 3am and in the midst of cleaning up two dead bodies.

Haan sighed then took a deep breath. 'I was sleeping down-stairs in the side sitting room.' She noticed the quizzical flick of Chester's eyebrow. 'That's room number six.'

They were currently in room fourteen. Each of the rooms of Bastian Fischer's ultra-modern, ultra damn big mansion had been assigned a number for the home security detail, of which Haan was in charge. Kind of. Haan guessed it was easier than calling them lounges one to ten, or whatever, and as there were plenty of rooms it would be hard to categorise otherwise. Numbers were easy. This room – fourteen – was some sort of mini meeting room that contained a round glass table that seated ten.

'Why were you sleeping downstairs?' Chester asked.

'Why not? Barton was upstairs in thirty. I like it down here.'

Haan and Barton had been the only ones home, given that

Fischer – and Chester, some sort of sidekick to him – had been out of the country.

'Okay. And next?'

'We found the gas canisters they used to put us under. They fed it into the air con from the outside, though to get to the maintenance room they'd already managed to sneak onto the property without the cameras picking them up. Probably a remote hack, before they then hardwired in from the maintenance room. That allowed them full control of the security system to actually get inside the house.'

'I'm asking for your recollection, not what you've deduced since.'

'Fine. My recollection is I went to sleep on the sofa in six. Just after midnight. I woke up when I realised some bastard was leaning over me.'

Haan paused now as she put herself back into that moment.

'And?'

'When I opened my eyes there's some fucking mountain over me huffing his nasty breath into my face. I acted on instinct. He was all tooled up. Black combat gear. Balaclava. I saw he had a knife. I grabbed it and stuck it into him. It was his weapon I attacked him with, you realise? He screamed. Went to attack me. So I pulled the knife out and used it to tear a hole from his pelvis to his ribcage. He fell on the floor. I pushed my panic alarm. Lockdown. Shutters crashing down everywhere. The gas knocked me out before I could leave the room.'

'So that's two lots of gas for you tonight. You must have a sore head.'

'Tell me about it.'

Chester's eyes narrowed now as the two continued to stare each other out. Haan said nothing more. Even though she felt she had no reason to be in trouble for what she'd done, she knew she was on trial here.

'It would have been more useful to have him alive,' Chester remarked. 'A woman with your training–'

'I saved myself, and gave the best chance of triggering the alarm quickly and catching the other intruders.'

'You didn't know there were other intruders at that point.'

'It was a logical conclusion. I figured the guy hadn't broken into this place just to stare at me asleep.'

Though the question, then, was why *had* they broken into Fischer's home? Haan could take several guesses.

Chester kept silent for a few beats. She got to her feet and smoothed down her jacket and trousers. 'Okay. Talk me through the rest of it.'

Haan didn't show anything, but was relieved the 'meeting' was finally over. She stood up as Chester moved over to the tripod and hit the button on her phone to stop the recording. She took her phone and headed around the table and knocked on the door which was unlocked and opened by the suited guard on the other side. One of Chester's guys. She had a whole army of them it seemed. The cavalry.

'So after you came around,' Chester continued as Haan stepped out of the room behind her, 'the second time, that is. What next?'

Haan looked at her watch. 'We're only talking about an hour ago. The alarm system was still going. I had to reset it. Once the shutters were up, I did a sweep. Found the other body by the front entrance. Crushed by the barrier. I woke Barton up. Then I tried to make contact.'

'Tried?'

'The signals were still jammed. That's how they got past the outer cameras, and it's why you couldn't get through to us. It's only because of the wired failsafe that the alert from me setting off the panic alarm got through to you at all. But there was nobody else here at that point, so I didn't know that for sure. I had to get into the forest before I could call you.'

'Meanwhile Barton?'

'Barton's got a nasty gash on his head. I'm guessing one of the intruders knocked him out when he was stirring. The gas they fed into the air con couldn't have kept us under for long, and with it wearing off I think they had to quickly change plan. But anyway, I got Barton to do a more thorough sweep outside. This was only just before you arrived.'

'And it was lucky I was close by. Bastian had wanted me to travel ahead to get the house ready otherwise I'd still be with him.'

Lucky? In some ways, Haan would rather have had the extra time alone to figure things out properly.

'Barton found the gas canisters in the maintenance room,' she said. 'Found the equipment they'd left by the electrical box. That's how they got into the system. We turned off the jammers. Disconnected everything. Then you lot showed up.'

Chester gave Haan a cold glower at that closing remark. They reached the end of the corridor and the grand marble-floored entrance hall to the mansion. Two men in white suits were busy cleaning away the last remnants of blood and flesh and bone from the floor by the entrance; the normally pristine white tiles were still covered with ugly streaks where one of the intruders had been crushed by the heavy metal shutters as he tried to make his escape. When Chester had arrived the body had still been there.

One thing was certain, the guys in white weren't forensics technicians from the police. The police hadn't been called yet, and Haan wasn't sure they would be. Not while the questions of who the intruders were, and what they wanted in breaking into the home of one of the world's richest men, remained unanswered.

'Somehow the barrier got one guy there,' Haan said. 'Quite how that panned out, who knows.'

'You haven't checked the CCTV yet?'

'I can't. The system's still in some sort of suspended state. It's in lockdown, other than to top-level access. I can't get to the cameras, can't open the vault–'

Chester sighed, not hiding her irritation, as though the set up and the pitfalls of the system were Haan's doing. She took out her phone and turned away as she made a call. To Fischer? Or just one of his other lackeys? Was there another lackey in between Fischer and Chester? Haan hadn't thought so.

The muffled conversation lasted barely a minute before Chester turned back around again.

'Give me your control pad.'

Haan handed her the tablet she'd been holding. Chester typed away. There was a noticeable mechanical murmur a few moments later from within the walls, the floor, the ceiling, as though denoting the security system, so ingrained in the house's fabric, had switched state once more.

'Pull the camera feeds up.' Chester handed the tablet back. 'Show me what happened.'

Haan took just a few seconds to do so. There were four cameras – all hidden – in the entrance hallway and she brought them up on a split screen. At 11pm the previous night the feeds showed an empty space. Haan hit forward and the screens pulsed as the timestamp raced. Just after 1am the feeds went blank. Haan hit play and stared at the black screen.

'They weren't just jamming the signals, they blocked the cameras,' she said. 'Likely when the system was in maintenance mode.'

'But the cameras would have come back online when you hit the panic button.'

Haan fast forwarded again and sure enough, a few minutes

after 2am the screen flicked back into life. She pushed play again. On the screen the hallway remained empty, as before, but the front doors were now wide open. Just seeing that, knowing what those wide open doors meant, made Haan's insides churn with rage.

A few seconds later, Haan watched as the hallway quickly filled with wispy gas, triggered by her pushing the panic button.

Then came the figures through the fog.

Not one man, but two.

Haan and Chester exchanged a look, then watched in silence as the carnage unfolded over a span of just a few seconds. It was difficult to catch it all through the smoke, but one thing was abundantly clear, and it filled Haan with dread.

Chester didn't need to prompt Haan's next move. She closed out one of the hall cameras and opened up the one from the porch outside the front entrance. She watched, teeth clenched, heart pulsing, as one of the men pulled himself under the barrier – through the gap created by the shutter smashing into his accomplice.

'He didn't take the van,' Chester said.

The van the idiots had arrived in was still out on the gravel by the front door.

'He didn't have the key.' Haan expertly switched from one camera to another, following the man's flight across the grounds.

'He's got a nearly two-hour head start on us,' Chester said, and her accusatory tone was back, suggesting it was Haan's fault that this guy had got away.

Was it? Even if it wasn't, if Chester – and Fischer – decided to blame her, she was well and truly screwed. She had to fight against the nagging voice in her head that was already planning how to tackle Chester, her guards, and leg it out of there.

Was that really an option?

'What's in that bag?' Haan uttered these words as much to

herself as to Chester as she watched the guy sprinting toward the perimeter wall, backpack over his shoulders.

'Nothing heavy, that's for sure,' Chester declared. 'Now the vault is back under control, we can start a full inventory. We'll figure out what's missing, if anything. We'll get it back.' She looked at her watch. 'Fischer's on the plane now. He'll be here before midday. Make sure you have *all* the answers before then.'

Haan swallowed, nodded. Then another thought struck her. She quickly exited out of all the outdoor camera views and opened up the ones from the library, and the anteroom that led to Fischer's crowning glory – the vault.

'Before you moved them, I searched the two bodies, their clothes, the bags they had. There was no key for the van.'

'Our runner might have had it after all then,' Chester said. 'Perhaps he thought it was too big a risk to take the vehicle.'

'Or...'

Haan left that dangling as she found the right time on the cameras. Just past 2am.

'There were four of them.' Haan stared at the screen.

'Two dead bodies. One runner. So what happened to number four?'

Chester sounded even more pissed off now – but not for long, as the answer became evident just a few seconds later.

Haan looked from the screen and up to Chester, relief washing through her, even if she wouldn't show it. The sides of Chester's mouth turned up slightly, making her face look crooked and sinister.

Was that supposed to be a smile?

'Looks like we've got a live one.' Haan's eyes moved from Chester to the corridor behind her, beyond which was the library, and the anteroom where the fourth intruder remained silently imprisoned.

'Get him out of there and make him talk,' Chester said. 'I

want everything. Names, addresses, co-conspirators. Do whatever it takes. Anything.'

Haan nodded. She felt nothing about the chilling reality of interrogating this man. She was only glad she was no longer under the spotlight. 'And the runner?'

'Use our little trapped rat to find out who he is first. Then we'll turn the screw. Before long we'll make him wish he never made it out of here alive.'

7

R yker had slept surprisingly well, considering how much he had on his mind. Perhaps because before he'd fallen asleep, he'd already decided on his plan of action.

After fixing a light breakfast his first port of call was to check on the three phones that he'd pilfered from the dead men in the Range Rover the previous day. The devices remained wired to his desktop computer which hummed away contentedly. Smudges of blood remained on the plastic and glass cases of the phones. He realised he didn't really feel bad about having taken the devices. The dead men didn't need them anymore, and he was sure they weren't the good guys. He also didn't feel bad about taking the phones without regard for official procedures – whether that be the police's or MI5's. He had a very good reason: Ryker trusted himself more than anybody else. He wouldn't let crucial evidence that could help him identify Parker's kidnappers get lost in the bureaucratic system. He wanted control, and he wanted answers. Now.

. . .

Yesterday, as he'd stared into the wreckage of the Range Rover, his primary reason for taking the phones was to try to track down Parker. Now it was all about figuring out who had killed him and why.

Ryker sat down on the desk chair and fired up the computer. He'd already easily bypassed the basic security settings on the phones and was using imaging and analysis software on his desktop to take full copies of the hard drives which he could then interrogate. Much of the initial process was automated though he would need to spend time in front of the screen to move the analysis forward, not least in cross-referring the results that his software spat out against the government and other information databases he had access to. That could wait.

Ryker left his machine to it and set about getting himself ready. He closed the door to his apartment less than ten minutes later.

He made his way down the stairs and out onto the street which was already bathed in bright sunlight which reflected fiercely off the glass-fronted apartment block he'd been staying at for the last six months. Not home. Ryker struggled to find anywhere that he called home. In the years he'd spent officially working with the JIA he'd lived a nomadic life, travelling the world, assignment after assignment, and even though he was now essentially a freelancer, and finally had the opportunity to settle in one place, he wasn't sure he'd ever fully adjust to what others would call a 'normal' life.

His eyes were busy as he walked the short distance down the street to where he'd parked his car. He saw nothing untoward and was soon in the driver's seat and heading off to central London. The traffic was heavy though relatively free-flowing and after parking up Ryker made his way on foot.

Eventually, he arrived on a street of plush Georgian terraces in Mayfair. The buildings here were all worth several, even tens of millions of pounds. Swish offices, luxurious and gargantuan apartments, and ultra-exclusive five-star hotels. Handsome, historic, expensive. But then right at the end of the street was the McLelland hotel, a multi-storey hulk of a building that was a blend of stone and industrial-looking grey metal, interspersed with mammoth floor-to-ceiling windows. To say it looked out of place was an understatement. Yet despite its drastically conflicting style to everything else around it, the ultra-modern block was obviously high end, topped off by the gold-plated flagpoles jutting out over the pavement, and the smartly-suited bell-boys standing in wait by the grand revolving doors.

Ryker carried on past them. Took the left turn at the end of the street to continue around the edge of the hotel. When he was at the head of the alleyway that led to the service entrances for the building he quickly glanced about him before heading on down.

No one here. The hum and whir of air conditioning and industrial extractor fans filled his ears, the smell of grilled bacon and sausages permeated his nose. He sent the text message and by the time he was approaching the third door along the way, the handle was already turning. The thick metal door clunked and was pushed open from the inside. A smartly-dressed man – immaculate black suit, and immaculate coiffed hair to match – poked his head out. He didn't look pleased.

'Come in.' He couldn't hide the nerves in his voice as he looked behind Ryker.

Ryker stepped inside and the man – Ciro Garcia – closed the door behind him with a thunk.

'You okay?' Ryker asked.

'No. Not really.' Garcia barely met Ryker's eye. 'Spying is one thing, but...'

'But what?'

'What if my manager finds out?'

'Why would anyone find out?'

He looked even more worried all of a sudden. His gaze dropped to the floor. 'What would it mean for my family?'

Ryker reached out and put his hand on Garcia's shoulder. 'They'll be fine. I'll make sure of it.'

Garcia still didn't look too convinced. He fished in his pocket and handed Ryker a key card.

'Have you seen him?' Ryker needed to be sure.

'No. I already told you that. He hasn't been here for more than five days.'

'But?'

'Some of his people are still here, yes. Or they were. This morning? I honestly don't know. But... what exactly are you going to do?'

'Don't worry about me. You go on about your normal business.'

'Normal? Nothing about this is normal.'

Ryker smiled, then turned and headed along the corridor. He meant what he'd said to Garcia. He'd look out for him. That was the deal. For the past two months Garcia had been a key source of information about Yedlin's whereabouts and the people Yedlin met within the hotel. Garcia was not only being paid handsomely, but the UK government was fast-tracking his family's immigration papers in return. Ryker would make sure that was followed through on, particularly as he was asking Garcia to risk much more today.

He carried on to the service lift and headed up as far as it went – the ninth floor. He then made his way along to the main elevator bank, where just one of the four lifts completed the journey to the tenth floor. Up there, more than ten thousand square feet of space was occupied by just one huge suite. At several thousand pounds a night, the tenth floor had been block-booked for a six-month period and paid for up front by a private wealth advisory company owned by a prominent Russian oligarch, though it had long been known that Yuri Yedlin was the benefactor of that payout. He, occasionally his wife, and more usually a whole cohort of associates, had been staying in the five-bedroom suite on and off throughout that period. This was the first time Ryker had actually set foot in the building, but it felt familiar from the information he'd been relayed which had included countless CCTV images of Yedlin and those closest to him coming and going.

They'd kept close tabs on Yedlin for weeks, but no one had seen or heard of him since the Parker meet had gone wrong. Ryker hoped to find some clues that would point to where Yedlin was now. Phones, computers, diaries, whatever was here Ryker would take. It was time to step up from basic surveillance.

The lift doors opened onto the tenth floor to reveal a glossy white and grey and black inner atrium. Ryker stepped out. He wasn't in a hotel uniform, but he was dressed smartly, in suit trousers, a white shirt and shining black leather shoes. He wanted to at least not look entirely out of place, and give himself the opportunity to blag his way out of a tight spot if he were to come across anyone. There was no one here though. At least not on the outside of the suite.

Ryker moved to the huge oak double doors. He knocked, just in case, then pressed the key card against the pad on the wall. A green light flickered and the magnetic locks released. Ryker pulled open the right-hand door. Listened for a second. All quiet. He stepped inside. Shook his head at what he saw. This wasn't a hotel room. More like a gold-plated, diamond-encrusted palace. He'd never seen anything quite like it.

He progressed with caution. Looked through each of the many rooms. No one home. In fact, no sign of anyone staying here at all. Every bed was made up. No cups or glasses had been used. No clothes or other belongings in the drawers or wardrobes. No toothbrushes or toiletries in the bathrooms, other than those provided by the hotel, neatly arranged by the sinks and baths.

Ryker returned to the wide entrance area. Garcia had said Yedlin hadn't been seen here for days, but he'd said nothing about this place having been cleared out. The suite was fully paid up for another month. So why had Yedlin and his crew shipped out? And when exactly?

Garcia could certainly help to answer the second of those questions. Ryker turned for the door. Pulled it open. Saw the figures in front of him. Gun in the hand of the one on the left.

Ryker lunged forward, but he was out-positioned. He'd walked right into the trap. The shot was fired before Ryker even reached them. Not a booming shot. More of a thwack. The dart plunged into Ryker's neck.

He crashed into the gunman and they both clattered to the floor. Ryker hit him. Again. And again. But within seconds he was drifting, his shots already weaker than they should have been.

The second man, somewhere behind, got hold of Ryker, further impeding the counter-attack. Ryker was hauled off, and shoved to the floor. There was nothing more he could do. He lay on the polished stone, struggling against the hold the men now had on him, but his movements became weaker and weaker by the second.

Soon, he was out cold.

8

Ryker didn't know where they took him. Didn't know how long he was out for before he came to. All he knew, when he opened his eyes and his brain calibrated, was that he was shackled to a chair, his head covered by a sack of some sort. There were at least two men in the cool room with him, he figured. Ryker could hear their calm breathing, though they hadn't yet spoken a word. At least not since he'd woken.

Maybe his trip to the hotel to track Yedlin had been foolhardy but then again, he was used to putting himself front and centre to get answers. That approach often got him into trouble. Trouble which so far in his life he'd always managed to overcome. It was a risky approach, but he operated in a world where risk was ever-present; the constant dilemma was in balancing that risk with the chances of getting the answers he needed.

Like walking into Yedlin's private space, on his own, unarmed, with his trust placed wholly in a low-paid hotel worker who himself was living through turmoil. Garcia had no loyalty to Ryker. He was looking out for himself and his family. Perhaps Yedlin, or one of his associates, had simply offered a better deal.

A knock on a wooden door. The creak as the door was opened. Footsteps. The door closed again.

Then, 'Okay, take the sack.'

A gruff male voice. It sounded a little familiar. Not Yedlin, but the accent was thick and distinct.

A few moments later, the cloth sack was pulled from Ryker's head and he squinted as he looked around the sparsely-lit space. The closed door was directly in front of him. What was behind? A grimy window, though it was letting next to no light in – was it painted over? A single bulb dangled overhead, a concrete floor lay beneath his bare feet. Bare feet. Ryker looked down. Still clothed, except for his socks and shoes. Interesting. His legs were secured to the legs of the chair he was sitting on. His wrists were tied to the chair arms – rope. He tried to shift his weight. The chair was secured to the ground.

He took in the three men in the room with him. All were dressed in black. All had balaclavas covering their heads. Two were standing either side of the closed door. The third was standing in front of Ryker.

'Now, how about–'

'Where's Yedlin?' Ryker asked. His words were a little slurred. The after-effects of the tranquilliser.

'No. Why don't we start with you.' The leader sounded perturbed. 'Who are you?'

Ryker huffed. 'If you don't know that already, that's your problem.'

The man turned and rattled off something in his native tongue to the men at the door. Ryker didn't speak it fluently at all, but he knew the language was Hebrew. And he had recognised the voice from somewhere.

The man on the left opened the door and stepped out and returned moments later carrying a fabric pouch.

ROB SINCLAIR

Ryker laughed. 'Seriously? Let me guess. Some nice shiny metal tools in there?'

The leader stepped forward and threw a fist into Ryker's gut. It was a powerful shot that sent Ryker's brain spinning as the oxygen was forced from his lungs. He needed several seconds to regain his focus, by which point the man was kneeling in front of him.

'I get it,' he said. 'You think you're strong. I know the type. I see the scars on you. What were you? Army? Marine? SAS? Or just some dumb idiot heavy. Whatever the answer, I like your bravado. I like the challenge.'

Ryker shook his head. 'Eli.'

The man paused.

'Eli Benado. That's your name. Thirty-nine years old. Ex-Mossad.'

Silence. Except for Benado's now heavier breathing. Anger?

'You think you're clever,' Benado said. 'But you've got an unfair advantage. You already knew me. What I want to know is why. Why did you come after us?'

Interesting. Did Benado not see Ryker as an undercover agent, but someone who'd been sent to capture or even kill Yedlin? If that was the case, was it because they were behind Parker's death and were wary of a revenge attack, or because they believed they were targeted by the same people who'd killed Parker?

'This is one of my favourites,' Benado said. He was still on the floor and Ryker couldn't see his hands at all. He felt pressure on his right foot. 'You know who I am. You know who I worked for. Perhaps you even know what I did for Mossad.'

There was a sudden sharp and horrific stab of pain in Ryker's big toe. He clenched his jaw and grimaced. The pain didn't stop. It got worse, sending a rush of nerve pulses all the way up his leg into his spine, but Ryker didn't let out even a murmur.

Benado cackled. 'You're strong. But you don't need to prove anything to me. Don't hold back. Let it out if you need to. Scream. Or just talk. Tell me who you are, and what you were doing at the hotel.'

Another shock of pain, more amplified than before and this time Ryker did shout out.

Another laugh from Benado. 'Can you believe this?' He brought his hand into view. 'Toothpicks. A big man like you, and look at you, all worked up about toothpicks. You see, the key is to hit the right spots. The spots where the nerves are tightly bundled together. Under your nails, that's the spot. But you have to move it slowly. Millimetre by millimetre, prolonging the sensation.'

Benado paused as he stared at Ryker. What was he doing?

'Okay, I think I'm going to have to show you what I mean. Better for you to see this.'

Ryker held his body tight as he glanced from the toothpick to Benado's exposed wrist. His watch. A mistake? Ryker could see the time was quarter to twelve. Fifteen minutes. That's all he had to hold out for.

Benado called to one of the other men, who came forward and grabbed Ryker's left hand, laying his fingers out straight. Ryker couldn't help but watch as Benado lined the toothpick up and then ever so slowly slid the point under the nail of Ryker's index finger. The pain was instantaneous and Ryker locked every muscle in his body and ground his teeth together. As the toothpick sank further and further, he resisted the urge to howl.

'Hurts more now you can see, doesn't it?' Benado said.

Ryker didn't say anything. Minutes passed – at least it felt like minutes – as Benado slowly pushed the toothpick deeper and deeper. But he didn't stop when the point was fully wedged under the nail, he kept going, the wood sinking into Ryker's flesh as blood seeped out onto the chair arm.

'This is the worst part, right?' Benado said. 'Looks like a bug crawling under your skin.' He cackled and his chums followed suit.

Ryker squeezed his eyes shut and tried his best to remember all the tricks for channelling and ignoring pain. Tricks that had once been second nature to him and that he wished still were.

'Of course, this is only the start,' Benado said, holding up another toothpick. 'Toothpicks are just a taster. Hopefully enough to make you realise how bad it could get, and that it's pointless to resist. Now. Let's see. Still plenty more to go before we move on.'

'Wait,' Ryker said.

Benado paused. His eyes fixed on Ryker, who could sense the man's smile behind the balaclava.

'I work for the UK government.' Ryker was annoyed that his voice sounded more anguished than he'd expected. 'MI5.'

'No. I don't think so. I know MI5. They don't have people like–'

'I'm working *with* them,' Ryker insisted. 'It's no lie. We were after Parker. Yedlin too.'

'Don't expect this nonsense to scare me off, I–'

'They'll be here soon,' Ryker said.

'Nobody is coming for you.'

'My phone. Where is it?'

Benado said nothing.

'I had to check in with my boss. If I don't call...'

Benado laughed. 'Seriously?'

But then came the chirp from the corner of the room. Of course, they hadn't ditched Ryker's phone. Benado was an ex-spy. Information was key, a phone a source of intelligence. And he'd thought Ryker was nothing more than a heavy. But MI5, with their capabilities...

'It's noon isn't it?' Ryker said.

Benado said nothing. The call went unanswered. The room went silent as though everyone was waiting to see if the phone would ring again. It would, eventually. That was the way Ryker had set it up, with the preset call seemingly routed through a government number.

'You made a big mistake.' Ryker felt and sounded more with it now, even with the toothpicks still wedged in his flesh. 'You should have dumped the phone.'

Benado began an exchange with his men, rattling off words in Hebrew at speed.

'It doesn't matter that nobody answered,' Ryker said. 'The fact the phone rang is enough. It's on. It's receiving a signal. They'll already know the location. You don't have long.'

Benado straightened up and the men moved over toward the door where their hurried conversation continued.

The phone rang again.

Ryker laughed. 'They're already here. Probably traced us as soon as you took me. They're not calling to check on me. They're calling to negotiate. This is your last chance to save yourselves.'

Benado turned around. All three men strode toward Ryker. One went behind him. A thick arm came around Ryker's neck and squeezed tightly. Ryker struggled but could do nothing. Benado pulled out the toothpicks then he and the other man went to work on Ryker's restraints.

Ryker bided his time, waited for the chance. There had to be a chance.

His right wrist was freed from the rope. A handcuff was slung over in its place. Then his left foot was freed. Another metal click – another set of cuffs. Ryker's left wrist came free, but was quickly slung into place in the cuffs. Not ideal. But workable.

Finally, his second ankle was freed.

This was the moment.

Ryker planted his feet and pushed up to stand, roaring with effort as he countered the force of the man holding his neck. He hauled his knee up, catching Benado under the chin, and hammered his clasped fists down onto the head of the man who'd been untying his wrists.

Both were sent sprawling, but they weren't out of the fight. And Ryker still had a brutishly strong arm around his neck, choking him.

Ryker clasped his wrists over the arm, heaved and leaned forward and swivelled, sending both of them crashing down on the ground. The grip loosened and he threw his feet and his elbows into whatever flesh of the man he could find as he squeezed himself out of the hold.

He rolled away. Saw the boot coming toward his face. Benado? It didn't matter. Ryker grabbed the boot. Jumped to his feet and sent the man flying. The man's head made contact with the floor. A horrific squelchy smash. Now he was out of the fight.

But there were still two left.

An elbow, arcing for Ryker's temple. He ducked, avoided the blow, then barrelled forward. With his wrists still bound, Ryker somehow scooped the man off his feet. Okay, so this was Benado. Ryker had already noticed the ex-Mossad agent was smaller than his two beefy accomplices, and Ryker easily carried his weight.

He crashed Benado into the wall, then with him pinned in place, grabbed Benado's head and cracked it off the mottled plaster. Once. Twice. Three times until Ryker sensed movement behind him.

He let go and Benado slumped to the ground. The arm came

back around Ryker's neck. Squeezed. Even harder than before. Ryker rasped for breath. The man twisted or leaned back, trying to take Ryker off his feet.

No chance. Ryker heaved again and leaned forward, the strain on his neck almost unbearable. But he kept going. Then, with the attacker's feet off the ground, he propelled himself backward. Awkward clumsy steps, teetering as he carried more than four hundred pounds at speed. Four hundred pounds of battering ram. Heading straight toward the window.

The glass was obliterated. Momentum carried both men out and into the open air. They were in free fall, Ryker staring up to the blue sky above. The man's arm loosened around his neck, but Ryker grasped hold of it and held him close. One second passed. Two. Ryker had no clue how far up they were.

Crash.

Three storeys. Survivable. At least for Ryker. The man beneath him, however, direct contact on the ground, plus Ryker's weight slamming down on him...

The arm flopped from Ryker's neck a moment later.

He achingly got to his feet. Looked back up to the window they'd fallen from. Was sure he could hear voices from within. More men?

He glanced down to the man by his feet. Blood was pooling around his head. Ryker quickly checked his pockets. No luck. No key for the cuffs on his wrists. No anything. Except for a decent watch on his wrist. Still ticking away. Ryker took it.

He stared ahead. Past the chain-link fence of the industrial yard. A row of warehouses stretched into the distance. To Ryker's right, traffic noise. To his left, green space.

He set off for the warehouses at a sprint.

9

The day that followed the botched heist at Bastian Fischer's mansion passed by in a blur for Daisy Haan, not least because of the lack of sleep of the eventful night before. After Chester's no-holds-barred instruction, the first port of call was to release the intruder from the anteroom outside the ultra-secure vault. Haan recruited Barton, head wound and all, plus four others from the dark-and-dirty security team overseen by Chester to pull the guy out of there and restrain him.

Perhaps so many guards was overkill. The guy was on his feet when the door was opened, his balaclava lying discarded by the door as though he accepted it was now pointless. He growled and shouted as the guards closed in but that was about as much defence as he could muster. The guy had been in the windowless and airless anteroom for hours, and it was clear he was oxygen-deprived and lethargic. He was soon on his knees, dragged out of there.

They took him to the basement. Of course. Stage one was figuring out who he was. Stage two was figuring out who the dead men were. Stage three was figuring out who the runner was.

Haan soon left the others to it. It didn't require the whole team to beat the crap out of the guy. Instead, she spent the next few hours trawling over the site, trawling through CCTV, counting down the hours until the boss himself arrived home. She needed to have some answers. As friendly and happy and charismatic as Fischer always appeared to be, the very fact that he kept someone like Chester close to him, the very fact that he had a security team that operated above the law and would sooner capture and torture an intruder rather than handing him over to the police, was evidence enough of Fischer's dark side.

What Haan had found in the intervening hours was both intriguing and worrying. Worrying in that this heist team had been well prepared to say the least. Haan wasn't a computer expert, but she was no slouch either, and it didn't take her long to figure out the modus operandi was exactly as she'd first guessed.

The crew had tapped into Fischer's home security network on two fronts. Firstly, they'd attacked wirelessly. Which made sense, because the system was mostly wireless. This had given them some base-level access to the security system, and they'd blocked the CCTV cameras from talking to the hub, in such a way as to not alert the hub to the fact that the cameras had been compromised. Clever.

With the cameras down, they'd been able to sneak onto site, likely over the perimeter wall as the outer gates would have remained shut at that point. An electrical maintenance cupboard at the side of the house had been the next point of attack. Gaining access to the electrical system through there had allowed the team to hardwire into the security system and take full control. This had, in turn, allowed them to bypass the finger-print scanners and keypad security on the outer gates to get their van in, and those on the doors to the house to let themselves in, which ultimately got them as far as the anteroom to the vault.

The vault had been the sticking point, apparently. Retina-scanning, facial and voice recognition. Had that been beyond this crew? Or had they simply ran out of time with the sedative gas that had knocked out Haan and Barton quickly dissipating? Perhaps they'd incorrectly measured the concentration needed, because she certainly wasn't fully under when the guy came to check on her, and when he'd tried to move her she'd woken, gutted him and tripped the failsafe. The falling barriers had killed one of the crew and trapped another.

But one had got away. What about him?

Haan had retraced his path across the gardens, visible on the CCTV. She'd used the dogs to follow his trail through the surrounding pine forest. They'd kept on the man's scent for a good two miles, twisting around the hilly terrain as he headed back east and toward the nearest town. Or village really, as it contained little more than fifty residences, and nothing but the most basic of conveniences and entertainment choices.

The dogs had lost the trail about a half mile out from the village. Perhaps because of the numerous small streams they'd had to pass. Given the route, the village was the obvious immediate destination for the runner.

Regardless, she'd called off the outside search for now. She could have spent some time going around the village door to door, asking whether anyone had seen the man. The one very good reason she hadn't was because she was well aware that Chester, and by extension the boss himself, Fischer, weren't planning on making any official complaint about the break-in. Despite the deaths, the police would not be informed, and nor would anyone else from outside Fischer's inner circle. They wanted to find the culprits themselves. Deal with them in their own way. These people – these criminals – had to know that Bastian Fischer was not fair game.

It was already dark by the time Haan made it back to the mansion. The security lights in the gardens remained blaring with the whole place still on high alert, not that they were expecting another heist team to suddenly rock up.

Other than Chester's security detail, no one else – cooks, cleaners, maintenance, whatever – had been allowed on-site during the day, and wouldn't be until risks had been fully assessed and dealt with.

Risks...

Haan moved through the expansive marble atrium at the main entrance. It didn't show any indication at all that a man had lost his life in this spot just hours earlier. Apparently the 'security' team weren't too shabby at cleaning away mutilated dead bodies. Multitalented, you could call them.

She moved on through the service wing of the ground floor and through the PIN-code-locked metal door at the back of the pantry. Stairs led down. Lights were on below and as Haan descended a shrill scream cut through the air. She tensed up. The idiot wasn't talking. At least, he wasn't talking enough.

The basement – at least this basement, as opposed to the other two under different parts of the house, one of which was something of a man cave, the other an elaborate and state-of-the-art wine cellar – consisted of a large open space with three doors off it. Each door was made of thick metal, and the rooms beyond were built from even thicker reinforced concrete. The idea, as far as Haan knew, was that this area could be used as a secure bunker, should the need ever arise. Plan for the worst, she guessed. As it was, this ultra-secure, ultra-soundproofed space was ideal for quite different purposes...

Another scream. Louder now. Haan traced it to the door at the far end, which was slightly ajar. She moved over to it and pushed it open a few more inches. And held inside whatever response might otherwise have come out as she stared into the room.

In the middle of the space, facing away from her, the captive was on a metal chair. Naked. His head bowed. His wrists were zip-tied to the chair arms, his ankles similarly secured to the chair legs. Beyond the man, suited in white plastic coveralls that were speckled and splashed with red, was Barton. Haan could tell it was him from his six-foot-six-tall frame, even though Barton's face was covered with a black balaclava. What was the point in that?

Also in front of the captive were three gurneys. On two of them were blood-soaked white sheets, beneath which Haan assumed were the remains of perhaps the two luckiest of the heist team. Lucky because they'd at least been afforded quick deaths. Their corpses were surely only in here to put extra pressure on the man in the chair.

On the third trolley were a multitude of metallic tools, several of them already bloodied.

Haan stepped in. Spotted Chester two yards to her right. Still suited, looking as serene as she did serious.

'Where have you been?' she whispered to Haan as she reached forward and pulled Haan back out of the room, out of earshot of the captive, as though it would matter if he heard the two women speak.

'I lost the runner's trail,' Haan said. Her insides curdled a little when another horrifying scream pierced her ears. Inside the room Barton stepped back, his thumb and forefinger pinched together as he held up a small blood-dripping piece of flesh. 'But he definitely went down to the village. If you give me some time, I should be able to figure out how he got away from there.'

'Make sure you do that discreetly.'

'I know that. Has he said anything?' She indicated the poor sod in the room.

'Not a word. Not a word of use anyway. Just the expected bravado from a man too stupid to recognise his own peril.'

The matter-of-fact way in which Chester said those words stirred something deep inside Haan.

She heard footsteps behind her. She turned to see one of Chester's goons, Carney, lugging a huge holdall down the stairs. Haan focused on the bag, trying to recall when she'd seen it before earlier in the day.

Of course.

'The plasma cutter?' Haan said.

'I'll leave you to it.' Chester smiled wryly. 'I'm not so sure I want to see this.'

Chester made herself scarce. Barton came out of the torture chamber. Even with the fabric of the balaclava covering much of his face, Haan could tell he felt in his element. The two men took the hefty pieces out of the bag and began to set up the machine. Haan, technically the most senior person left down here, decided to take charge.

An appeal to sense, she hoped.

While Barton and Carney were busy, she scooted into the room, and went to kneel down in front of the man. His face was bloodied. Red dripped from his chin, from his several mangled fingers where flesh had been cut and torn free. There were slashes and gashes to his limbs too.

'Look at me,' Haan said, her voice stern. The man barely reacted. 'Look at me,' she repeated, more forcefully this time.

The man lifted his head slightly.

'I know what that is out there,' she said, indicating over his shoulder even though he was clearly too weak to turn and look for himself. 'A plasma cutter. The one you brought with you. You know that thing would never have got you into the vault?'

A mumbled response from the man, and he slightly shook his head.

'You must have known that. So what was it for?'

Haan knew that as well as the vault, Fischer's house contained at least three other more standard safes for everyday valuables. Had the heist team known that too?

'I know about these things,' Haan said as Barton and Carney hauled the industrial machine into the room and in front of the captive. 'Would you believe I've actually used one before, myself? Though perhaps not like this. They cut at more than twenty thousand degrees. I've seen what they can do to metal six inches thick. The beam cutting through it like it's jelly. Can you imagine what twenty thousand degrees does to human flesh?'

Perhaps the sight of the cutter in front of him was the reality check the man needed. He sobbed, mumbled, shaking his head more vigorously.

'What's your name?' Haan persisted. 'Tell me. It's a start. A sign of trust. Tell me your name now and I promise I'll get them to take that thing away.'

Another mumble, though a little more clear now.

'What was that?'

Haan leaned closer to him. Watched his dried, blood-caked lips.

'Fuck... you.'

She clenched her jaw. Turned to Barton, who was already powering up the cutter. He flicked a switch and an arc of bright blue superheated plasma pulsed from the tip of the gun. Barton cackled in delight.

'What's your name?' Haan said, turning back to the man. She sounded a little more desperate now, even if that hadn't been her intention.

The man's lips stayed shut.

'He's had his chance,' Barton said. 'You should step back for this.'

Haan straightened up, only realised then that her legs were weak and wobbly. Barton edged forward.

'You don't wanna talk?' he sneered. He crouched down. 'Let's see what you think about that when your foot is melted to the floor.'

Haan stepped back as Barton held the gun close to the man's toes.

He flicked the switch.

The man's scream was instantaneous, and rattled around inside Haan's stomach. Within seconds what had been a foot was little more than a bubbling, smoking, pulpy mess of melted flesh and bone. The man's whole body quivered and spasmed. Despite the devastation, Barton held the cutter in place, circling the beam around and around.

Haan was far from squeamish, but the sight was beyond horrific. She turned away. As she did so, she caught Carney's eye. He glowered as though he'd read her reaction, but said nothing before looking back to the carnage.

But Haan... she couldn't look again. She wouldn't.

Nor did she need to. The man's continued harrowing screams said it all.

Screams that invaded every corner of Haan's mind, and which she was sure would forever haunt her.

10

It took Ryker only a few minutes to sneak into one of the warehouses and find the tools to snap the chain between the cuffs on his wrists. A dusty old first aid kit allowed him to quickly tend to his wounds, and first, using the pilfered watch as barter with a black-cab driver on a nearby street, it took him less than an hour to make it back to his car, and finally his apartment, barefooted and bleeding. He needed only a few minutes more once inside to pick the lock on the cuffs to properly free his wrists and his ankle. After that he was finally able to make the call to Winter.

Yet another call where Winter seemed seriously pissed off. Yet another call where Ryker hung up.

Not long after and his phone – one of several replacements he had in his apartment – was ringing again.

'We found the warehouse,' Winter announced.

'We?'

'The police. Along with MI5. It's abandoned, though the property belongs to a private landlord company. We're still trying to figure out who's behind that.'

'But what was at the warehouse?'

'Other than a few shards of broken glass?'

'Seriously? No bodies?'

'Thankfully, no.'

Ryker huffed. He was sure the man who'd fallen from the window was dead. Benado? If he was alive he certainly wouldn't have been in much of a state to have cleaned up that place so quickly. So who had?

'Talk to me,' Winter urged.

Ryker had already explained the basics the first time. Had told him all about the hotel, Garcia, Benado. Ryker's finger and toes ached as his brain whirred. His injuries were minimal, but that feeling... At least Benado hadn't had a chance to really get started.

Ryker balled his fists. 'I think Yedlin's on the run.'

'Possibly,' Winter replied.

'Most likely, I'd say. The questions Benado asked me. They thought I was there to take out Yedlin. They're worried. I think whoever took out Parker is also after Yedlin. He knows too much.'

'About what?'

'That's what I need to figure out.'

Ryker hung up. He hadn't meant to be rude but his mind was in overdrive now. He got up from the dining table, grimacing as he did so. He had no serious injuries but his bones and his joints and his muscles all ached from his morning's ordeal. He downed some painkillers then headed over to his computer.

Finally. Something.

Ryker had thought tracking down Yedlin would get him answers. But he'd gone after the wrong people. Parker was dead and he now increasingly believed Yedlin was on the run from the people who'd killed the banker. It was those people who Ryker needed to find. And now he had his first thread to pull on.

His software had been running through the morning,

pulling and deciphering the data from the mobile phones. Ryker took a couple of hours, as the painkillers took hold and his body recuperated, to go through and branch out on the initial results. It had been apparent to him, even from the first glance at the data, that these were burner phones with little saved activity, but with the resources available at his fingertips – namely the many databases and other information privy to the UK intelligence services – Ryker was able to hone in on areas of interest.

The recent call lists from the phones had five numbers in common, and with access to phone usage data garnered by the UK Government's GCHQ, Ryker was able to get an insight into calls both made and received from those numbers, and from the three burner phones. This widened the pool of phone numbers of interest several times over: in all, there were more than 200 numbers that one of those eight phones had either called or received calls from. But that was all GCHQ could offer. Numbers. There was no immediate access to the identity of the account holder for each number, or anything as useful as that – at least not without specific and substantiated data requests which Ryker had no time for or interest in. But the key was in starting wide, and then narrowing down.

As you'd expect from burner phones, none of the three phones had any downloaded apps like Facebook or Instagram, and at first glance the internet browsing histories appeared empty. At first glance. Because the users had more than likely been operating on what they thought were 'private' browser settings. What they probably hadn't understood was that even in private mode, the phone's hard drive still had to do the same work in searching and opening and processing web pages. And all of that work left its mark on the hard drive – at least until the data was overwritten by subsequent use.

One thing Ryker could see was that each of the three phones had used a messaging website accessed through the Tor network. Highly secure, highly secretive. Ryker would have to do a lot more work if he was to piece together the discussions that had taken place. But one of the phone users had been less careful than the others. He'd also accessed an Instagram account on the phone, through the internet browser rather than an app. Maybe because of boredom. Maybe stupidity. Either way, Ryker now had a basic profile for the dead man – a handle, an email address, a picture – even if he didn't yet know his full name. The account belonged to the man who'd still been breathing when Ryker had first crouched down by the smashed-up Range Rover. The information meant little on its own, but searching the Instagram account in more detail, Ryker soon found what looked like a close acquaintance of the man. A girlfriend perhaps. Maria Kohler. A young woman who, judging by her many pictures, lived in London.

Now all Ryker had to do was to find her.

11

Ryker set about gathering what he needed. He'd already had plenty of adventure for one day, but saw no point in sitting on what he'd found. He wanted more. More answers.

Before he headed out, he stood at the tall window in his lounge with a long glass of iced water, pulling together his thoughts. Across the way he could see various other residents milling about behind their apartment windows. Eating, watching TV. A young couple on the top floor of the block to the left were have a shouting match, though there wasn't a whisper of what was being said through the thick glass.

Down below, the street was busy as workers arrived home from work, or headed out for exercise or an early evening drink. Ryker's car was just in view, off to the far right. He was about to pull away from the glass when something caught his eye. A flash. Was it a light or just a reflection?

Ryker's eyes settled on a white van, parked three cars in front of his. There was definitely someone in the front seat – he could see the driver's arms and torso – but from this angle, the roof of the van was covering the man's upper body and head. So where had the flash come from? There was nothing obvious in the man's hands and the van had no side windows.

Ryker stared for several seconds. The man in the driver's seat remained still. One hand on the wheel.

There was nothing else to see.

Time to go.

He headed down, pushed the exit button to unlock the outer doors to the building and stepped out into the heat. The temperature had ramped up in the few hours Ryker had spent inside. He stared across the road, to the spot where the van had been. Not there anymore. Looking left and right, there was no sign of it heading away in either direction. Nor was there any sign of anything or anyone else untoward.

Ryker shook his head at his own paranoia. How many years had he lived like this? He'd like to say it was simply a natural reflex. A subconscious defence that undoubtedly had saved his life many times. Recently though, and he couldn't put his finger on exactly why, he'd been seeing his suspicion and paranoia more as a burden.

Had this morning's events with Benado unnecessarily heightened his angst, or was it reasonable to assume that the Israeli and the rest of the crew working with Yedlin would be looking for Ryker now?

That was fine. He'd be prepared. But really, he just wished he could find the off switch every now and then.

The journey across London to Stratford took a little under thirty minutes, despite the heavy traffic. Here, ongoing regeneration had long ago swallowed up the 2012 Olympic park. For all of the new-build apartment and office blocks in the area, the address Ryker found himself outside of was a run of bland red-brick terraces from the 1960s. Three storeys tall, the terraces looked to be split into modest apartments. Ryker was looking for 12c, which he assumed was on the top floor.

He parked up a few hundred yards away then casually walked back along the road, on the opposite side to the homes, next to a poorly-kept recreation ground that was nonetheless busy with dog walkers and young parents with babies and toddlers.

On the pavement itself, there were few people about, although further ahead, past the row of terraces, and by the entrance to a much taller and ageing concrete apartment block, a group of young men were milling. Ryker was too far away for them to take notice of him.

He was fifty yards from 12c when he spotted the door opening as a young lady walked out. Ryker recognised her face from the many pictures she regularly posted online.

Maria Kohler was tall and slim, her face caked in thick and pale make-up that made her look somewhat washed out. Her eyes and lips were painted dark, her hair was black. Nothing too extreme, it was something of a watered-down goth look, although she was wearing tight-fitting and trendy-looking gym gear.

Ryker walked past her, checking over his shoulder a couple of times to see her heading off in the opposite direction. Up front, he was getting closer and closer to the group of men, and with each step now could hear their chatter a little more loudly, even if he still couldn't hear their words. There was nothing to suggest they were acting in anyway untoward, though their very presence – the big group, laddish banter, smoking whatever, most of them with hoods over their heads – would be intimidating to most pedestrians.

Ryker wasn't intimidated. Though he didn't want to draw their attention either. No point in asking for trouble. Which was why, when he was happy they weren't looking, he crossed the road to double back. But as he did so, one of the group looked over and when he locked onto Ryker his eyes narrowed. Ryker paid him no attention and kept going. There was a slight hush for a few beats. He didn't let up. Another few seconds, across the other side of the road and walking away, he glanced over his shoulder, as subtly as he could. He didn't move his head around so far as to put eyes on the group behind him, just far enough to make sure none of them had decided to break free and follow him.

They hadn't.

Why would they?

Ryker shook his head. Better safe than sorry though.

Satisfied that he remained incognito, Ryker headed through the open gates to the terraces' small car park, up the external stairs, then along the open-air walkway that ran along the front of the building. He kept his cap pulled low, his head down the whole way. He'd noticed the building itself wasn't covered by CCTV, though as with most parts of London, the street was.

He reached 12c and checked left and right. No one about. He knocked on the door. From what he had seen of Maria Kohler online, he believed she lived alone, but it was better to be cautious.

No answer, and he could hear nothing from within.

Thirty seconds later Ryker had successfully picked the single lock and was pushing open the door.

No alarm. Good news.

He stepped in and quietly shut the door behind him. Without lights on, the apartment was gloomy, even despite the sunshine outside – a far cry from the much more modern construction he was living in that, if anything, received far too much sunshine at times. At least this place was nice and cool as a result.

Ryker did a brief search to satisfy himself that he was indeed alone. He was. The apartment was small, probably a similar size to his own, but this one felt far more cramped and outdated with low ceilings, small windows and cluttered furniture. It was also a mess. Clothes everywhere. Make-up, shoes, handbags. The life of a glamorous twenty-something. What there wasn't, was any obvious evidence of a male presence.

He spent a few minutes searching through cupboards and drawers. Nothing of interest. He guessed it wasn't like twenty-somethings kept hard-copy photos or address books or anything as old-fashioned as that to tell the stories of their lives. Everything important was in electronic form, online. So Ryker grabbed the most obvious source of information: an iPad plonked on top of a sofa, covered in a ruffled blanket.

The iPad needed a thumbprint or a four-digit PIN for access. Not to worry. Ryker knew there were plenty of hacks that could get him access to distinct areas of the iPad. The most simple was by activating the voice-recognition and requesting access to message data or call lists. But Ryker wanted access to everything. So instead he took the lead from his pocket and connected the iPad to his own phone. The software on his phone took less than a minute to bypass the security and unlock the iPad screen. And he wasn't even using proprietary government-owned hacking software this time, but one of dozens of simple programs that anyone could download from the internet for free. The majority of people had no idea just how vulnerable their electronic equipment – and by extension their private lives – really were.

Ryker took a seat and spent some time roaming. Emails. Messages, both iMessage and WhatsApp. Twitter. Facebook. Instagram, SnapChat.

It didn't take long. Less than thirty minutes, and Ryker had not only got the names of three of the men from the previous day but also alternative phone numbers for them – likely ones that were properly registered in their names.

Thomas Podolski was the now dead young man who'd been dating Maria Kohler, and whose Instagram profile had started this whole search. Lukas Kahn was one of the men who'd been in the square with Parker. As was Emre Tufan. Tattoo man. Given he was the one who'd stood front and centre, communicating with Parker, he was the one Ryker was most interested in.

A raucous car engine outside caught his attention.

iPad still in hand, he got up and headed to the front window. He pulled aside the net curtain an inch to peep out. A bright-blue Ford Focus, modified almost beyond recognition, pulled up on the street outside. The stereo boomed away, the exhaust rumbled. The back door opened.

Maria Kohler stepped out. Then another person. Ryker smiled grimly when he saw the man's bare arms, inked as far as the eye could see.

Mr Tattoo. Aka Emre Tufan.

12

Ryker tensed, his body readying for action. Was Tufan going to head this way? Did Ryker want him to?

As the pair outside had an awkward-looking conversation – a few nods, a few shakes of the head – Ryker scanned the car. He caught a glimpse of the two men in the front seats but didn't recognise either from the day before, or from his clandestine research.

Tufan gave Maria an even more awkward embrace, and then sank back down into the rear seat of the Focus.

Ryker clenched his teeth. Tufan could wait. Maria was walking toward her home, head down, while the driver of the Focus heavily revved the engine, sending vibrations through Ryker's body. The souped-up car shot off down the street at deafening volume.

Maria seemed oblivious to the racket, or perhaps she was used to it.

She would be at her front door within thirty seconds or so. Ryker could scarper down the back fire escape before she arrived... or...

He casually moved into the lounge at the back of the apartment. He closed the screens on the iPad and put the device back where he found it. Then he moved out of view of the doorway. He heard the lock turn and the waft of air flow in as the front door was pushed open. When it was closed again he heard something of a desperate sigh. Two shoes plonked onto the floor, then soft footsteps pattered across the hall toward the lounge.

Ryker moved across the doorway, hands held up to show they were empty and that he was no threat.

Still, Maria jumped in shock. Then froze. She was already teary, but now she also looked petrified.

'It's okay,' Ryker assured her. 'I'm not here to hurt you.'

She recovered her composure remarkably quickly. Perhaps it was something in Ryker's conciliatory tone. Still, he was more than a little surprised that she hadn't screamed or bolted or both.

'Who are you?' Her voice was shaken.

'I need to talk to you about Thomas. Thomas Podolski.'

At the mention of the name she shivered and her bottom lip quivered though she again recovered her composure in a beat.

'I just found out he's dead,' she said. 'He died yesterday. I can't believe I only just found out. I thought he was off partying.'

This time her non-British accent came through more strongly. A tear fell from her eye and rolled down her cheek, though she didn't make any attempt to wipe the trail away.

'Quite a way to ruin a workout,' she continued, before huffing as though annoyed at her own choice of words.

'I'm sorry. I just need to ask you a few questions about him.'

'Are you police?'

'No.'

She didn't seem to like that answer. 'Why me?'

'Because you knew him.'

'I'm not the only one. Who are you?'

'I'm trying to find out what happened to him.'

'He was killed in a car crash.'

'There was more to it than that.'

'What does that mean?'

'It means I'd like you to tell me about him.'

She huffed again – incredulity?

'Don't you want to figure out *why*?' Ryker urged.

She held his eye for a moment, though didn't say a word.

'Why don't you come and sit down.'

He took a step back into the lounge. She hesitated, but then cautiously walked forward, her eyes narrow, never once leaving Ryker as she moved.

Ryker sidestepped over to a rickety-looking armchair, though he didn't take the seat. Maria, too, remained standing. Ryker indicated the sofa.

'I'm fine,' Maria said. 'You won't be staying long. Will you?'

'Maria, I'm not going to ask for any kind of sob story. Frankly, I don't care how you and Thomas met, how long you've been seeing each other, how much you loved him or how sad you are he's dead. The thing is, he was involved in something bad. And I need answers about how he got involved.'

Emotions flitted across Maria's face as she processed this – from distress to anger to worry – but she still didn't say anything.

'I think you probably know something about what Thomas was caught up in,' Ryker said. 'That man in the car just now, for example, Emre Tufan. He and Thomas were involved in some bad shit.'

Maria shook her head in denial but didn't say anything.

'Who do they work for?' Ryker asked.

'I don't even know what that means.'

'Maria, I won't play games with you, if you don't with me. You watched the news in the last twenty-four hours?'

She looked puzzled. 'Kind of.'

'You saw what happened by Tower Bridge?'

Now she looked shocked. 'Emre didn't...'

'He didn't tell you that was how Thomas was killed?'

'No... he...'

'I was there too,' Ryker said. 'The problem is, your boyfriend and his friends *weren't* supposed to be there. I need to know why they were.'

'The news said that was about terrorists.' Maria was shaking her head. Her confusion seemed genuine to Ryker.

'National security is how I think the news termed it.'

'This makes no sense.'

'Who was Thomas working for? And Emre?'

She didn't answer, though it was obvious from the twitch in her face that she did know something.

'Maria? All I need is a name. You won't come to any harm for telling me.'

'How could you possibly know that? You're standing here because my boyfriend is dead. Did you tell him the same thing?'

'Whatever you tell me, it won't come back to you. I promise. And if you tell me what you know, you'll never see me again.'

Tears were rolling down her face. He appreciated that his timing was lousy. But he was here now. She glanced at the fitness watch on her wrist, then looked up to the ceiling, hands on hips. She was struggling. She'd just found out her boyfriend was dead, and now a mysterious intruder in her home was asking her questions she didn't want to answer. At least the seriousness of the situation wasn't lost on her.

'Thomas was just a young man,' Ryker said. 'Twenty-three years old. Whatever he was doing, whatever he got involved in that ended up with him being killed yesterday, he was put up to it by someone else. I need to know who.'

Maria shook her head. Bit her lip. Then, 'He's just... I've never even met him before.'

'Who?'

A sigh. 'It's just a name. That's it. I've heard the name. I've heard people talk about him.'

She checked her watch again. Ryker eyed her with suspicion.

'Maria? What's the name?'

There it was. In the near distance. Muffled, but distinct. The rumble of the Ford Focus. Getting louder by the second.

Maria initially looked relieved, but tensed up when she caught Ryker's eye.

He got it. He'd thought it a little strange that a woman alone in her house with an intruder had calmed so quickly. Hadn't attempted to cry out for help or to run. Now it made sense. She'd always known Tufan and his crew were returning.

'Gone to get milk or something?' Ryker said.

Maria didn't answer. Ryker took a step toward her.

'Don't you move another step,' she warned him.

'You have no idea what you're doing. No idea the mess you could find yourself in.'

His thinly-veiled threat caused her tough exterior to crack just a little.

'You want me to come back here?' Ryker hissed. 'Because I will. You and your little friends won't stop me. I *don't* stop. Not until I get what I want. Your boyfriend knows all about that now.'

He took another two steps toward her. She cowered back until she bumped against the wall. Nowhere else to go.

Outside, a car door opened. Then another.

'I'm not afraid of them,' he continued. 'I'll happily sit and wait here for them. They'll come inside. Then I'll deal with you all, one by one. I'll get what I want. Or... just give me the name now, and I'm gone. No harm to anyone.'

He stepped forward again. He was close enough to reach out

and grab her. She was quaking on the spot, even if she was trying to look strong.

'Akkan,' she said.

'Akkan?'

'That's all I know,' she said, her voice even more shaky now, even though she was seconds from being saved. Or so she hoped.

Footsteps outside the front door. Ryker glanced past her, along the corridor. He saw the silhouette of a figure slide across the frosted glass of the door. A knock.

Time to go.

Ryker screwed up his face in determination. 'Don't tell them anything.'

His words were hard, and carried just enough menace to make his point clear, he hoped. Maria gave no response.

Ryker darted across the room, into the kitchen. As he reached the back door he heard Maria thudding along the corridor.

'Emre! Emre! Hilfe!'

Hilfe. Help. Ryker rolled his eyes. He'd thought he might get out of there quietly. Now that option was gone, and he was faced with an age-old choice. A choice he'd had to make a thousand times in his difficult life.

Fight, or flight.

13

Ryker would nearly always fancy his chances in a straightforward fight, even when the odds were stacked against him. The events of the morning were testament to that. Yet he'd also long believed that it was better to walk away from a confrontation, if possible, as any confrontation had the possibility of going awry. Some risks were worth taking. Some weren't.

This one wasn't.

He'd already come out on top from this visit, and he'd already taken a hell of a battering that morning. No point in adding to that. He'd now put names to faces from the previous day, and perhaps even more importantly, he had a name for who Podolski, Tufan and the others were working for. Perhaps the man who'd had Parker killed.

So rather than standing his ground, Ryker slipped his cap back on and unbolted the back door. At the same time, he heard the front door opening. Maria was shouting in a frenzy of German. Then there was shouting from a man. Two men.

Thudding footsteps entered the apartment and came his way as Ryker flung open the back door and raced out onto the metal gangway at the back of the properties. He cursed under his breath. The stairs were right at the other end of the building.

Ryker darted along, not bothering to look back. He didn't need to. He could tell that the men were already out and chasing after him by the bounce and vibration on the metal platform.

There was more shouting. At least there were no gunshots.

Ryker reached the stairs. He grabbed the handrails either side, lifted his legs and slid down in one smooth motion. He turned the corner at the halfway point and did the same again and again until he was on the ground floor.

Now he did glance above. The men had only just reached the top of the stairs. Sure, they were angry, but they weren't exactly tooled up for this.

Ryker darted across the small yard area that was largely filled with industrial bins. He scaled the wall at the far end with ease and found himself in a narrow alley. Legging it to the left, he took a series of left and right turns, along streets, alleys, some wide, some narrow, all the while checking over his shoulder. Intermittently, he heard shouting. High revs of the Ford Focus. But he saw no one.

After five minutes, puffing for breath, his leg muscles heavy with lactate build-up, he finally came to a busy shopping street dominated by low-end clothes stores, electronics stores and charity shops. There were plenty of people about to lose himself among. He took off his jacket and dumped it in a bin. Did the same with his cap at the next bin. No sign of Tufan or anyone else suspicious behind him. He was a good half mile at least from Maria's apartment, and he figured that the chasers had by now given up, headed back to Maria and found out what had happened.

Ryker paid five pounds to a street seller for a new knock-off baseball cap, different in colour to the one he'd just dumped.

Then, when he was sure he was in the clear, he doubled back to head toward his parked car.

He kept his eyes busy. After several minutes of steady walking, he turned onto a wide street that ran parallel to the one Maria lived on. He continued to glance behind him. He was approaching the next turn when he saw them. Two men. Two men Ryker hadn't seen before. Not Tufan; with his tattoos he was remarkably conspicuous. Both had their faces covered with caps, much like Ryker. Both wore smart-casual clothing, hands in the pockets of their jackets. Ryker himself had worn a jacket to Maria's, not because it was chilly out, but because he'd wanted to be ready for a quick change of appearance if necessary. It had been necessary. But there was another reason why someone would wear a jacket even on a hot sunny day like this. Concealment.

So who the hell were these two?

Ryker kept on going. All he wanted now was to be back in his car and heading away. He took the next right, onto a street where both sides were lined with terraces almost identical in look and style to Maria's. He turned off the pavement and stooped behind a red-brick wall.

He waited. Glancing out every now and then.

He hadn't wanted a confrontation... but...

He remained in place. But there was no sign, or sound, of the two men.

Ryker stuck his head right out. No. They were gone. Which was even more odd. He was sure they'd been following him, even if he had no clue who they were.

He moved away. Kept on going. Took the next left onto the street where his car was parked. He could see it, 200 yards in the distance.

Again, he looked behind him. The men still weren't there.

He was soon approaching his car. Up ahead, there was no

sign of the Focus now, outside Maria's house. Everything felt uncomfortably serene.

He unlocked his car and got in behind the wheel. Closed the door. He waited for several seconds. He looked up front, checked in his mirrors. Still no sign of the men, or Tufan or anyone at all who caught his eye.

But then, after a few moments of quiet, a white van emerged and pulled to a stop at the edge of the last street he'd come from.

The same van as when he'd left his apartment earlier?

Ryker hadn't caught the plate then, and couldn't see it now because of the angle, but it wasn't unusual to see a white van in central London. In fact, there was another approaching him from the front that very moment. That van went past. Ryker followed it in his mirror. The other van remained stationary.

Ryker pulled out into the road. He didn't put his foot down, just crawled away. The van remained where it was. For about ten seconds. Then it, too, pulled out. Ryker built up his speed to twenty-five as he headed past Maria's house. No sign of anything untoward there. Outside the tall apartment block the group of youths remained, though they barely glanced as the car passed.

The van remained a steady distance behind. Ryker took a left and then pulled over to the side of the road. A few seconds later he watched in his mirror as the van came to the junction. It seemed to pause there longer than necessary, but then turned right and headed away.

A few seconds later it was swallowed up in London traffic.

Ryker let out a deep sigh. He didn't like this. There were too many coincidences. Why was he being followed? Whoever it was, it didn't seem they were that bothered about being spotted.

Did they want him to know they were there?

Ryker took a circuitous route back across London, on even higher alert than normal, but nothing else caught his attention. He thought about heading back to his apartment. Thought about calling Winter and arranging to properly talk over his action-packed day. He decided against both, and instead pulled up in the small car park belonging to the South Greenwich Hospital. He was back here again for more than one reason. Of course, he wanted to see Moreno, but he also knew this burgeoning investigation would benefit from her input, particularly now that he had several names and profiles that needed further investigation. Something Moreno was vastly experienced in.

Ryker headed from his car toward the entrance. Standing outside the doors was a man casually smoking. He locked eyes with Ryker for a second before looking away. Ryker carried on past, and through the maze of corridors, up the stairs, to where Moreno's room was located.

As he stepped from the stairwell, he spotted someone coming out of Moreno's door. A smartly-dressed woman. Ryker didn't recognise her, but something about her demeanour caused him to react. He jerked to his left and pushed open the door to a small vending area. It was empty inside and Ryker moved in and held the door almost closed, leaving just an inch for him to peep through.

He waited, expecting to see the woman heading past.

She didn't.

Ryker frowned. He opened the door and stuck his head out to look along the corridor. No sign of the woman at all now.

Why had she gone the other way? She was in for a hell of a walk to find the exit from there.

Ryker stepped back out and moved along to Moreno's room, looking back and forth. No sign of anyone else. Ryker knocked on the door but didn't wait before trying the handle. Unlocked. He pushed the door open. Moreno was just pulling herself up from the sofa.

'Hey,' she said. 'Two times in twenty-four hours. Is it my birthday?'

Her jovial words belied the anxiety on her face.

'You okay?' Ryker asked, still holding the door.

'Yeah. Are you?'

She looked more concerned now.

He closed the door, his brain whirring. He wanted to ask the obvious and simple question, *Who was that?* For some reason he didn't.

He moved through the room as Moreno settled back down on the sofa. He went past her and to the window.

'Busy day?' he asked.

'Not really.'

'You've not been out?'

'Not yet.'

'No visitors?'

He looked out of the window, down below.

Moreno didn't answer. He turned back to her. Saw she was glaring. She knew him better than most people. She knew he was prying.

'Just the doctor,' she said.

'Which one?'

'A new one. I don't think you know her.'

Ryker held her eye. He didn't buy it, and her unimpressed expression suggested she realised that. Ryker looked out of the window again. He spotted a man and a woman strolling across the gardens at the front of the hospital toward the main road. He was pretty damn sure it was the woman he'd just seen leaving Moreno's room, and the man he'd seen smoking by the entrance.

Ryker faced Moreno. He wanted to be angry, but he saw the look in her eyes. Anguish.

'You okay?' he asked again.

'Not really,' she said.

'You want to tell me about it?'

'Not really.' She laughed, but it was forced. 'Just come over here.'

She patted the seat next to her. Ryker hesitated for a second but then moved over and sat down. Moreno shuffled over and nestled her head against his shoulder, the delicate smell of her skin tickled his nose. He put his arm around her and she sighed.

'I don't know what I'd do without you,' she said.

Ryker didn't say anything. He was too busy thinking about that man and woman. He had no clue who they were.

One thing he did know: Moreno was lying to him.

14

Picturesque and historic Baden-Baden, at the north-western border of the Black Forest mountain range, was the nearest city to Bastian Fischer's remote home, though with under sixty-thousand inhabitants it was hardly a sprawling metropolis.

Dating back to Roman times, Baden-Baden had more recent significance as the headquarters of the French occupation forces in the aftermath of World War II, though its spectacular land-scape meant that even more recently its most important role was as part of the Black Forest tourism industry, which the city was increasingly geared to cater for.

And that was one of the main reasons why Haan and Barton were there now. Some fifteen miles from Fischer's home, Baden-Baden would have been a perfect spot for the heist team to base themselves and to carry out their preparations. There were hotels here, plenty of food outlets, easy access to Wi-Fi, to road networks, rail, air. And car rental shops, which were of partic-ular interest to Haan.

The heist team had left their getaway van at the scene. Not intentionally, Haan believed. The problem for them was that when Haan hit the panic alarm, the keys for the van were in the pocket of Mr Melty. At least that was the gruesome name that Barton had given to the man who'd been trapped in the ante-room and who was now languishing in the basement. Haan hadn't spoken that ridiculous name at all, even if Barton and the others thought it was hilarious.

Mr Melty. They still had no clue who he really was. The poor bastard remained captive in Fischer's home, somehow clinging to life, as stubbornly as he was clinging to his and his accomplices' identities. The 'doctor' had suggested the captive needed at least forty-eight hours to recuperate before they could restart interrogation. At least if they wanted him to survive the interrogation. Haan did. Because she wanted answers, not to get off on someone else's suffering.

'Open it,' Barton said in his stilted German, shoving the luckless young man he was holding in the back.

The guy whimpered and stumbled toward the door. Henrik Bach was twenty-six years old, and the assistant manager of the Baden-Baden branch of Zuerst Rentals. The getaway van had been riding on fake plates – obviously – but Haan had used the VIN number to trace it to Zuerst Rentals. Taking a rental vehicle to a heist was a decent call really. The idea would have been to take the van back to the shop as soon as possible after the heist, switching vehicles back to whatever the crew had really rode to town in. Back with its genuine plates, the rental company would be none the wiser as to what their vehicle had been used for, and in using a rental there wasn't the problem for the heist team of dumping the getaway vehicle, that could then easily be found and searched by the police.

'I...I,' Bach stammered as he scrabbled uselessly. It was a miracle he hadn't pissed his pants. Maybe he had. It was too dark out to tell.

Barton grabbed Bach around the back of his neck and slammed his face up against the still-locked shutter.

'Don't fucking mess with me,' Barton growled.

'Give him a chance,' Haan said, looking around her. The yard behind the store was pitch black and there were no lights on in the buildings overlooking here, but still... there was a time and place for Barton's over-the-top macho routine, and this wasn't it.

Though his fingers were fumbling all over, Bach somehow managed to unclasp the padlock, and Barton let go of his neck, reached forward and clattered the shutter upward.

Subtle, Haan thought, but didn't say it.

Bach managed to unlock the back door with a bit more focus, though as he pushed it open the blips from the premise's alarm sounded out.

'Turn it off,' Barton said. 'Or–'

'I think he gets it by now,' Haan said, which earned her a scowl from Barton, clear enough even with the balaclava covering his head.

Bach had soon disabled the alarm and Barton and Haan stepped inside. Haan shut the door behind her and Barton flipped on the lights.

'Get us logged in,' Haan said to Bach. 'We'll do the rest.'

Bach nodded and feebly walked them through into the small office-cum-cupboard at the back of the shop that had just two desks and two computers in it. It took a couple of minutes for the system to boot up. Bach was quivering in his chair the whole time. Haan could understand why. It wasn't like she'd have been too keen on being woken up at 1am by two black-clad figures, hunting knife pressed up against her skin.

At least Bach lived alone, which meant no one else had to be involved.

'Is that it?' Barton said, when Bach stopped typing.

'I... I signed in to my account.' He looked up to Haan, his eyes pleading.

'Thanks,' Barton said.

He drew back his fist and sent a stinging hook onto the side of Bach's head. Bach crumpled and Haan reached out to catch him as he tumbled from the chair.

'What the fuck!' she shouted to Barton.

'We don't need him now.'

'Says who? What if we come to a roadblock?'

'I thought you knew how to do this shit?'

'I do–'

'Then do it. If we need him I'll wake him up. Piss on him or something. You should be glad I haven't killed him already.'

'And you damn well won't, you dumb prick.'

Barton looked ready to explode but he said nothing.

'Tie him up or something,' Haan said. 'Your punch wasn't that good.'

Barton grunted but then got to it.

Haan took Bach's seat and was soon diving deep into the records on Zuerst's system. It took only a couple of minutes to find the documents for the van rental. The van had been taken out just two days ago. Paid for in cash for a week. There was a name and address attached to the rental, and a scan of a driving licence. No doubt the licence was fake, but it was something at least, and the picture could certainly prove useful – unless, of course, it wasn't their guy at all. Would a teller at a car rental shop really scrutinise the face on a licence to make sure it was the person standing before them?

Far more useful to see the face of the man who actually signed the documents.

Haan would get to that. First, she performed three further searches. One for all previous rentals of that same van. She downloaded the file with the results onto a thumb drive. Second, a search for all other rentals of similar vehicles. A much longer list, but it could prove telling. Finally, she searched for any other rentals in the same name. Interestingly, there were two others. One was ten days ago. The other over a month ago.

Well planned, just as she expected.

'Anything?' Barton said, hovering over Haan's shoulder.

'Plenty,' she said, without further elaboration.

She could imagine Barton's eye-roll to that, though didn't bother to turn for confirmation. She was too focused. And was soon opening up the recordings from the shop's CCTV system. She'd already deduced that the shop was running a modern but basic system that linked directly into the company's local server. All recordings were stored on the hard drives in this very room. Haan needed only a couple of minutes to find the right day and time. She hit play.

On the screen Bach was behind the counter. The renter was already inside. He had a cap on, and his head was down, his back to the camera.

'He's not stupid,' Barton said.

'Just be patient.'

Haan switched the view to the camera that was behind the counter, which was lower down than the other one. She rewound fifteen minutes, and the shop was empty. She hit play and waited. Two minutes. Three minutes. Four minutes.

'Are you actually just going to sit there?' Barton asked.

Haan ignored him. Seconds later, on the screen, a figure approached from outside. He opened the door and stepped in. Haan hit pause just at the moment the man went to greet Bach. His head wasn't raised exactly, but it was lifted to eye level, enough to see his chin, his jaw, his mouth, nose... eyes...

Haan froze. Then zoomed in on the picture.

This couldn't be happening.

'It's not one of the guys in the basement,' Barton said. 'That's our runner. Bastard.'

Haan agreed. It definitely wasn't Mr Melty or either of the two dead men.

'We're going to nail this fucking prick,' Barton added.

Haan said nothing. She couldn't. Instead, she simply continued to stare into the achingly familiar eyes of the man on the screen.

15

Secrets – or the potential of secrets – had kept Ryker awake in the night. He hadn't asked Moreno who the mystery woman was. Hadn't tried to call her out, or put pressure on her to see if she would come clean of her own accord. Instead, he'd ignored her apparent lie entirely. But he hadn't really moved on either. And he'd left the hospital without discussing his findings with her or asking for her help as he'd intended.

He felt a little bad that his reaction to her being secretive was to hold back on her. For the past twelve months, since Africa, Ryker had been Moreno's safety net, and she'd been the closest thing to a genuine and close friend that he'd had in years. Yet the reality was that they knew very little of each other and their dark pasts. That would likely never change.

He tried his best to move on. Armed with the information he'd gleaned from the phones and from Maria Kohler, Ryker spent much of the morning further researching his targets, both in public records, and also in data held by the UK government and its various law enforcement and intelligence agencies. As expected, his digging didn't go unnoticed. Most of the highly-restricted databases he was accessing sent out automatic alerts to ensure user integrity, which was why Ryker was soon on the phone with Winter.

By midday, he was in his car on his way to a hastily-arranged rendezvous with the JIA Commander – at Winter's behest. Ryker had agreed. Better not to rock the boat too much, but he wasn't planning on stopping long. He had somewhere else to be.

As with the previous day, Ryker remained vigilant as he travelled across London, though this time there was no indication that anyone was following or otherwise watching him.

Ryker parked his car on the side of the road and paid for an hour at the meter. As long as Winter was on time, he wouldn't even need that long.

He walked the short distance across St James's Park, as ever bustling with tourists and locals alike. As he walked, he had glimpses of Buckingham Palace, a couple of hundred yards away, people swarming around the gates like they did day in, day out, whatever the weather.

Like many places in London, it was easy for Ryker to be anonymous here. But that would be the case for people intent on spying on him too, and as Ryker headed across the grass to a bench overlooking the twisting lake in the centre of the park, he couldn't shake the feeling that he was being watched, even if he didn't spot anybody who looked particularly suspicious.

He'd beaten Winter to it, and took a seat on the bench. A middle-aged woman was sitting there too, tightly clutching a bulging oversized handbag on her lap. The woman paid Ryker no attention. If she was still there when Winter arrived, the two men would take a walk.

Ryker spotted Winter across the other side of the water a couple of minutes later. He kept his eyes busy as the commander hobbled around the edge of the lake and then up the grass to Ryker's spot.

Ryker realised he could have gone to meet him halfway to

save him the effort. Oh well. It was Winter who'd asked to meet, and he who'd suggested this spot in this park.

As Winter neared, the woman must have sensed that she was about to be outnumbered, and she groaned as she got to her feet to saunter away down toward the water, grumbling under her breath.

By the time he arrived, Winter was breathing hard and his forehead glistened with beads of sweat.

Ryker smiled. 'Still working hard on the rehab.'

'Very funny,' Winter replied, his tone not particularly friendly. He slumped down onto the bench next to Ryker. 'So come on, what have you got.'

Ryker reached into his pocket, took out the phones and dropped them onto Winter's palm. No surreptitious exchange. What was the point?

Winter shook his head. 'Seriously?'

Ryker shrugged.

'You realise since this operation went tits-up, I've been fielding non-stop push back from MI5, and have been holding firm with them that whatever went wrong with Parker was not down to us. Not down to *you*. That *you* are in fact the experienced investigator I originally claimed you to be.'

'Thanks.'

'I'm not asking for your thanks. I'm trying to understand what the hell went through your mind when you figured it was a good idea to steal evidence from a very public crime scene. When you thought it was a good idea to go chasing after Yedlin without so much as a word to me, possibly killing a man or three in the process, and very nearly getting yourself tortured to death.'

'That's cheap coming from you.'

'And what the hell does that mean?'

Ryker looked Winter in the eye.

'If the UK government thought that its police forces were adequately equipped for every type of investigation, what's the point of having the likes of the JIA?'

'I'm not arguing against the point of the JIA,' Winter replied. 'I'm arguing about objectivity and bloody common sense. You're not on a secret undercover mission in some backwater corner of the globe. You're running a very public operation on home soil. I'm sure it didn't escape your attention that the scene you took these phones from was filmed by several bystanders and made the national news just minutes after–'

'I get it.'

Winter sighed. 'You say that. But your actions suggest otherwise.'

Perhaps that was true. Ryker did understand that Winter wanted him to see what he'd done wrong, but his taking the phones from the crime scene had jump-started the investigation as far as Ryker was concerned. If it was public perception of the police or MI5 or whatever that bothered Winter, he obviously was talking to the wrong person. The only problem Ryker saw with his actions was that those phones would likely never be admissible evidence in a court case now. Ryker had never been tasked with building a court case. Such a finality had rarely been a consideration throughout his long and fraught career.

'I've got names for all of the dead men,' he finally said. 'Plus two others who were in the car with Parker. And I also think I know who they were working for.'

Winter shook his head, but didn't say anything. Was he still incredulous or quietly impressed?

'What I don't have is any hint of a link between these people and Parker or Yedlin.'

'And we still haven't had a sniff of where Yedlin might be,' Winter said. 'Despite your efforts.'

'My best guess would be anywhere but England right now. What about Garcia?'

'I had MI5 haul him in to interview him. It didn't take long. Money. Simple as that. They offered him more.'

'And his family?'

'He chose this path.'

Ryker said nothing. Did he feel sorry for Garcia and his family? A little. Would he intervene? Probably not. Not if it was simple greed which had led Garcia to turning.

The two went silent. Ryker watched a young couple strolling in front of them. They were hand in hand though weren't talking to each other at all, and the woman had a thin scowl on her face. Something about the two didn't look right, though they continued away casually and were soon well out of earshot.

'So?' Winter said.

'What?'

'Are you going to give me anything?'

'I already did.'

'Names?'

This was the sticky part. Ryker did trust Winter, mostly. Not one hundred per cent, in every instance, but enough for him to still be working with him. But that didn't mean that he would reveal his full hand at the first opportunity. Of course, Winter had the resources at his fingertips to assist Ryker here, but he also remained inextricably tied to the big machine. Winter had bosses who needed answers, who he had to keep sweet for the sake of his own career path. There wasn't anything necessarily wrong with that – Winter was no different to the vast majority of other people on the payroll of any company or organisation. But it did mean that Ryker wasn't sure he wanted to give Winter everything, all of the time. Not if there was a chance that the information could be passed along to MI5 or to the police, and for Ryker to then have them stepping on his toes.

If he needed help, he'd ask for it.

But he also couldn't say nothing.

'I'll send you the names. The guys in the Range Rovers were mostly of German and Turkish descent, although they were all UK citizens.'

'Germany? Turkey? What's that got to do with–'

'Parker and Yedlin? Perhaps nothing. These were all young guys. Oldest, twenty-five. Most likely they were nothing more than hired help.'

'Yet they were hired for something pretty damn high profile.'

'They probably couldn't have cared less what it was all about. They probably weren't even told.'

'Plus there was that man and woman in the square–'

'I've got nowhere identifying them,' Ryker said.

'No. Nor has anyone else, as far as I know. Which says a lot, don't you think?'

'I agree. And most likely it means they weren't with the Range Rover guys at all.'

'So who was paying our young German friends?' Winter asked.

Ryker thought about that one. 'When I find out, you'll be the first to know.'

He held Winter's eye for a few beats. Winter didn't seem convinced but he didn't question Ryker's answer either.

'Anything else?' Winter said.

'No. But keep me in the loop with what you're hearing on the official side.'

Winter sighed, though he had a slight smile on his face. 'Talk about a one-sided arrangement.'

There was an awkward pause before Winter rose to his feet. 'Stay in touch.'

He headed away, back the way he'd come. Across the water Ryker still had one eye on the couple who'd passed by him and

Winter. They were still strolling, paying no particular attention to Ryker. They still looked like they didn't belong.

Ryker looked around him. No. No one was spying on him here. He was pretty damn sure of that. Alone. Anonymous. That's what Ryker was in this world. And thinking back to the less than satisfactory time with Moreno last night, that fact filled him with a certain dread.

He looked at his watch. It was time for his next stop. Despite what he'd told Winter, Ryker had a very good idea who had paid Tufan and the others for their services. What Ryker didn't know was how on earth the man named Yunus Akkan fitted into the story of Parker and Yedlin.

There was only one way to find out.

16

Like many parts of London, the cluttered area of Shoreditch was a clashing neighbourhood that included plenty of up-and-coming trendy locales, yet poorer and more run-down parts were never more than a street or two away. It was the latter where Ryker was walking.

Having already a grasp of the immediate area from satellite and street photos, he felt an eerie familiarity as he walked alongside a row of bland mid-twentieth century terraces. Run-down businesses took up the ground floors, and he slowed as he approached one of the more obviously-used establishments; a Turkish café called Mehmet's. He glanced through the windows as he walked by to scope out the inside. Quiet. He decided to head in.

A bell above the door tinkled as he entered, causing most of the half-dozen punters in the place to glance over. One man held his gaze on Ryker far longer than the others, a heavy-set man in his thirties with a thick-and-scrunched-up face. He was sitting in the corner on his own with a small cup of coffee that was dwarfed by his meaty fingers. The man wasn't Akkan, nor anyone else that Ryker recognised from his online research, but certainly someone to keep his eye on, he decided.

The café was something of a middle ground between fast-food outlet and restaurant. Functional tables and chairs were topped off with more lavish furnishings that gave flashes of the Middle East. Most of one side of the modest space was taken up by a glass counter that contained both desserts and a multitude of salads and other accompaniments to the savoury food items. As Ryker browsed one of the menus at the counter he realised most dishes consisted of grilled meat. Despite the tempting offerings he ordered only an Americano from the pot-bellied man at the counter, then took a seat at the back of the café, in the opposite corner to the gruff customer who by now had his eyes set on a folded newspaper.

Ryker soon had his coffee and took out his phone as he waited, and hoped for a lead. He hadn't just happened across this place. Research on social media had shown this to be a regular hang-out for Tufan and his crew, and a little more digging had revealed that the owner was Yunus Akkan's uncle.

Akkan himself, from what Ryker had deduced, was a forty-something local thug, likely one with gangster tendencies. Or was it desires? Akkan was born in London to Turkish parents, known to the police as a petty criminal with a string of offences that had started in his teens, from car theft to burglary to assault and drug possession. He'd spent five years of his earlier life in jail, though had been a free man, and apparently law-abiding, since the age of twenty-eight.

Ryker didn't quite buy the law-abiding part. He hadn't yet met Akkan, but felt he knew the type well enough. Most likely he was something of a local gang leader, who kept his nose relatively clean, with runts to do his dirty work. The immediate area around here had large immigrant populations from all corners of the world, it had for decades, and it was common for the unscrupulous to make easy money by terrorising those within their own hard-up communities. Ryker could imagine a younger Akkan, poor family in a poor neighbourhood, drawn into a life of crime like so many others, fighting through his formative years to make a name for himself and rise through the ranks.

One by one, Ryker spied on the scattering of people within the café as he waited. Other than the man in the adjacent corner, the others all seemed innocuous enough. Still, Ryker covertly took pictures of them with his phone to check back on later.

He had only a lukewarm sip of his coffee remaining when he finally got the action he'd been hoping for. Mr Gruff across the way had already checked his watch four times since Ryker had taken his seat, and on the fifth occasion he put his paper down onto the table, got up, his jaw pulsing from being clenched so tightly, and moved through a bead curtain into a back room.

Someone was late.

In the next few minutes all the other punters left, except for two teenage girls who took up stools in the front window. As if the others had known welcome time was over.

Ryker heard them before he saw them. Laddish voices, shouting and heckling. As the three men stepped into the café and the bell tinkled, though, their conversation died down to a hush. Ryker looked over each of them as discreetly as he could. He recognised one of the three: Tufan. Ryker, fork in one hand, phone in the other, clicked away on his phone's camera as the three held a brief conversation with the waiter before moving toward the back, Tufan in the lead.

He'd only seen Ryker with a baseball cap on the previous day, though there was still a chance that Tufan might recognise him now. Nothing he could do about that. He exited the camera and dropped his phone to the table as the men neared. Bowing his head slightly, he flicked his eyes up to keep watch. All three gave him the eye as they passed.

Tufan pushed through the beads and headed out of sight. The next man followed. The third man paused. Ryker lifted his head. The guy, all of twenty years old, fresh-faced but with a sneer that he must have practised for hours in the mirror, had his deep glower locked onto Ryker.

'What?' Ryker said.

The kid was about to bite back when the waiter shouted over in a jumble of Turkish – a language Ryker only had a basic grasp of. The young man looked over and shot back a short, angry retort, before he once again set his eyes on Ryker and snorted, as though Ryker was beneath his lofty status in life. Without another word he moved off through the beads to disappear into the back with the others.

Ryker downed the remainder of his coffee as he listened, but all he could hear were distant muffled voices.

He realised the waiter was staring at him.

'I'm sorry about that,' the man said.

'It's fine.'

'Perhaps you should go before they come out.'

Telling, yet perhaps kindly advice to which he didn't reply.

The waiter hesitated a moment before getting back to whatever he was doing behind the counter. Ryker got up from his chair. His eyes moved to the bead curtain to his right. A small part of him tried to drag him over there and through the beads to see what was beyond.

No need. Not yet.

Ryker made his way toward the exit.

'See you again soon,' he said to the waiter as he passed. No response. Just a look, somewhere between apprehension and confusion.

Ryker opened the door and stepped out. He headed right, walking casually along the street as he slipped a cap over his head. He pushed his hands into his jacket pockets and carried on. The row of shops soon came to an end and gave way to dilapidated and mostly derelict industrial units. There were few people around. A hundred yards from the café, Ryker ducked off the street and into an alley. He looked out, back up the road. Stood and waited. And waited.

Twenty minutes passed. No one went in or out of the café in that time. Several pedestrians sauntered past him, though he received only a few disinterested glances.

Anonymous. Again.

It was more than half an hour before anyone emerged from Mehmet's. Ryker watched as the three young men headed out, one after the other, Tufan now in the middle. Once they were all outside they congregated for a moment, chatting, lighting up cigarettes, before they set off. In Ryker's direction.

Ryker pulled back into the alley. The men passed by, oblivious to Ryker's presence. He leaned out and watched them heading away, and when he was satisfied they were at a safe distance, he set off in tow.

Less than five minutes later the men had led Ryker on a traipse through what were surely some of the least salubrious parts of the least salubrious parts of the East End. They ended up on a narrow lane with more potholes than tarmac, lined on either side with derelict, industrial, grey-brick buildings that loomed high. Ryker waited at the top of the lane in the doorway to one of the buildings and watched as Tufan and the others carried on.

The lane was a dead end. At least, as far as Ryker could tell there was no through road in sight. But there was a building. Smaller and with two storeys, it looked like some kind of old workshop with a plain door as a side entrance and a much larger metal roller door that was currently pulled down. Above that door was a faded sign that Ryker couldn't make out.

The men reached the property and stopped. They milled for

a few moments until there was a loud clunk and then rattle as the roller door lifted. Ryker took his phone out and as discreetly as he could, he snapped away, though at this distance he'd be lucky to get a decent glimpse of anything from the pictures. What he could tell was that the building wasn't empty. There was racking and tooling all over – a garage perhaps? And a fourth man inside who Ryker didn't recognise, not from so far away.

Ryker expected Tufan and the others to disappear inside. Instead, all four men remained waiting. Then the sound of a high-powered car engine caused Ryker to jolt. He swung his head to the left to see a hulking Mercedes SUV pull into the lane.

Ryker threw himself back as far as he could, up against the padlocked door to the building. The Mercedes shot past, its dark glass making it impossible for Ryker to tell if anyone inside had spotted him. He didn't move for several seconds as he strained his ears. The Mercedes came to a stop. The engine was shut down. Doors opened then closed.

Ryker risked a peek.

Three more men had arrived. All tall and stocky, suited up like nightclub bouncers. Even from so far away Ryker knew these men meant business by the way Tufan and the other youngsters looked sunken now, tails between their legs, their previous bravado on the wane.

Of the three men who'd emerged from the Mercedes, one stepped forward to Tufan. As he did so he fleetingly glanced over his shoulder. It was enough for Ryker to catch a glimpse of his face.

Enough to realise this was the very man Ryker had come to find. Yunus Akkan.

17

The exchange outside the garage continued, though Ryker couldn't hear, or even read the mood of the conversation from such distance. Akkan remained facing away from Ryker, though the other two from the Mercedes, standing guard, were looking this way and that, and frequently back toward where Ryker was standing. He was sure he hadn't been spotted yet, but if he stayed where he was, there was a good chance he would be as the Mercedes left. Plus, at this distance Ryker couldn't hear a thing, and he was too far away to take any useful pictures.

It was time to get a closer look.

Ryker fished in his pocket and seconds later was picking the rusting padlock securing the door he was standing by. The mechanism would have been easy enough had it not been so weathered and he had to jerk and tug with force to get the pins released. Doing so wasn't exactly silent, and every few seconds he peeped out to the group further down the lane. The conversation was still in flow, giving no indication they had become aware of Ryker's presence.

Finally the lock popped and Ryker creaked the door open as quietly as he could. A waft of dusty air burst into his face as he slunk in through the narrow gap and closed the door behind him.

He paused as his eyes adjusted to the darkened space. Whatever building this was, or had been, he hadn't come in through the main entrance, but what looked like a little-used service entrance or even fire escape – there was nothing in front of him but a mottled concrete floor and a ditto staircase.

Ryker headed for the stairs and climbed all the way up to the fourth and top floor. He eased open a door that led onto a narrow and dark corridor. Rough carpet underfoot, a series of doors off to his left and right. Ryker carried on, peering in through the mostly glazed doors as he headed to the far end of the building adjacent to the garage.

It was apparent that this place wasn't derelict at all. Rooms were filled with all manner of clutter; mainly boxes and old-looking office equipment. While the building was decrepit, this floor at least was being used as some sort of storage dump, it seemed.

Ryker carried on along the corridor until he reached the final door on the left. He tried the handle. Unlocked. He pushed the door open, then crept into the dank space. A box room. Metal racking covered two walls and was filled with dusty computer equipment – desktop towers, keyboards, monitors. Had someone just left this stuff here and forgotten about it?

Ryker moved to the warped and paint-peeling sash window which had a rusting steel grate on the outside of it. He crouched down, just far enough to have a view of the gathering still in flow below.

Even through the glass Ryker could hear their voices more clearly now, was even able to make out some of the words, though he was pretty sure they weren't speaking English. He could see that the building they were standing in front of was indeed a garage, and more cavernous than he had previously realised. The vaulted roof stretched a good fifty yards, and from his point of view, several vehicles, in various states of repair or modification or strip-out, were visible.

Ryker took out his phone and began snapping again. Over the next couple of minutes he got good clear pictures of all seven of the men's faces. Every now and then Tufan and his chums would break into smiles at something Akkan said, though it seemed forced, and their discomfort – or wariness at least – remained apparent.

Then the conversation took a turn. The faces of the young men dropped. One of Tufan's crew rattled off an angry flurry of words, gesticulating as he did so. Even though he hadn't been the focus of the tirade, Tufan seemed to take offence at this, turned and threw his fist into his friend's gut. The young man doubled over. A knee went down onto the ground, his head bowed as he tried to regain his breath.

Tufan looked to Akkan as if asking whether his friend had been punished enough for whatever error he'd made. Akkan's verbal response was less than friendly. Akkan's two bouncers strode over and grabbed the young man under his arms and hauled him upright.

What the hell were they going to do with him now?

Akkan nodded over to the garage. His bouncers nodded in turn and began to drag the man there.

A clattering noise echoed through the air. Ryker jerked back, away from the window just as all eyes turned his way. He held his breath. He hadn't made the noise, but was sure it had come from the building he was in.

After a few seconds of silence, Ryker was about to poke his head up above the parapet when he heard another noise. Not as loud or distinct now. Shuffling. Footsteps?

Ryker didn't risk a peek outside. Instead, staying low, he moved back toward the doorway. He poked his head out to look along the corridor. No one there. He stayed on the spot, looking and listening. He was sure he hadn't imagined the sound before, but all was eerily silent now. Ryker stayed there for only a few seconds more. Whatever the noise was – an occupant downstairs , or even just a rat – he was sure there was no one on this floor, and he was more concerned to find out what the group outside were doing now.

Ryker edged back through the room to the window. No one was in sight, and the roller door slammed shut just as he glanced across. The Mercedes's engine purred into life. So not all of the men had headed into the garage. Then the car swung around and the revs peaked as it shot off down to the end of the lane. Ryker cursed under his breath. There was no way he could follow the car, though he at least had another registration plate to trace.

Ryker pulled away from the window, and even more cautiously than when he'd arrived, headed back along the corridor to the stairwell, tense and alert for any sound, any movement. He saw and heard nothing.

Outside in the lane he looked left and right. Deserted.

Should he go closer to the garage, have a look around?

He was about to when a police car edged into view at the end of the alley. What the hell? Just a random patrol? Ryker was already in view of the car's occupants, so he took what he believed was the most sensible option and walked toward it, away from the garage.

He'd found Akkan, but most likely the boss had headed away in that car, and there was no point in drawing the attention of the police, why ever they were here. Akkan would be back, and so would Ryker.

The passenger in the police car momentarily caught his eye, but moments later the car had edged out of view, and by the time Ryker was at the end of the alley, it was nowhere to be seen.

He pulled to a stop again to look around him, still in two minds as to whether he was done here or not. The road remained quiet – why would any pedestrian come this way? Yet down the street, beyond the lane with the garage, and poking out of an adjacent road, was the nose of a white van. The other way, about the same distance from him, two men stood in the doorway of a crappy-looking red-brick building, casually smoking.

That made up his mind. He would be back for Akkan soon enough, but these men... that van... Ryker wanted to know what was going on.

He crossed the road, his eyes flitting between the two men on one side of him, and the white van on the other. The engine wasn't on, but someone was in the driver's seat. Ryker couldn't see the person's face.

He flicked his gaze back to the two men the other way. One of them quickly looked from Ryker and to the ground, then gave a forced laugh as though his mate had said something funny.

Ryker decided they were the best bet. He set off toward them, walking with purpose. He was soon closing in, and with each step he took, the two men – were they the same two as he'd seen near Maria's house? – seemed to tense a little more, as though undecided about their next move.

When he was only ten yards away the men stubbed out their cigarettes, turned their backs on Ryker and walked off.

As before, whoever these spies were, they were hardly inconspicuous – so what was their game? Ryker increased his pace a little. A diesel engine rattled to life behind him. The van? Ryker glanced over his shoulder. No, the van was nowhere to be seen.

Up front, the men were increasing their pace to stay ahead of Ryker, though they hadn't once looked back to check on him. As though he was of no concern. Other than the fact that they were walking away, there was certainly no panic or alarm that they'd been made.

The men took a left turn, then soon after, a right. Ryker was still ten paces from them. They were approaching another junction and it was impossible to tell yet which way they intended to go, though he knew that if they carried on along this route they'd soon be heading into a more populated area. Was that a good thing?

Ryker contemplated bursting into a sprint to close in on them and knock them to the ground. It'd be the quickest way of ending this farce and figuring out who they were.

He was seriously considering it when he heard the revving diesel engine somewhere in the near distance. Seconds later the white van burst into view at the junction up ahead and came to a rocking stop. The side door slid open and the men raced forward.

Ryker sprinted too.

The men jumped into the back. The van was already moving as the door was slid shut again.

Ryker could do nothing, too far away to lunge forward and make any attempt to either stop the men, the van or whatever. He growled in frustration as he came to a stop, and watched the van shoot off into the distance.

Then he frowned. A different registration to the van he'd seen just moments earlier. Which meant that there was more than one vehicle tailing him.

What the hell was going on?

Ryker hesitated for only a few seconds. One thing he did know: he wouldn't find answers by going home.

He turned to head back to the garage.

18

Two days. Two long days since Haan had sat at that computer screen in the car rental shop staring at a face she thought she'd never see again. Two long days during which she'd done her best to appear active in identifying a man she already knew.

But what was her endgame?

And what was Adam Wheeler doing here?

Barton was driving. Haan was staring out of the passenger window as the forest blasted by. Neither of them had said a word to the other for nearly an hour, pretty much since they'd left the train station at Stuttgart, the nearest metropolis to Fischer's home.

Haan had never believed that Stuttgart was where Wheeler would have fled to. Wheeler was from England – which itself was intriguing, and the heist team being English hadn't so far been considered by Fischer's team. After escaping Fischer's home, Wheeler was much more likely to have travelled by car or van to the nearby French border so he was at least out of the country and away from any immediate efforts of the German police. The German police, who still had no clue there'd been an incident. But Wheeler wasn't to know that and may well have believed that they were his biggest threat.

Unless Wheeler knew exactly what type of a person Fischer really was.

Still, France was Haan's best guess. The sensible thing for Wheeler would be to lay low in France for a few days, until finally making the trip back to England – if he ever dared.

Stuttgart, though, was a well-connected city. Trains, planes. If you wanted to get away from the area fast, Stuttgart was the best point to do it from. Which was why Haan had planted the idea for Barton to persuade Chester that it was worth trekking there. After all, Chester had a close acquaintance within the Stuttgart Stadtpolizei who was able to help them gain access to the train station's CCTV cameras through (semi-) official channels.

But to no avail. There'd been no sign of Wheeler arriving into Stuttgart at any point, or of him making an escape on the train network through there. Because he had never been there in the first place.

'There's always the airport,' Barton said.

Had he really taken that long to think of that?

'Our guy is running, on his own,' Haan said. 'Flying is by far the hardest form of travel when you're on the run.'

Then, as Barton humphed, she wondered fleetingly whether it *was* worth putting some effort in checking the airport, just to provide further delay.

But then, why was she delaying at all? It wasn't as if she owed Wheeler a thing.

Perhaps she should just turn all focus to France. That was the best bet. Wheeler had gone to France – and he'd come into Germany from France. Most likely he'd have come to the Black Forest by car or van, which, from England, meant the Euro-tunnel or a ferry. Yet he wouldn't have come to the Black Forest in an English-plated right-hand drive car. Too obvious once he was driving around Western Europe. Which meant he'd have rented another vehicle close to either the Eurotunnel terminal or ferry port to take him to the Black Forest. Searching that area was the first step. Finding when and how he'd come to Europe, and following his movements from there and into the Black Forest, second.

Of course, Barton and the others weren't yet thinking about that, because they didn't know the missing link to the heist team had come from England.

Haan shook her head. Too much.

She bunched her fists to channel energy and glanced over at Barton, worried that he'd somehow been a party to her thoughts.

Barton took no notice of her. Just carried on weaving the car along the bumpy track.

Not long after and they arrived outside the gates to Fischer's mansion. Barton wound down his window and typed the code into the PIN pad then placed his thumb onto the reader. The pad flashed green before the brushed-metal gates silently slid out of sight into a cavity in the outer wall.

Haan's heart thudded a little harder in her chest when, after Barton pulled past the gates, she spotted the dark-blue helicopter sitting on the grass.

Fischer was home.

That was all Haan needed.

Barton pulled up in one of the staff parking bays at the side of the house, out of sight from the front, and the two of them headed back toward the main entrance. Two sentries stood guard there. Not an everyday necessity before the break-in, but since then, Fischer – or was it Chester? – had insisted on additional security. Most of these new guys were just hired help, from local security firms, guys who were more used to guarding commercial premises through long and boring nights. They weren't part of the core team. Not part of the elite, either in their training or their remit.

'*Guten Tag,*' Barton said with a nod to the two lumps. Neither smiled, though they stepped aside without question and Barton input his credentials into the keypad on the door. He and Haan stepped into the cool air-conditioned interior.

'Want me to check on the basement?' Barton said.

'No. He's fine down there,' Haan said. 'We were told to wait until tomorrow, that's what we do.'

The poor sod was barely clinging onto life. He was on a drip, under twenty-four-hour watch in case of the need for further medical intervention, but Haan really didn't see how they'd ever get anything useful out of him now, even if they kept him breathing. Had Barton been given free rein, the guy would have been dead already.

That certainly would have been a kinder fate.

'So what now then?' Barton asked.

Haan didn't get a chance to answer. Kathy Chester pounced. She slid into view from the corridor to the right of the winding marble stairs, gliding high on four-inch heels. Her tight-fitting skirt-suit clung to her body in all the right places. Ultra-effort, even for her. Well, the boss was around after all.

'You're back,' Chester said, glancing at her watch as if to say *where the hell have you been*?

'We are.'

'Anything? Though I'm presuming if there was, you would have called.'

'Not really, we–'

'Actually, hold it there.' Chester held a hand up. 'You can fill in me and Mr Fischer together. He wants to talk to you anyway.'

The way she said it did not bode well. Haan's stomach tightened a little.

'Of course,' she acquiesced.

Chester spun. Haan and Barton made to follow her. Chester stopped and waved dismissively at Barton.

'Not you.'

Barton opened his mouth to retort, but said nothing as he sulkily headed off.

'Come on,' Chester said to Haan before turning.

Haan gulped, then set off in tow.

19

Haan followed Chester along the corridor, past room six – the little-used yet gargantuan sitting room where she'd instinctively gutted one of the intruders three nights ago. Despite her misgivings about the brutal treatment of the captive in the basement, and about the involvement of Adam Wheeler, she didn't feel bad about killing that guy. Who knows what he'd have done to her if she hadn't acted so swiftly and decisively? He'd brought it on himself.

But then, wasn't that the same for Wheeler? Why was she protecting him? Or was she only protecting herself?

They carried on working their way through the mansion, not a further word spoken between them. Haan was reminded of all those gangster movies she'd watched when she was younger. The betrayer being escorted to see the boss. Sometimes their fate was already known, sometimes they were there under false pretences, but in either case there was nothing they could do to escape the inevitable ambush when they walked through the door into the don's lair.

Finally, they came to the very last door in the corridor. The one that led into Fischer's prized library. Chester knocked.

'Come in,' came the call from the other side.

Fischer. Even in those two words his voice was sharp and commanding, full of confidence, though not overbearing. Chester opened the door and stepped to the side to let Haan through first.

Haan's body was tense as she moved forward. Her eyes flicked left and right as she stepped over the threshold. She wanted to feel relief when she realised Fischer was alone in the room, but she wouldn't feel relaxed just yet. Not when the air of deceit was so thick.

Behind her, the door closed with a thunk. Chester moved over to one of the floor-to-ceiling bookcases at the side of the room and propped herself up.

'Nice to see you, Daisy.' Fischer smiled firmly, yet pretty convincingly.

Such was his style. For all Fischer's unabashed confidence, arrogance, and hard-nosed business dealings, he wasn't a bulldog. At least to the outside world, he was charming and cordial, always had been whenever Haan had met him. Yet she knew the truth, knew what really went on behind closed doors, and because of that, his outward niceties took on a whole other-worldly ghastliness.

'Please, take a seat,' Fischer said.

Haan tentatively crossed the room and sat in a black velvet armchair opposite Fischer's plush, ruby-coloured, wingback leather armchair.

In his fifties, Fischer was clean-shaven with a tanned face and cropped light-brown hair that was barely greying or receding. He was smartly-dressed, though there was a casual air about his whole persona. His deep-blue eyes were fixed on Haan. She suppressed a shiver, and tried to avoid his eyes by looking around the room.

The library was like something out of an 18th century grand

country mansion, with wood-panelled walls and sturdy, built-in, dark-wood bookcases filled with all manner of books from new to old. Very, very old, in some cases. And probably very, very expensive.

The most interesting thing about this room, though, was the bookcase over by where Chester was standing. Because the first four books on the fifth shelf up weren't books at all. They were a false panel with a switch. That switch enabled the whole left-hand side of the bookshelf to swing open and reveal a metal door which led to the anteroom for Fischer's vault. The same anteroom where the man in the basement had found himself trapped when the heist had gone so badly wrong.

What lay in the vault itself... that was something Haan was not privy to. She could only imagine the treasures – art, jewellery, bullion – given the effort put into keeping that place locked up and secure.

Fischer gestured to the shiny mahogany coffee table between them upon which sat a cafetière with a single cup and saucer, and a tumbler of what looked like Scotch.

'Would you like a drink?' he asked, his knowing eyes still firmly fixed on Haan. His smooth English had a clear Germanic twang to it, like a baddy from a 1980s action flick.

'I'm fine, thank you.'

There were a few moments of awkward silence. At least, for Haan. Fischer held her eye.

'I hear you've been having issues getting to the bottom of who robbed me,' Fischer said.

'We will get there.' Haan winced.

Robbed. Not tried to rob. Haan was one of the few people who'd now been let in on the truth. She'd since been told that while the looters hadn't achieved the aim of getting into the vault, where much of Fischer's physical wealth was stored, they had managed to break into a safe in the master bedroom, taking with them nothing but pieces of paper.

However, these were pieces of paper upon which were printed several dozen strings of digits and numbers. Seemingly random, those strings of digits and numbers equated to the IDs for cryptocurrency wallets that held virtual assets to the tune of more than two hundred million dollars.

Two hundred million dollars now missing.

'I remember when I first interviewed you for this role,' Fischer said. He leaned forward and took the tumbler in his hand, sipped, and placed it back down again. 'I'll admit, I was a little wary.'

Haan's eyes narrowed. 'You were?'

'Too good to be true. You know the saying.'

'Yeah.'

'That was my immediate thought.'

He leaned back in his chair. His demeanour was slowly changing, second by second. The usual outer cheer was dropping away, replaced by something more flat and stoic.

'You don't have anything to say?'

Haan looked around to Chester, who was at the bookcase, arms folded as she glared at Haan.

'I'm sorry you felt that way.'

He sniffed. 'My point is that here was a young woman who had everything I needed. Well educated, speaks five languages fluently, you were a martial arts champion at nine years old, spent several years in the army before becoming a close-protection security specialist. You had the brain, the training, and you'd been there and done it all.'

'You're saying those are bad things?' Haan asked.

'Absolutely not. What I said was it was too good to be true. And when I met you that first time... I mean, wow, you're a striking young woman too. You're articulate, engaging.'

'A hell of a lot of flattery.'

Haan's slightly snarky tone elicited a hint of a smile from Fischer but his seriousness soon returned.

'I couldn't quite believe it,' Fischer stated. 'You even had that dark streak to you that's so important for a boss as unflinching as Kathy.'

Something of a snide look from Fischer now. Well, of course, all of Chester's team had to have a dark streak to them. Just look at some of the things she got them to do.

'If I'd asked someone to come up with the perfect candidate, every single attribute I could possibly need for my personal security team, then you, Daisy Haan, would be it.'

'I'm sensing this isn't actually a good thing, though,' Haan said.

'It is, and it isn't. Seriously, it's almost as if you were put together specifically for this role. A perfect fit, some kind of manufactured robot.'

He smiled at his own words. Haan didn't find his challenge remotely funny, and the hard look on her face showed it. And concealed the worry curdling her insides as to where Fischer was going with this.

'And you must know how thoroughly we screen potential new recruits. After all, that's an area you now take an active role in yourself.'

'I do.'

'And I hear you're damned good with computers. Hacking, researching.'

'One of my many talents.'

'Indeed. So I'm sure you'll be a huge help as we try to trace my missing money.'

Haan briefly looked to Chester again. 'You know I will. But you'll also know cryptocurrency transactions can be nearly impossible to trace to individuals without additional indicators.'

Fischer rolled his eyes. 'But nearly impossible is not the same thing as impossible is it?'

'No. It's not.'

'Good. Back to my point, do you know what we found when we screened you?'

'Nothing you didn't like, I'm presuming, seeing as I got the job.'

'Apparently so.'

Fischer paused the bizarre conversation as he sipped from his coffee cup. He held Haan's eye the whole time.

'I paid a visit to our friend,' Fischer said when his cup was drained.

His comment hung in the air. Seconds passed, each one more uncomfortable than the last.

'Which friend?' Haan said eventually.

'Downstairs. What a mess.'

'Him, or the situation?'

'Both. Not a nice thing to see.'

He shook his head solemnly.

'We are doing everything we can to figure out who those intruders were,' Haan said.

'Oh, absolutely, I'm sure you will. It's just that I heard... no, it's best not to spread tittle-tattle.'

He looked away. Pure nonchalance.

'Sorry?' Haan's hackles raised – exactly as she was sure he'd intended. She couldn't give a crap who Fischer was, she wouldn't sit there with all these unspoken accusations, even if a growing part of her was terrified at where the conversation was going. 'I'm working my ass off trying to get results for–'

'You are? Oh. Okay.' He shrugged. 'Well, that's great. A woman with your experience, your capabilities, I mean... the biggest surprise to me, the biggest *problem*, is that we're now more than forty-eight hours after the event and you have the grand total of piss all to show for it.'

Haan gritted her teeth, but kept silent. Now his barriers were down. Was this the real Bastian Fischer? The one the general public never got to see?

'Which makes me wonder. *Why* haven't we got any results yet? What are you not doing that you should be doing?'

'I'm not sure what you were told, but we have plenty of results. We know our runner's face. We're searching for a name that fits. Same for the rest of his crew, but it does take time to do this quietly, and believe me, it's much harder to check these things, even through our channels, when we're using photos of corpses.'

Fischer looked from Haan to Chester now, as though Haan's response was a little unexpected. But which part?

There was a buzzing sound over by Chester. Haan glanced over to see her lifting her phone from her suit pocket.

'Sorry, just give me a minute.'

She turned and moved to the corner of the room as she answered. Haan switched her gaze back to Fischer who was now giving her a hard glare. Neither of them said a word, and the knot in Haan's stomach continued to build. Even though Fischer was hardly being direct in whatever accusations he was trying to lay on Haan, she reckoned her chances of walking out of this mansion alive were diminishing by the minute.

But why now?

'Great work,' Chester said into the phone as she came over to Fischer's side. He looked up at her expectantly as she ended the call and pulled the phone from her ear. She stared at the screen.

'We have a result,' Chester told Fischer. 'Our runner.'

She looked at Haan. More of a glare really. A ping on her phone.

'Here he is,' she said, turning the screen and holding it out for Fischer. 'Adam Wheeler. British national.'

Fischer took the phone, his eyes fixed firmly on what was no doubt a profile picture of Wheeler.

Chester shot Haan another look. 'This didn't come through the face recognition request,' she said.

'No?' Fischer said.

He and Chester shared another look. What on earth? So how had they found Wheeler? What did Chester have going that Haan wasn't part of?

After a few moments, Fischer handed the phone back then fixed his gaze on Haan once more.

'Adam Wheeler,' he said. 'Does that name mean anything to you?'

'No,' Haan lied. 'But I'll get onto finding him straight away.'

'You do that,' Fischer said. Haan got to her feet. 'But, Daisy? It's time to convince me just how good you are. Because you know what happens around here to people who make mistakes.'

20

Ryker was surprised when he turned back into the lane to see two vehicles parked outside the garage. The same Mercedes that he was sure he'd witnessed leave minutes earlier, plus a dark-grey Range Rover.

His mind flitted back to the scene on Monday morning when Parker had been whisked away. Two Range Rovers, both pristine black. One of those Range Rovers had crashed and was now in the custody of the Met. Or MI5. The other Range Rover was still missing. Was it possible this was the same one? A quick respray and change of plates to make it useable?

As Ryker carried on toward the garage, he took a couple of pictures of the vehicles. When he reached the Mercedes he stared through the windscreen to the bottom corner of the dashboard. The VIN number was clearly visible. Ryker took a picture. He moved over to the Range Rover. Looked in the same position. This time the VIN was blacked out.

'What are you doing?'

Ryker spun around to see a man standing at the now open side door to the garage. The same man who'd come from inside earlier, to greet Tufan and his friends. Ryker peeled away from the Range Rover and moved toward him.

'I need my car fixed.'

The man looked dubious, and his eyes flicked from Ryker to the street beyond.

'What car?'

'It's broken down.'

'We're not a recovery service.'

'Then what are you?'

Ryker was now only five steps from the man. He paused. The man was clearly wary. Why hadn't he run back inside to raise the alarm?

'We're a private business. We only deal with clients we know.'

'Like Yunus Akkan?'

Now the man screwed up his face. 'Who the fu–'

Ryker drove forward and grabbed the man around the neck. He swept his legs away, spun him around, sunk down and pulled him into a sleeper hold. Ryker squeezed and held on tight as the man writhed and spluttered, the pressure on his carotid artery starving his brain of oxygen. The man's legs scrabbled on the ground. Within seconds his movements became sluggish...

He went limp. Unconscious.

Ryker glanced along the street. No one to be seen. He dragged the man over the threshold and closed the door softly behind him. With two cable-ties from his pocket, he hog-tied the man. If he woke up, he'd be able to shout out, but at least he wouldn't be able to run for help.

Ryker straightened up. He was in a corridor, with three doors leading from it on the right and one at the far end. His heart rattled in his chest, his breathing a little heavier than before the one-sided altercation. He took a few moments to compose himself.

Muffled voices in the distance. Beyond the door at the end of the corridor, which was slightly ajar – the door to the garage, he thought.

Then another noise. Not muffled at all. A man shouting. Howling in pain.

Ryker cautiously moved forward. Another pain-filled shout. This time followed by laughter. Then a booming, anger-filled voice.

Ryker passed the first door on his right. A kitchen. Second door. Office. No one inside. All the while the sounds from the garage were getting louder and louder. He passed by the final door on the right. Another office space, empty. The garage door was only a few yards in front of him now.

Ryker glanced over his shoulder. The bound man lay unmoving by the front door. That was good. Ryker continued moving. He soon came to the last door, that was open all of three inches. He pulled up against the wall. Then peeped through the gap. He could see nothing but shelving and car parts.

He reached forward tentatively and pushed the door open three more inches. A scream of pain caused him to freeze. Steeling himself against what he was about to see, he moved his head into the widened gap.

His eyes fell upon the bundle on the floor covered with a bloodied tarpaulin. It didn't take a genius to figure out what lay beneath.

Ryker pushed his head another inch inside. Saw three men on their feet with their backs to him. They were gathered over a workbench of sorts.

A workbench upon which lay a man. Naked.

His skin glistened red. His head... little could be seen of it because it was stuck between the jaws of an industrial vice.

One of the men rotated the vice's lever a half-turn and there was a sickening cry of pain.

Ryker tensed. Then the man at the workbench took a side-step. Ryker's eyes widened. Two more men were now in view. One was glaring down in disgust at the man in the vice.

Yunus Akkan.

In front of him, on his knees, hands tied behind him, blood covering his cloak of tattoos... Tufan.

His weary eyes flicked up. He spotted Ryker. There was a pause as both men eyeballed each other. Ryker didn't contemplate running. Yes, it was best to avoid confrontation if possible, but he wasn't about to run off to save his own backside while two young men were tortured to death. Only two men, because Ryker was sure the third, under the tarpaulin, was already dead.

Tufan opened his mouth, and bellowed like a strangled cat.

21

Ryker burst into the room. He grabbed the first thing he could reach from a shelf to his left. A weighty monkey wrench. That would do.

Two yards in and Akkan had spotted Ryker. Infuriated, Akkan backstepped, dragging Tufan in front of him as a cover. Akkan's three minions had all turned to Ryker. One began shuffling back too. Whether to protect the boss or because he wasn't up to this, Ryker didn't know, and he didn't care.

The remaining two...

Both big. Both ham-fisted. Both snarling and snapping like angry dogs. The one on the left reached behind him and pulled a handgun from the back of his jeans. Ryker raced forward, and in the second before the gunman could fire, arced his arm back and hurled the wrench.

As the tool spun through the air, the gunman ducked and threw up his arm. The wrench clattered into his forearm. Ryker smashed into the man, took him off his feet like an NFL lineman, and slammed him into the concrete floor.

The gun clanked away.

Ryker lifted his arm and threw his fist down onto the man's throat. The guy's eyes bulged as he rasped for breath. Ryker hit him in the same spot again.

He was about to jump to his feet when he realised the third guy, the one backstepping with his boss, was now pointing a gun at Ryker.

Too late to attack him.

Ryker grabbed the choking guy he was on top of and rolled them both over just as the gun was fired. Three shots boomed. The man's body pulsed as the bullets tore into him. Luckily his frame was thick enough to stop the bullets boring through and into Ryker.

But Ryker knew he needed to act before the guy had unloaded the whole magazine.

The loose gun was right next to Ryker. He reached out, grabbed it. Took aim and fired. A leg shot sent the gunman down. The next shot caught him in the shoulder. Ryker adjusted and fired at the last of the goons who was racing toward him, knife in hand.

Wrong weapon for this fight, which was no doubt why he'd chosen not to attack already.

Ryker fired again. Two more shots. One to the knee, the other in the gut. The latter wasn't Ryker's intention, but the guy had twisted too much from the first shot.

Ryker heaved the now dead lump off him. Blood smeared onto his own jacket and jeans as he did so. He hauled himself to his feet. The other two men, still alive, were on the ground, groaning in pain. Ryker didn't put them out of their misery. No need. They wouldn't be getting up any time soon.

He looked over to Akkan. A few yards further away now. No gun. But he did have a knife in his hand. He still looked angry. Tufan, at his feet, looked petrified.

'Probably best if you put that down, don't you think?' Ryker said as he knelt down and grabbed first the knife, and then the gun from the fallen men. He tossed the knife and emptied the gun of its remaining ammunition before stuffing the weapon into his jacket.

'You're dead.' Akkan's accent was thick, his voice dripped with hate. 'My people will tear the skin from your face.'

'Is that before or after you put my head in a vice?'

Akkan growled but didn't respond. Pointing the loaded gun at Akkan, Ryker stepped over to the workbench and turned the handle two, three, four times. The man on the bench barely moved as the pressure on his head was released. His body quivered as he struggled to find the strength to breathe. Perhaps it was already too late for him.

'You like torturing kids?' Ryker turned back to Akkan, trying to keep his bubbling rage under control.

'Kids? You know nothing.'

'Actually, I figure I know a fair bit. But I'm hoping you can fill in the blanks.'

A burst of movement from Akkan. But it wasn't a move on Ryker. Instead, he grabbed Tufan, hauled him up and placed the knife against his throat.

'Really?' Ryker said.

He acted calm, disinterested, as if he couldn't care less if Akkan slit Tufan's throat, though he was determined to get the young man out of here alive if he could.

Ryker knelt back down by the two writhing goons. A pistol-whip to the skull of each quietened them down a bit, and made the task of hog-tying them all the more easy.

When Ryker straightened up again, Akkan had a curious look on his face. As though he couldn't understand what to do about Ryker's nonchalance.

'Put the knife down and let him go,' Ryker ordered.

Akkan didn't respond.

'I get it,' Ryker said. 'The kids fucked up. They were supposed to bring Parker to you, quietly, but you had no idea Parker was under surveillance.'

Still not a word from Akkan, though the twitching in his face showed that Ryker was bang on.

'I was there,' Ryker added. 'In the square. And I'm the reason one of their cars crashed.' He looked down to Tufan. 'I'm sorry your friends are dead.'

Akkan was shaking his head in disgust.

'The police, MI5 too, are all over this now. You're trying to cut ties. You want to make these kids disappear so the trail doesn't lead back to you. But first you want to make them suffer, and to understand how they messed up. Were they supposed to get Yedlin too? Except this mess wasn't their fault. And you're too late. I'm already here.'

Ryker took a step closer to Akkan who shuffled back a little, but he was already nearly upon the front end of a car under repair, nowhere left to go from there. Ryker stepped forward again.

'What I don't understand, and what I need you to tell me, is why Parker. Where were you taking him? Who was paying you?'

Akkan looked a little smug now. 'Like I said, you know nothing.'

'Then it's about time you started talking.'

Ryker lifted the gun. He was about to fire a shot. Although Akkan thought he was covered by Tufan, there was plenty of the big man left for Ryker to aim at. But he didn't fire. Instead he stood and listened.

A car engine. Perhaps more than one. Then doors opening. Footsteps. Talking. Purposeful.

Backup.

Ryker glared at Akkan. How had they got an alert out?

It didn't matter. What mattered was that Ryker had already

had enough odds-against action recently. The longer this went on, the more people wound up dead, and the greater the chance that he was one of them.

So it didn't take him long to decide what to do next. He squeezed the trigger, and fired a single shot.

22

The bullet nicked the outside of Tufan's arm on its trajectory toward Akkan, who wasn't so lucky. The bullet sank into his side, he jolted, and the knife came away from Tufan's throat.

Ryker rushed forward. Tufan was falling to the deck. With his hands tied it would be a painful contact for his face, but Ryker ignored him. Instead he raced to Akkan, who was hunched over, trying to recover. Ryker wound back and delivered a ferocious uppercut that sent the hefty Akkan up into the air and to the floor with a thud. The knife flew from his grip.

Outside, the voices were louder and more angry, followed by banging on the roller door. The metal shook and quivered.

Ryker looked over to the side door he'd come through. Still open. He strode over, stuffing the gun into his jeans and grabbing an iron crowbar as he went. He kicked the door shut.

Then he moved over to the nearest racking on the adjacent wall. He climbed up the side. Two shelves, until he had enough height to lever the crowbar into the bracket holding the racking to the wall. He pulled, heaved and roared with effort, and the fitting came loose.

Ryker jumped down, dropped the crowbar and grabbed hold of the racking with both hands. He yanked back, knees bent, body stooped forward, using all of the muscles in his arms, shoulders and back.

There was a crash somewhere outside. The door next to Ryker was still closed, but was the backup already in the corridor?

Ryker heaved again and heard a crack as the remaining wall fixtures came loose. The racking lurched forward. He jumped back, out of the way as the steel frame and all its contents plummeted to the floor. He turned and threw an arm up to protect him as screws and rivets and all manner of small car parts clanked to the floor and burst through the air.

The ruckus was over within a couple of seconds. Ryker uncoiled and looked over to the door. Then jumped when the handle came down and the door was flung open.

Crack. It made it all of four inches before it smashed up against the fallen racking. No one was getting in through there.

The men behind the door were shouting and heckling. Baying for blood. They'd find another way in soon enough. Ryker needed to get away. Even if he called for backup now, it wouldn't arrive in time.

He caught a glimpse of movement in the corner of his eye. He turned to see a figure gunning for him. It took his surprised brain a beat to realise what he was seeing. Tufan, torso bloodied, racing toward Ryker, snarling, with a knife in his hand.

Tufan pulled back the knife, ready to slash. Ryker shimmied to the side, caught the arm midway between wrist and elbow and twisted. Tufan went down to his knees.

Ryker peeled the knife from Tufan's grip and, using the heel of his shoe, thumped Tufan onto the floor.

Ryker opened his mouth to say something. But what was there to say? Tufan was a world-class fool. Not only had he got himself mixed up in a scheme way beyond his aptitude and experience, but even after Akkan had been about to stick his head in a vice, even after Akkan had held a knife to his throat, he still wanted to be part of the crew, still saw Ryker as an enemy.

'Try that again, and next time you won't ever get up,' Ryker hissed before launching his foot into Tufan's side.

A gunshot rang out. Ryker ducked. The bullet fizzed and clanked as it ricocheted around.

Ryker spun. The gap in the doorway wasn't big enough for a man to fit through, but it was easily big enough for a gun barrel. At least from where he was positioned Ryker wasn't in the firing line. But across the other side of the room, Akkan was. Akkan, who was groggily trying to pull himself up. Akkan, who Ryker wasn't yet finished with.

Ryker pulled his gun back out and fired off the remaining bullets in the magazine as he rushed back to the fallen gangster. The covering fire gave him a few seconds. Ryker tossed the now empty gun, grabbed Akkan by the shoulders and dragged him behind the workbench, out of view of the door.

On top of the bench the tortured youth remained in position. He was no longer breathing.

More shouting from the door. More gunfire. Ryker instinctively ducked, even though he was in cover. But he couldn't stay here forever. The others would find a way in. The roller door was the most likely avenue.

Ryker looked down to Akkan. His face was still creased in anger, though it seemed he didn't have any real fight left in him. Ryker grabbed the back of Akkan's neck and dug his fingers into the bundle of nerves there. Akkan squirmed in pain. Ryker sunk his knuckles into the bleeding gunshot wound on Akkan's side. Akkan moaned as the flesh squelched under Ryker's force.

'Why Parker?' Ryker held Akkan's eye. Akkan squinted in agony. Ryker dug a little harder. 'Why Parker!'

A slight and slow shake of Akkan's head.

'You want me to put you up there?' Ryker nodded to the workbench. 'In your experience, how many turns does it take to get what you want?'

Akkan did now hold Ryker's eye. But he still said nothing.

Ryker pulled back his hand, balled his fist then thumped the wound on Akkan's side as hard as he could. Akkan shrieked.

'Who paid you!'

The roller door clattered. Ryker looked over. Still closed. Mere seconds now before Akkan's crew would come blasting through. Ryker didn't have time to sit trying to persuade the boss to talk. And despite his obvious pain, the gangster knew that.

Ryker looked behind him. At the back of the warehouse was a fire escape, but there was also a metal staircase leading up to a mezzanine level. A small office sat in the corner of that level. Ryker thought back to the previous day. When he'd been in the building opposite, spying on the garage from above. There was another fire escape at the top level. A metal gangway at roof height that connected to an adjacent almost identical warehouse behind this one. Perhaps that building was owned by Akkan or associates too, but regardless, it was a better option to go out across the top than to rush outside at ground level straight into a bunch of angry Turks with guns.

'We're going,' Ryker decided.

He grabbed Akkan under his armpits and hauled him up. Akkan deliberately pulled back his feet to fight him.

'Really?'

Ryker let go and shoved him down. Akkan's face smacked into the floor with a crunch and a squelch.

'Let's try again.'

Ryker grabbed him to pull him up and as Akkan's face

scraped up off the concrete, blood dribbled from his mouth and nose to a pool on the floor where a tooth now remained.

This time, Akkan did put his feet down, though he wasn't going to make it easy; Ryker grunted and strained as he dragged Akkan to the back of the warehouse. They were a yard away from the stairs when there was another clatter from the roller door. Ryker glanced over his shoulder. Still shut. But for how long?

'You won't... get away from here,' Akkan spluttered through laboured breaths and a mouthful of blood.

'If I don't, you don't.'

Ryker pulled Akkan to the first step. Akkan stumbled and went down and his shins smacked into the edge of the metal stair.

'Lift your feet properly or your bones'll be mush by the time we get to the top.'

Akkan seemed to realise his fighting would only result in more pain. Ryker pulled them both up and they were soon at the top. Off to their right, the office space. Dead in front, a short gangway leading to a door.

Was there a hit squad ready and waiting on the other side?

A crash down below. Then shouting, louder than before. But no onrush of footsteps. Ryker glanced behind. The roller door was six inches off the ground. They'd be inside within seconds.

Perhaps Akkan realised this, perhaps he didn't. Either way, Ryker thought it would help if he provided a quick reminder of what he wanted. A jab to the wound on Akkan's side did the trick and they were soon moving again.

They reached the door. A traditional fire escape with a push-down bar. Ryker leaned forward and depressed the bar and the door swung open.

An alarm blared.

Not the worst result in the world. How long before the fire brigade, or even the police arrived?

Another crash from down below. Ryker didn't turn to look this time. He dragged Akkan out into the open air where the rain was now pelting down in thick, heavy drops.

A half-flight of stairs faced them, leading to the top of the roof. Ryker stared across. Sure enough the suspended gangway led to the next building along, and then down to a similar fire escape door in that building. But beyond that was a row of terraces. Was it better to stay up here and try to make it across to the roofs of those buildings?

Ryker hauled Akkan up. When they reached the top Ryker looked to the street below. No sign of the crew. No one to take potshots at him. But he was overcome with doubt. How was he going to get away, particularly if he wanted to take Akkan with him? Whether Akkan realised this, or whether both men were simply drained, Ryker didn't know, but it was blindingly clear that the struggle to keep Akkan moving became harder with each step they took.

Ryker paused to catch his breath. He again looked down, beyond the gangway to the ground below.

'Tell me who paid you,' Ryker said.

He looked to Akkan. Was that a grin on his face? Ryker swung his arm back and launched his elbow into Akkan's face. The blow sent him sprawling to the metal. The whole structure wobbled and creaked.

'Tell me who paid you!' Ryker grabbed Akkan by the scruff of his neck.

A gunshot from behind Ryker. Then a flurry of shouts and footsteps. The men were inside. Within seconds they'd realise where Ryker was. Ryker couldn't take Akkan a step further. There wasn't time.

'Tell me!' Ryker snapped.

Akkan said nothing. Then he jolted.

Shit. Ryker heard the click-clack. A flick knife. Where had that been hidden?

Akkan pushed up and Ryker grimaced as the knife slashed across his arm. He reeled back as Akkan found the strength to rise to his feet, hunched down like a wrestler ready to attack.

He wound up to slash Ryker again, but Ryker burst forward and blocked the arm before the blade came anywhere near him. He barrelled into Akkan. Expected to take the boss off his feet. Instead they both remained upright, grappling, Akkan strong as an ox and still trying to stick the blade into Ryker.

Ryker heaved and shoved Akkan back against the four foot metal railing. The gangway swayed and shook. The railing creaked and strained.

Ryker pushed again, his whole concentration on the knife hand, desperately trying to keep the blade at bay. Another shove.

A shove too far.

The railing faltered. There was a snap and the metal rungs peeled away.

Momentum sent both men teetering...

Ryker let go. Akkan swooshed the knife through the air. The blade missed Ryker's neck by a fraction. Akkan wouldn't get another chance. The panicked look on his face said it all.

Ryker, still flying forward, reached out and grasped hold of the broken rail. Akkan had nothing to grasp. The knife came free, his hands flailed uselessly.

He plummeted down.

Ryker's grip slipped on the sopping wet metal. One hand came free and his body tumbled over the edge just as there was a sickening splat beneath him.

He reached out and caught the edge of the gangway. One hand. His fingers slipped... he threw his other hand up and somehow got a hold. He readjusted the grip of his first hand, and dangled there, both hands now holding on tight.

Groaning with effort, Ryker found the strength in his arms to heave his body back up. He rolled out onto the gangway and took a breath as he looked up to the sky, rain pounding down as he tried to compose himself.

He shuffled to his side and glanced down below. Akkan's body lay sprawled, his eyes gazing upward as blood wormed out from beneath him to join the puddles of rain around.

Inside the warehouse, the men's voices were very close, and that snapped Ryker back into focus.

He found the energy to jump back to his feet. Then he turned and ran.

23

Haan had no choice. Fischer and Chester wouldn't tolerate any further delay, and with Adam Wheeler's identity known, there was little she could do to stop the machine. At least she had no indication that Fischer, Chester, or anyone else knew of Haan's and Wheeler's shared past.

Could she keep it like that?

It had taken forty-eight hours to track Wheeler down to Frichebois, a small town less than twenty miles over the border into France. Haan's hunch had been right. Wheeler had been careful, but not careful enough. A CCTV camera on a main road out of Baden-Baden had captured a glimpse of Wheeler in the driver's seat of a van as he made his escape from the area not even twenty-four hours after the botched heist. A lot of digging and a bit of luck had shown that car entering France, and ultimately arriving in Frichebois.

They'd found that van, but without him in it. Wheeler could have since moved on, in another vehicle to another location, but after doing stake-outs around the town for all of twelve hours they'd spotted him.

A surprising mistake, in many ways. While Wheeler

undoubtedly had many talents, evading capture was clearly not his strongest point.

And so, having utilised little more than old school spying and tradecraft, here they were. Haan, Barton, and Klein, on the streets of Frichebois, stalking their prey.

Wheeler – dressed casually in jeans and a black jacket – was a little under six foot and of unremarkable build. Usually clean-shaven, he now had several days of messy stubble, mousy brown, as though he thought the basic change of appearance was going to help his predicament. About a hundred yards ahead of Haan, he was entering the vibrant farmers' market which was already in full swing on this warm, sunny morning. He was striding quickly, trying to appear calm, though Haan reckoned he knew he had a tail.

Did he expect to lose them in the chatter and bustle of the market?

Haan was soon within the crush too. People shuffled in every direction, no natural flow to the haphazard movements. Stall owners yelled out the natures of their fresh goods, their prices, while buyers jostled for position. Haan wormed her way through them, her pace painfully slow, but too much shoving and pushing would only cause a scene; there was no point in giving Wheeler the opportunity to scarper.

Up ahead, Wheeler was becoming more and more nervous, looking over his shoulder every other step. Haan checked the map on her phone. Where was he going?

She turned to Barton.

'Keep on him.'

Haan abruptly turned off to the left, heading around the back of the stalls where the pavement was more open and far less crowded. She ducked down an alley and was almost at a jog as she rushed around to try and intercept Wheeler. Moments later she emerged at the far side of the market. Stopped and looked around.

No sign of Wheeler. Had he already gone the other way?

No, there he was, looking nervous as hell as he came out of the crowds. With folded arms, Haan stared right at him. It only took a couple of seconds for him to clock her. By then, he was all of five paces away.

His eyes darted left and right. He glanced over his shoulder, then back the other way.

'Adam,' Haan said. Calm, yet purposeful. She paused and took a half step toward him. 'Don't run.'

Wheeler shuffled back, his body twisted so he was at an angle to her. A fighter's defensive pose, even though he surely wouldn't try to beat her at close combat.

'Why don't we get a drink?' She could tell he didn't know how to take that. 'You still owe me one, right?' She gave the smallest of smiles now. 'And we have so much to talk about.'

He shuffled back again. Edging closer to the crowds once more. Then he turned and he must have spotted Barton and Klein behind him because his face dropped even further.

'You've got nothing to say to me?' Haan asked. 'Come on, this way.'

She indicated to the café right next to where they were standing. Behind the glass front she could see a dozen tables inside. Half were taken. Regular-looking people drinking coffee, eating cakes and sandwiches. No trap in there. Haan wanted to do this quietly and quickly.

She moved first. When she did, Wheeler flinched, even though she'd only turned to take a couple of casual steps toward the door.

'Last chance, Adam.' Haan was stern now.

At the door, she turned to face him. One hand on the handle. The other pulled back, resting just above her hip. The butt of the concealed handgun inches from her fingers. He'd surely get the point.

'You either come inside and talk, or you force me to–'

'Okay,' he gave in.

They took seats by the window, away from other customers. A small and scratched wooden table, chairs opposite each other. Barton and Klein remained outside. Not too obvious, but obvious enough for Wheeler. He sat back in his chair, as though trying to keep his distance. Haan remained perched, one hand on the table, the other out of sight on her lap.

She briefly wondered what the patrons thought when they'd glanced at the two of them walking in. Just another couple out for a morning treat?

A young waitress came over and took their order. Wheeler's eyes never left Haan's. Despite her dark purpose of being here, seeing him sent her mind back in time. A time of innocence? No, not at all, yet completely different. They had undoubtedly changed, even if his pinched hazel eyes still drew her in like they had back then.

'You know it was a really shitty thing to do.' She was surreally placid, despite what she was about to do to him.

The man in the basement... that was brutal, but the trap they'd laid for Wheeler... something else indeed.

And it was all down to Haan. Yes, part of her hated what she was doing, but by and large, she knew it was the only way to get through this. She couldn't afford a slip-up. Not with Fischer scrutinising her every move.

'It was nothing personal,' Wheeler said. 'You know that.'

'Are we talking about the same thing here?' She offered him

a snide smile. 'I'm talking about you standing me up. How long ago was that?'

'Ten years. And I didn't stand you up.'

'No, you really did. After first using me for your own ulterior motive, I should say. You have a habit of using others?'

'You have a habit of working for scumbags.'

'Ouch.'

Except she wasn't hurt by that. Not in the slightest.

'You really tracked me down just to talk about our past?' Wheeler asked.

'So you do remember at least?'

'I remember.'

'Good. Yet you still haven't apologised.'

The waitress came over with the drinks. Haan glanced at her briefly. Her fresh face looked worried. Like she knew that something wasn't right with this picture. She left the coffees – both long and black – on the table, then hurried away.

'I heard about Liz,' Haan remarked.

Wheeler grit his teeth, anger rather than worry evident for the first time. Liz was Wheeler's wife. Dead wife. She'd died of cancer while he'd been stuck in prison.

'Heard about Liz? No, you didn't hear about it. Who would you have heard it from? You would have known nothing about what's happened to me for the last ten years. What you mean is you've been doing your homework on me. Spying. It's what you do.'

Haan's brain rumbled. What did he know? When planning the heist, had he realised that she was part of Fischer's team? Was that one of the reasons for his involvement?

'Still, I'm sorry. For her. For you. Your daughter.'

'I'm guessing you also know exactly where I was when she died.'

Haan nodded.

'Want to know how I ended up in there?'

'Not really.'

'Shame. Because that would help to explain why we're both here now.'

She shook her head. 'It's a bit late for that.'

'Is it? Don't you ever ask your–'

'I saw a movie the other day.'

They both paused. Wheeler waited for her to expand on her offbeat interjection. She took a slow sip from her cup. He still hadn't touched his.

'You saw a movie?' Wheeler said.

'*The Meg*. You heard of it?'

'We didn't get to watch many movies in jail.'

Haan shrugged. 'Anyway, it's about a damn big shark – a megalodon – terrorising the seas.'

'Sounds frightening.'

'Old-school monster movie. Our action-man hero, well he devises this ludicrous plan. Rather than sending a couple of massive torpedoes up this behemoth's behind and getting the whole thing over with quickly, he's diving into the water alongside it, with nothing but a handheld harpoon. So he can shoot a tracker onto the fin.'

'Sensible.'

Haan smiled. A genuine cheeky smile now. For a split second it was almost like they were back in time, a decade ago, two carefree twenty-somethings, sitting together having a normal conversation over coffee, the air of attraction strong even if it was built on a pack of lies. The strange sensation passed in a flash even though her smile remained.

'It was complete nonsense.' She feigned disgust. 'But what got me even more, as the hero jumps into the sea in nothing but a muscle-stretched wetsuit, he's got this fancy-looking Bluetooth headset in his ear. And I'm thinking, what was the point in that?'

'Maybe it was waterproof.'

Haan laughed. 'Maybe, right? So our guy dives under, how in the hell is he going to be talking on the goddamn phone even if that thing's waterproof?'

Haan paused. Wheeler looked confused, like he didn't know whether to answer the question or not.

'You know what?' Haan took another sip of coffee.

Wheeler shrugged.

'I realised it didn't matter. Not at all. You see, the point of the scene wasn't the Bluetooth headset, and it had no bearing on what happened next. So asking myself why he had it was absolutely pointless.'

She paused again, waiting for Wheeler to get it.

'Okay?' he said.

'Just like it doesn't matter why you lied to me all those years ago. Why you ended up in jail. And it doesn't matter why you broke into that house and stole what you did from my employer. It doesn't even matter that none of the rest of your crew made it out of there alive.'

The mood had instantly darkened and Wheeler was stiff as a rock now.

'The only thing that matters, is that you did it,' she said. 'And now you'll have to pay the price. But first, you need to give back what you stole.'

'What I stole?'

'Yeah.' She looked to her left, as though wracking her brain. 'You didn't get into the vault. I know that. But you didn't leave empty-handed either, did you?'

The look on his face gave away the answer. Then his features screwed in disgust.

'You have no idea, do you?' he remarked bitterly. 'They haven't even told you. You're just the dog sent out sniffing.'

Haan clenched her fists.

'I'm right, aren't I?'

'Actually I do know,' she said.

That shut him up.

She looked to her left again. 'I believe at today's market price, the Bitcoin now missing is worth... a little over two hundred million dollars.'

'I... c.... I can't–'

'This is how it's going to work.' She reached down with her free hand and Wheeler tensed up even more until he saw her hand come back onto the table clutching nothing more than a mobile phone. 'Give me the details for the digital wallets where you transferred the Bitcoin. You'll transfer it all back. Then we can talk some more about recompense.'

'But? That's... there are dozens of different keys. I don't have that information on me.' His bravado had deserted him now. He was petrified.

'I thought you might say that.' Haan wasn't put out. 'So where's the data? A phone? Tablet? Laptop?'

'Laptop,' he said after an unnecessary pause. Which most likely meant it was bullshit.

'Which is where?'

'The apartment I've been using.'

'Give me the address. My friends outside will go there now. We'll wait here.'

Haan glanced outside to where Barton and Klein were standing, looking in. Barton had been against this apparently soft approach. He didn't look too happy. Haan had wondered more than once whether it was him who'd been suggesting to Chester that she was disloyal.

Back to business.

'I'm sensing you might need an extra prompt here,' Haan said. Her heart rate ratcheted up a notch. Could she really do this? Who had she become? 'I thought a smart man like you would understand how deep you're in here. But...'

Before she could talk herself out of it, she tapped away on her phone and put the handset to her ear. She said nothing, but after a few seconds, held the phone out for Wheeler.

He took it from her and placed it to his ear. She could just hear the gruff voice on the other end coming through the speaker.

'Is this Wheeler?'

'Yeah.'

'You hear that?'

The man went silent. The background noise was barely audible to Haan but it would fill Wheeler's head with horror. The distant sound of traffic, drowned out by chatter and the whoops and calls of children playing.

'You hear that?' the man repeated.

Wheeler was mute.

'You know where I am?' Another pause. 'That little playground on the end of Fenton Park. A regular hang-out from what I've seen. She really does love that zip wire. It's Charlotte, right?'

After a few moments of silence, the call went dead.

Wheeler's hand shook as he placed the phone back on the table.

'She'll be fine.' Haan showed no hint of care now. She'd stepped over the line, could she ever go back? 'He won't hurt her, won't touch her at all, *if* you do what I've asked.'

Wheeler still said nothing. Was likely imagining his daughter. All of the wonderful times he'd spent with her, all of the dark and sad times too. Nothing compared to the images he was no doubt seeing of what would happen to her in the hands of Fischer's crew.

'Tell me the address,' Haan said, her impatience showing for the first time.

Wheeler opened his mouth. Then paused. Closed his eyes. What was he doing? Seconds passed until he opened his eyes again.

'So?'

Wheeler didn't reply.

Then, from nowhere, he shot up like a jack-in-the-box, and sent the table crashing.

Haan, too surprised to react in time, tumbled backward as coffee went flying. Before she'd even hit the deck, Wheeler turned, and was sprinting for the door.

24

Hot coffee splashed over Haan as she crashed onto her back with a painful thud. She grimaced as the liquid stung the skin on her face, but she was up on her feet again in a flash.

Wheeler was already at the door. Outside, Barton and Klein hadn't reacted at all. What were they looking at? Wheeler crashed open the door, sped onto the pavement. Now Barton saw him. He jumped into action, snarling like a dog. Wheeler ducked right, away from him, and Haan lost sight of him as she hurtled past startled customers to the still swinging door.

She raced outside the moment Klein started running too. Wheeler was already ten yards away, aiming for the crowded market. Barton was giving chase, but for all his size and muscle, he wasn't the fastest unit. Both Klein and Barton weren't going to be able to manoeuvre well through the crowds if that was where Wheeler was headed.

Should she head around the backstreets again to try and intercept?

No. Don't take chances.

Up ahead, Wheeler was almost at the market. Pedestrians were slowly realising there was an impending commotion. Barton's hand disappeared into his jacket.

'No!' Haan shouted.

That got everyone's attention.

'Stop that man!' she screamed, pointing ahead to Wheeler. 'Thief!'

Not exactly subtle, but would anybody be brave enough to tackle him, without knowing what the hell was going on?

No. They weren't. There were murmurs of disquiet, but not exactly mass hysteria as Wheeler shoved and pushed into the crowds.

Barton's hand again went into his jacket. Again came out empty. He wasn't that stupid. Firing a shot into the air would get the crowds here to disperse, giving them a much better chance of reaching Wheeler quickly. But it would also draw attention, leave too much of a mark of their presence here in this town. That wasn't the plan, even if they had come armed today.

Seconds later Haan was in among the bustling marketgoers, nearly side by side with Barton, closely followed by Klein. Wheeler was all of ten steps ahead. Haan, shorter and slighter than the men, had the advantage now, and with a lot of pushing and shoving and squeezing and shimmying, she was soon closing the distance to Wheeler.

Not quickly enough, and the end of the market was just yards away. Wheeler got there. But he didn't immediately break into a sprint. Instead he veered left, toward the last stall stacked high with fruit. He bent down, grabbed the shelving and yanked back. The startled stall owner could do nothing as his prized produce – apples, oranges, huge watermelons – cascaded down, bouncing off unsuspecting pedestrians and splatting to the floor.

Now there was commotion, shouts of alarm. People stepped

back, trying to clear a path around the destroyed stall. Which only meant more people pushing and shoving toward Haan, Barton and Klein.

Haan broke free first. Sprinted in the direction Wheeler had fled. She reached the end of the street she was sure he'd taken.

'Shit.'

Wheeler was halfway down the tight street that was lined by two rows of quaint terraces. He wasn't moving now. Instead, he was talking to a uniformed Gendarme – a member of the militaristic Gendarmerie Nationale, the force responsible for policing rural areas like this. Wheeler pointed back in Haan's direction, but she had already ducked back out of sight. She turned to Barton and Klein who were quickly catching up with her.

'Police. Split up, now.'

'Who gives a fuck,' Barton snapped. 'Let's just get him and get back across the border.'

A typically brash comment for him. And it wasn't that Haan doubted they'd achieve that aim if they tried. But was it worth the risk, and the mess?

'No,' she decided. 'Split up. Head back to the car.'

She set off without waiting for a response. She'd barely taken a step when the siren from the Gendarme's motorbike blared.

Haan ran, heading away from the cop, away from the market. A quick look behind to make sure she was out of sight of the Gendarme.

No, no. Klein was already nowhere to be seen, but Barton...

The gun was in his hand. He lifted it up, taking aim straight for the Gendarme as he emerged from the street.

Boom. The bullet hit the policeman in the leg. He went down. Barton raced forward as the Gendarme writhed on the ground. Smack. Barton launched a boot into his face.

Now he wasn't moving.

What choice had Barton given her?

Haan turned and raced after her colleague. Headed on past the cop, onto the narrow street. No sign of Wheeler now. Barton, gun held in a double grip, was edging along the parked cars and scooters that lined the left side of the street. A few yards ahead was the Gendarme's motorbike, its lights flashing, its siren blaring, but no sign of any backup. Yet. There surely would be any second. Even a small town like this would have more than one officer, and once report of a gunshot got out, and one of their own the target... they'd descend en masse from every corner.

Haan needed to get hold of Wheeler before then, or this town would turn into a bloodbath.

She crossed over to the other side. She looked behind her. No sign of Klein. He must have heard the gun too, but was he intent instead on getting back to their van?

The bastard better not run and save himself, Haan thought. Would he dare?

'You see anything?' Haan shouted to Barton. She might have been ready to tear his damn head off, but that could wait. The priority was getting Wheeler and getting out of there.

Barton reached the motorbike and flicked a switch and the siren cut out. Haan's ears were ringing from the din, but it only took a couple of seconds before she heard a more distant siren, getting louder by the second. Barton glanced over at her, as if to ask, *What now?* Even though this was a mess of his making.

'He's not on this street anymore,' Haan said. 'Move. Quickly.'

Haan still hadn't taken out her gun. She wouldn't unless she absolutely needed to. Barton continued to hold his in a double grip as the two of them picked up their pace and headed along opposite sides of the street. Every time they came to a turning they both slowed, peered around the edge. They passed one, two, three, then four side streets.

No sign of Wheeler. No sign of anyone.

The siren was getting louder. It could only be a few streets away. Haan thought she could hear another one too. Behind them?

'Maybe we head back for the van,' Barton shouted over.

Haan didn't even respond. Was the irony lost on him?

'Wait,' she said.

She pulled to a stop at the top of the next street, shorter than the one they were on, which opened out onto a much wider road that encircled the town's small central park. The park's orientation meant that from here she could see a good 200 yards into the distance, along the road encircling the green space.

And there was Wheeler. At the side of the road by the park, head down, casually walking away now.

'There!' Haan shouted and pointed at the same time.

Barton growled and the two of them set off at a jog. Except they were jogging right toward the siren, Haan realised. They were a few steps from the main road when the strobes of blue were reflected in the windows of the nearby buildings.

'Put the gun away,' Haan said. 'Take it easy.'

She slowed down to a brisk walk. Was glad to see that for once Barton listened to her when he stuffed the gun out of sight.

They turned left onto the main road. Wheeler was still in sight. Still walking casually. Did he not realise they were on him?

'If we can lose the police, and stay close, he's going to take us right back to where he's staying,' Barton said.

It was a possibility. Or was Wheeler more clever and cunning than that? Was he luring them into a trap?

The Gendarmerie car came into view.

'Calm,' Haan warned, one eye on the fast-approaching vehicle.

It flashed past them. Two officers inside. Haan couldn't resist a glance over her shoulder. The car took a right turn, heading toward the market.

'Let's get this bastard,' Barton said, picking up a little more pace. Haan followed suit and they crossed the road. Sirens still hung in the air.

Haan looked over her shoulder again. A car, blue lights flashing, was poking out of the street she and Barton had just come from. The same car?

The passenger door opened. An angry-looking Gendarme stepped out, hand on the gun on his hip.

'Hey!' he shouted over to Haan and Barton, before ducking back into the car which suddenly shot forward, engine growling.

'Run!' Haan said.

She did. Barton didn't. At least not to start with. Instead, he pulled out his gun and fired off three shots. Thunk, thunk, smash. All three hit home somewhere on the car. Tyres screeched and there was an almighty crash. Haan looked back to see the car wrapped around a lamp post. She grit her teeth in anger.

Up ahead, Wheeler was now running.

Another police car came careening around a corner and sped right past Wheeler, heading for Haan. What was she supposed to do now? She was ten yards ahead of Barton already, she had to take action. She whipped out her gun, fired warning shots at the car. The vehicle swerved viciously, only narrowly missing startled pedestrians scuttling for cover.

The car rocked to a stop and two policemen jumped out. Haan fired two more shots to send them scurrying.

Ahead, Wheeler was approaching a roundabout. As Haan and Barton followed, they were steadily moving further and further away from their van at the other end of the town. What the hell was the game plan from here? Wheeler or freedom?

Thankfully that tough call was made a lot easier a few

seconds later when the high revs of a fast-approaching vehicle caught Haan's attention. She looked over. To the left of the roundabout. Saw a van, speeding along. Their van.

Wheeler noticed it. There was nothing he could do to avoid the collision as the van raced head-on for him. But at least he had seen it, otherwise he would have been obliterated. Instead, he dived to the side. The van caught a flailing leg which sent him spinning into the dirt verge. More screeching tyres as Klein pounded the brakes and the van skidded to a halt, smacking into a wire fence at the side of the park.

Haan was onto Wheeler within seconds. Grimacing in pain he was clutching his leg as he tried to pull himself to safety.

Klein jumped from the van. He slid open the side door then grasped Wheeler by the ankles. Wheeler bucked and shouted in anger and pain. So Haan booted him in the gut, after which Barton helped Klein haul him into the van. They all jumped in. Haan last. As she grasped the sliding door, Klein was already reversing back onto the road.

Another police car was approaching in the distance, but it was too little, too late.

Not for the Gendarmes already on the scene, though, hunkered down behind their police car. An officer jumped up, gun in hand.

Haan was pulling up her own weapon when a shot boomed right in her ear. The bullet clunked into the police car, sending the Gendarme bouncing back out of sight.

'Idiot!' Haan screamed at Barton, her ear ringing and stabbing in pain as he reached forward and grabbed the door to slide it shut.

He said nothing. Just gave her a snide smile as he sat back onto the bench on the opposite side. Klein put the van into first, slammed his foot down on the accelerator and they shot away.

They'd got Wheeler, and Haan was sure they'd get away from Frichebois well before the Gendarmerie gathered enough resources to hunt them down.

Job done.

But at what cost?

25

Ryker ran. But he didn't go far. Only far enough to ensure he was clear of the emergency services that were closing in on the garage. He'd heard the first sirens only seconds after getting moving. He figured Akkan's remaining gang members wouldn't fancy sticking around to meet the police either, and would scarper rather than pull out all the stops to capture Ryker. He was safe, for now.

He ducked into the entranceway of an abandoned brick warehouse. He was out of breath, his head pounding, a combination of the toil of fighting, hauling Akkan around, and his abrupt escape. He felt frustrated. For all the action, he'd come away from the scene with nothing. Akkan, his main lead in figuring out what had happened with Parker and Yedlin, was dead, and the police would be all over the garage premises. The police. Ryker was on the same side as the police, as MI5. Wasn't he? So why wasn't he on the phone with Winter to help get him access to what was now a crime scene? Was it the messy end to Ryker's visit to the garage that was holding him back?

No. There was something more than that. The suspicion that someone in MI5 or the JIA wasn't playing ball. The fact that he was sure he was under surveillance. The two mystery guests at the hospital last time he'd been to see Moreno – spooks, no doubt. Ryker was missing something in this picture, and he wouldn't get the answers by walking away.

Clenching his jaw, he looked down to his arm. There was a three-inch slash in his jacket, and blood was seeping through the fabric from the cut underneath. Not particularly debilitating, but it was painful, and he didn't like the idea of his blood dripping all over and leaving a trail. Especially not with what he had in mind for his next move.

He took the jacket off to inspect the wound. Not too deep, and actually the blood was already coagulating. Yes, there were patches of red on his clothes, but he couldn't do much about that now. And the wound would most likely need stitches... but that could wait.

Head down through the rain, Ryker circled back around. He was two streets away from the garage when the unusually high number of pedestrians became apparent. Curious bystanders, passers-by, who'd been alerted initially by the police sirens and, no doubt, social media. It was the same in any city in modern times. As soon as a major incident took place, camera phones were pointed and images and videos uploaded to the internet – way before police reports or news broadcasts.

At least the number of gawkers on the usually near-deserted streets meant that Ryker's approach back toward the garage was less obvious. He turned off to head down the street immediately before the lane that led to the garage. The office building he'd broken into the previous night was on his left. He'd entered on the other side before, through a little-used back exit. The front of the building had a grander entrance, with a wide staircase and columned canopy.

Not that it was any less run-down from this side. As before, his first impression was that this building was unoccupied, given the weeds sprouting along the bottom edge of the brickwork, the murky and dilapidated windows, and the lack of any kind of corporate logos or insignia anywhere. Oh, and the padlock on the solid wood doors.

Not a problem. Ryker was soon through the poor security and standing inside a dusty foyer that at one time would have been light and airy, with a polished stone floor and central staircase with wrought-iron banisters. Now the foyer was dank, dark and grotty-looking. But not abandoned. For one, there were noticeable bootprints in the dust.

Curious.

Ryker crept through the space, alert for any movement or sound. He headed up the stairs and found his way back to the computer storage room he'd been in earlier, overlooking the garage.

He crouched down at the window and peeped outside. Four police cars. A police van. Three ambulances. Police tape cordoned off the whole end of the alley. On the other side of the tape were well over a dozen bystanders, mostly youngsters. All but two of them had their phones held aloft.

Ryker checked his watch. A little over twenty minutes since he'd made his escape. This crime scene was still in its infancy as far as the police's work was concerned. The dead bodies certainly wouldn't have been removed yet, though Ryker wondered about the injured men; the goons he'd tackled, and Emre Tufan. Were they still inside, receiving medical attention? Had any of them been taken away already by the police? It wasn't unthinkable that the other gang members had taken the wounded with them, if they'd had time – or simply put them out of their misery. Better than them landing in the police's hands where they'd be nothing more than a risk to their crew's freedom.

Ryker watched with interest for the next thirty minutes. Two trolleys were wheeled out in that time. With the bodies covered, Ryker had no clue who was on them. He knew for sure that the kid from the workbench and Akkan were dead, but had the gang indeed killed their own in an attempt to keep themselves safe?

What Ryker didn't see was anyone being dragged from there alive. But ten minutes later he saw something else that was interesting.

A plain hatchback turned up and parked outside the police tape. Phones all around pointed to it as a man and a woman stepped out. Equally plain-looking as their car, the woman was slight and dressed in jeans and a leather jacket, the man tall and lanky, in cords and an open-neck shirt. They had a brief conversation with one of the uniforms at the tape. No ID was shown, though soon there was a wave of activity as three, then four, then six uniformed officers gathered together, passed beyond the police tape and slowly but assuredly pushed the onlookers further and further back. All the way until they were out of sight to Ryker, likely to the far end of the lane.

Ryker could take a good guess at what he was witnessing. The new arrivals had authority. Enough authority to get the uniforms to do what they asked. And what they wanted was to get rid of prying eyes. They didn't want the public getting full wind of what had happened here.

Ryker watched the man and woman for the next few minutes. The woman mingled among the police officers. The man mostly stood with his phone plastered to his ear. After a short while they recongregated. The man nodded then glanced over to the building Ryker was in. Ryker inched his head back to blend into the gloom behind him, but the man was soon looking away again.

Then another car arrived. Unmarked, and similarly plain. Two men got out of this one. Casually dressed. They joined the man and the woman and the four disappeared into the garage.

Ryker knew exactly who the four were. Not detectives, but spooks. The way they moved, the way they looked at the world around them. MI5 most likely.

How had they got the call to come here so quickly? And why? Their presence only added to Ryker's already growing suspicions. He was still mulling it over when noise from the corridor behind grabbed his attention.

A distinctive noise. Footsteps.

26

The sense of déjà vu wasn't lost on Ryker. The last time he'd been in this building he'd also heard a noise. Somewhere below. That time the sound had been indistinct, and ultimately he'd thought little of it. This time the sound was closer, and although not loud, he was sure it was the shuffling of feet. Like someone trying to walk very quietly to mask their presence.

Ryker darted to the door, moving across the room in absolute silence. He peeked out into the corridor, just enough to get a glimpse.

Nothing.

Yet he was sure of what he'd heard. He glanced up and down. All the other doors in the corridor remained closed.

What the hell?

Ryker looked back. Was it worth hanging around to spy on the garage longer? The most obvious answer was yes. In particular, Ryker wanted to know why the spooks were here, and what the end result of their presence would be. Would they be taking the survivors – Tufan? – with them? Had they already started an interrogation inside?

Another sound. Down below now.

No, Ryker wasn't hanging around waiting. He wanted to figure out what was going on.

As stealthily as he could, he headed back along the corridor. At every doorway, he stopped and pulled against the wall, and peeked through the glass to the room beyond. No sign of anyone.

He came to the final door before the stairwell, which, just like the storage room he'd been in, had a solid wood door, no glass. The door was closed. Was it worth a look? Or should he just keep going and down the stairs...

A quick look.

Ryker grasped the handle and pulled down, then painstakingly slowly pushed the door open. Not a creak or strain to be heard from his movement. He stuck his head into the gap.

The room was empty.

He sighed, then stepped back out into the corridor, and made his way down the stairs, checking each floor as he went. He reached the ground floor without any further indication of company.

So who had he heard? And why were they sneaking about? Had they already scarpered, knowing that Ryker had been alerted?

The exit was right in front of him. Time to go?

He froze. Something was stopping him.

He turned and headed beyond the stairs. A door there led into a downstairs corridor he'd not been through before. As he glanced into the first three rooms, his previous thoughts about the building's continued use were confirmed: all were in various states of occupation. Yes, the fixtures and fittings were basic at best, decrepit at worst, but two of the rooms had computer terminals set up – in one of them the hard-drive tower hummed away. There were lever arch files, papers arranged in piles on desks. Boxes. A lot of boxes.

No people though.

Ryker moved back into the room with the humming computer. He glanced briefly over the paperwork arranged neatly on the desk. Invoices. Consignment notes. He moved to a pile of stacked and sealed cardboard boxes, each one three feet square. He read over the labels. Addressees, couriers, senders. Ryker took it all in. Took pictures too – all the while listening out for noise that would suggest someone else still lurking in the building.

It was absolutely clear that whoever was using this space was linked directly to the building next door, and that the deliveries were for businesses linked to Akkan. Ryker had already done a great deal of research into the man's enterprises, many of which were incorporated overseas. Akkan himself had few official dealings with these companies, keeping them at arm's length, but a common naming convention united the businesses Akkan controlled: the initials KLL. The company name for the deliveries here was Karadeniz Logistics Limited. Karadeniz was the Turkish word for the Black Sea, by which Akkan's family originated.

So this building, these deliveries, were related to Akkan, but what *was* he receiving? The names of some of the suppliers indicated they were selling motor parts, and there was nothing particularly exciting about that. But not all of it was so obvious, the nature of the ordered items on some of the paperwork obscured by coded names and numbered stock items.

More interesting to Ryker than the fact that Akkan's businesses were being run from this building, was who he was doing business with. Ryker was about to move on when a label caught his eye. An unfamiliar company name. Ltd, its designation, except this wasn't a UK Ltd company – its address was Tel-Aviv.

Was this the link to Yedlin?

A scratching sound just outside the room. Ryker spun on his

heel, hunched down, ready for an attacker to burst through the door.

No one there.

Ryker waited, breath held. He was becoming increasingly annoyed. Was someone toying with him?

He could do one of two things. Continue to creep around – somewhat aimlessly really. Or burst out and finally come face to face with whoever else was here.

He opted for the latter.

Staying low, Ryker sped for the door and raced out into the corridor. Looked left, then right. That's where he was. Five yards away. And the man was ready and waiting, gun held up, pointed at Ryker.

Ryker didn't panic. He straightened up. Shook his head in disgust. Judging by the frown on his face, the man he was facing felt the same way.

'You?' Kaspovich exclaimed.

27

'What are you doing here?' Kaspovich seemed more angry than surprised that he was face to face with Ryker.

'What are *you* doing here?' Ryker shot back. 'And are you going to put that thing away?' He indicated the gun.

Kaspovich hesitated. He lowered the gun, but only a little. He glanced to Ryker's arm. The cut sleeve, stained red.

'So we've got you to thank for this mess,' Kaspovich remarked. 'I shouldn't be too surprised really.'

But was he surprised? What about the eyes that had been on him the last few days, Ryker thought. Was it all Kaspovich? All MI5? It made some sense. But was it Akkan or him who was under surveillance?

Kaspovich continued, 'A dozen police officers out there would be delighted to know I've just stumbled upon the man who's killed three people today.'

That was telling. Not just the threat, but the fact there were just three dead. So the goons and Tufan were either in police custody, or they'd escaped.

'A dozen police officers,' Ryker said. 'Plus four of your fellow agents that I counted.'

Kaspovich looked a little perturbed.

'So tell me, just how did you get to be here?'

'The problem is, Ryker, I'm not inclined to disclose anything to you anymore. From what I've been told, your assistance on the Parker investigation has been pulled.'

'Is that right?'

'You know how it is.'

'Actually I'm not so sure I do.'

Ryker's brain was tumbling. Winter hadn't said anything about Ryker being pulled from the investigation. Was this because of Yedlin? Something else?

Both men went silent. Ryker became more uncomfortable by the second, particularly with Kaspovich still holding that gun.

'Why are you in this building?' Ryker pointed outside. 'The action was all out there.'

And was it Kaspovich he'd heard snooping, or someone else altogether?

'One of the policemen said they thought they saw someone in here. Obviously anyone in here could be a potential eyewitness.'

'Then why is it you in here, and not one of the police officers?'

No answer.

'I didn't see you approach the others outside when they arrived. So where did you come from?'

Kaspovich's eyes narrowed but still, he said nothing.

'You don't know me that well,' Ryker started, 'but you should know enough by now to–'

'–realise that wherever you go, there's usually a pile of bodies and a trail of blood left behind?'

Ryker smiled. 'It's generally not me who starts these things. But people pull knives on me. Guns on me.'

He nodded to the gun.

'Very funny.'

'Not from where I'm standing. So what now?'

Kaspovich's eye twitched. Was he seriously contemplating shooting Ryker?

'I need you to come with me.'

'Where?'

'A safe house. While we figure out what went down here. You're going to need to be straight with me. And this is me being generous. There's nothing to stop me taking you away from here in cuffs and having you locked up in the slammer.'

'You got cuffs on you?'

'There's nothing stopping me from shooting you either.' His tone was snide now, as though he was bored of Ryker's insolence. 'So which is it?'

'Put that gun away and I'll tell you.'

Kaspovich rolled his eyes, but did lower the gun and stuffed it inside the holster strapped to his side, inside his jacket.

'So come on then, where's this safe house?' Ryker said after a few moments of tense silence.

'This way.'

Ryker moved to the side as Kaspovich approached, giving the other man the space to step past him. He kept his eyes on Kaspovich as the MI5 agent came forward. Kaspovich did a lousy job of pretending he was calm and casual. Ryker continued to mull over his options. Kaspovich was half a step from him when he made Ryker's next decision a lot easier. The movement was slight. Tiny. Perhaps Ryker read too much into it – he'd certainly been hoping for something. But he was sure Kaspovich's hand twitched, and his arm jerked just a fraction – a move for the gun, or another weapon as he went to pass Ryker?

Ryker would never know for sure.

He stooped down, spun and swiped Kaspovich off his feet. He reached out and grabbed the gun from the holster as the MI5 agent plunged to the floor.

Unfortunately for Kaspovich, his position in the corridor meant he cracked his head on the wall as he fell. He hit the deck and lay unmoving. Ryker straightened himself up. Stared down. On the brink, Kaspovich was groggy and barely moving. But he'd be fine.

It was time for Ryker to go.

28

The inevitable call from Winter came minutes after Ryker had tackled Kaspovich and fled Shoreditch. Ryker ignored that call, too busy contemplating what he'd say, and what he would do next. He ignored the next six calls too. Finally bit the bullet on the eighth, as he was in his car, sitting in the sprawling car park of a disused furniture store.

'No. No. Ryker? Even for you, this is something. Talk to me.'

Ryker didn't say a word.

'Ryker?'

'I was pulled from the investigation?'

'Even if you hadn't been already, what the hell do you expect! Every day this week, another Ryker mess to sort.'

'Is that really how you see it?'

'Don't you?'

'So it was your decision to pull me?'

'Does it even matter?'

'A lot.'

'It wasn't me who asked for it, no. But I could hardly fight it, could I?'

'Of course you could have.'

A sigh. 'Ryker, I know this can get cleared up, but only if you listen. You're a wanted man right now. MI5 don't like to be made to look like mugs.'

MI5? Or just Kaspovich?

'Come and see me,' Winter added. 'We'll get MI5 over. We'll sort this out the right way.'

'I'm not going to do that.'

'Why the hell not?'

Ryker thought for a moment. But he didn't offer an explanation. Why not? Probably because he wasn't sure whether paranoia was taking over.

'I'm going to sort this,' Ryker finally answered. 'But I'm going to do it my way.'

'You're operating on UK soil here, Ryker.' Winter's voice was even more stern now. 'I can help you, but if you go off on a personal mission without regard–'

'Yeah, I get it. I'll be on my own. You'll disown me, or whatever it is you want to call it.'

Silence. This was far from the first time they'd had a conversation along these lines, yet something about the conversation suggested this time was different.

Why?

'No. You won't just be on your own,' Winter said. 'This isn't a simple case of me and you, the JIA. If you go off on some rampage here, while the calamity from Monday is still in the public spotlight, it's not just the end of our ad hoc secret arrangement, you could end up in jail, and there's nothing I could–'

'I'll see you around.' With those words, Ryker ended the call.

Ryker fully understood his predicament. He'd just made a very clear move against Kaspovich, MI5, possibly the entire network of security services in the UK, and now he had refused to cooperate. But he wasn't about to back down and turn himself in for what had happened at Akkan's garage, hoping it would all work out. He'd seen enough people get burned by trusting the likes of MI5 and the JIA.

So what next?

He had two options. To lay low for a while, before reaching out to Winter again and trying to get things smoothed over once the dust had settled. Or to go underground. Cut ties. Fade into the shadows to get through this. He didn't know which solution he preferred, which was most likely to get quick results, nor what the ultimate ramifications of either would be.

He dumped his car not long after the call with Winter, and after sitting tight until the sun went down was now travelling on foot and by public transport. By changing his method of travel, it would be much harder for the police or MI5 to track him in real time. While on a cross-city bus he took the opportunity to upload anything of worth from the phone into the cloud before he turned the device off. He removed the battery and left the phone on the seat, when he got off at the next stop.

Would anyone track the phone's movement? In a way Ryker hoped so, it amused him to think of Kaspovich spending time chasing a dead end.

Ryker continued to stay on the move for the next few hours, until night-time arrived. Come 10pm, he was standing outside South Greenwich Hospital. He looked around before moving for the entrance, though he knew that any watchers would be much harder to spot in the dark.

He saw no one, and hadn't spotted anyone following him since he'd left Shoreditch. What did that mean? Had the surveillance ever been for him at all, or for Tufan? Akkan?

With the night shift in the hospital in full swing, and the outer doors to Moreno's wing locked up, Ryker had to await a security guard before he was let inside. No problems. Most of the staff, including the security team, recognised Ryker by now, though there was a feeling of unease. These workers weren't MI6, but they were still connected to the big machine. Would they report Ryker's presence?

He made his way up to Moreno's floor. Along the corridor. All was quiet in the rooms beyond. He knocked on Moreno's door. It was only 10pm but it wasn't unheard of for her to be asleep at this time, particularly if she'd had a gruelling day of physical rehab.

No response to the knock. Ryker tried the door. Unlocked. He pushed it open.

'Sam?'

Nothing. Ryker stepped into the darkened room and flipped the light on. No sign of Moreno.

He moved through, into the bedroom. The bed was made. No Moreno.

He headed to the bathroom. An image flashed through his mind. Moreno sprawled on the floor.

No. The bathroom was empty too. Except for Moreno's phone, sitting on the porcelain splashback next to the sink. He grabbed her phone and went back out. Checked the basics to confirm what already felt like the inevitable.

No overnight bag had been packed. Her laptop remained. Toothbrush, jewellery. He couldn't see a single thing that was missing.

Except for one thing. Moreno.

29

They were five miles into their escape from Frichebois when Haan made the call to stop. There was no indication anyone was on their tail, and the aim was to get to the border and back into Germany as quickly as possible. Klein pulled the van over. Barton got out to change the front and back registration plates to the German ones they'd had when they arrived in the country. That should help to keep the French authorities at bay.

While Barton was working on the plates, Haan made the necessary call to Chester, and was relieved to be put through to voicemail. She kept the message brief.

Along with the problems they'd left behind in Frichebois, there was one other sizeable problem with having to run out of the country so soon... Wheeler. And the digital keys for the Bitcoin he'd stolen. Was that information now languishing somewhere in the small French town? Not the end of the world, but it meant that Haan would have to organise for someone else to go back to Frichebois. First, she'd need Wheeler to open up about where he'd stashed the information.

Was that the reason Wheeler had ignored Haan's threat

against his daughter? Because he thought he had leverage? Before long he'd be in for a nasty surprise when he found himself in Fischer's basement.

'I can't figure out if you're braver than I thought, or just incredibly stupid,' Haan snapped at Wheeler after she'd stepped back into the van and taken her seat.

Wheeler was handcuffed to the railing underneath the bench she was sitting on, his body twisted awkwardly on the floor of the van. He grunted in pain as he tried to move into a sitting position. He half managed, leaning his back against the bench.

'Anything happens to Charlotte... Fischer will never see his money.'

So there it was. Leverage. Wheeler really thought he could call the shots.

'Just you wait.' Barton jumped back into the van and slammed the door shut. Obviously he'd heard Wheeler's dumb threat. 'When we get you back...' Barton snorted in delight as he plonked himself onto the bench opposite Haan. 'I'm looking forward to going to town on you. And your daughter? We'll do what the fuck we want, whether you tell us what we need to know or not.'

Wheeler didn't reply. Haan didn't either. If Fischer decided he wanted Wheeler to pay in the most grievous way, how could she stop that?

Klein took them back on the road. They carried on in silence. From the back of the van Haan gazed beyond Klein, out of the windscreen. She recognised the road they were now on. Within minutes they'd be back in Germany. Not long after that and they'd be deep into the forest.

'Home and dry,' Klein said when the border was disappearing behind them.

Relief washed through Haan, even if she wouldn't show it.

Nor would she show her disgruntlement toward Barton for his macho display back in Frichebois. His antics had made them a target of the French police. Who knew where that could lead. She'd have it out with him, would stick the knife in when she next spoke to Chester – and Fischer too? For now, she'd ride it over. She wouldn't show any sign of weakness, any problems in the camp, not with Wheeler in earshot. He'd likely jump on that in the blink of an eye.

'You must realise this can only go one of two ways for you now.' Haan prodded Wheeler with her foot.

He craned his neck to look up at her. 'Which two ways are those? From where I'm sitting, I'm screwed whatever.'

Fair point.

Barton smirked. 'Yeah, you are. But once we start taking pieces off you, like we did with your friend, you'll soon see sense.'

Haan glared at Barton but he clearly couldn't care less. She could tell he was relishing the thought of getting Wheeler to crack.

'The heist took a hell of a lot of planning,' Haan said. 'You know the strange part to me?'

Wheeler didn't say anything.

'Clearly you and your crew weren't just a smash and grab bunch of fools.' She caught Barton's eye as she said that, and could see the slight look of offence, as though she was insinuating he would be that kind of fool. Most likely true. 'You're an intelligent guy, Adam Wheeler. Intelligent enough to plan a heist against one of the most highly protected personal residences in the world. And intelligent enough to siphon two hundred million dollars without leaving a trace of where it went.'

Barton raised an eyebrow.

'So I'm absolutely certain that you're intelligent enough to have remembered every single letter and digit of the keys you used to make that money disappear, and every number of every bank account that money is now sitting in. More than that, I think you would have made several copies of the information in any case. Fail-safes. Perhaps hard, paper copies, but also stored electronically. A drive, the internet.'

'Sounds like you think you know a lot about me?' Wheeler glanced up to Haan.

Barton eyed her questioningly.

'If you give the information to us here, now,' Haan offered, 'you're going to save yourself a lot of pain. Believe me, you don't want to find yourself in the position of your friends.'

'Oh, that plasma cutter.' Barton grinned widely as he glared down at Wheeler. 'You're gonna love it when I turn your body parts to mush.'

He reached over and slapped Klein on the back. Klein didn't respond.

Wheeler laughed. The unexpected reaction jolted both Haan and Barton.

'Is he seriously laughing at the thought of his foot melting to the floor?' Barton sounded genuinely baffled.

'It's not going to happen,' Wheeler said.

'You won't–'

'Has she told you?'

Haan's insides tightened. Barton was glowering at her. Wheeler laughed sarcastically.

'No, of course she hasn't. She's too devious for that.'

'What's he talking about?' Barton was confused.

'He's grasping,' Haan said. 'Nothing more. You tried to beat him down with threats, now he's going to try and get us arguing with each other.'

She went to pull the gun from her inside pocket. Barton whipped his out first. Pointed the barrel at Haan.

'Are you serious?' she said. 'I was only going to smack him and shut him up.'

'Take your hand out. Now.' She did, but she left her hand within easy reach.

'What the fuck are you two doing?' Klein asked, glancing behind him.

Haan looked to Wheeler. She could see he was smiling.

'Tell me,' Barton demanded.

'Me? Why don't you ask her. Ask her about what she was doing ten years ago when we first met.'

Haan tried her best to show no reaction. This moment – the reveal that she knew Wheeler – had played out in her mind so many times the last few days. But what was she supposed to have done? Back in Frichebois, the priority had simply been to snare their prey. Perhaps she could have rendered Wheeler unconscious before now. Taped his mouth shut. Perhaps she should have just shot him dead and then worried about the ramifications of that – and getting Fischer's money back – after the event.

Why hadn't she?

All she'd done was walk into the inevitable.

'You've got one chance, Haan,' Barton threatened. 'One chance to tell me what he's talking about. Or else you're going to end up in the exact same position as him.'

'Who the hell do you think you're talking to?' Haan tried to sound in control. But she wasn't.

'I always thought there was something up with you.'

'Tell them,' Wheeler said to Haan. 'Tell them about Prague. About the job you were working on back then.'

'And you can shut the fuck up 'n' all.' Barton twisted the gun and fired. The boom in the confined space was deafening and the bullet clanked into the bottom of the van, all of two inches from Wheeler's groin.

'What the hell!' Klein shouted. He whipped his head around.

'Missed.' Barton rolled his eyes.

'What is going on?' Klein turned around again. As he did so, this time the van veered and sent both Barton and Haan sliding across the benches.

Haan saw her chance. She pushed off her heels and dived forward. Barton saw her coming, twisted the gun toward her. He fired but Haan had already grabbed his wrist and pushed his aim off and the bullet blasted into the side of the van.

'Seriously?' Klein shouted, the van veering again.

Haan struggled to hold Barton's gun at bay. Her other arm was pressed up against his neck, but he'd got hold of her wrist and would soon overpower her.

'If you don't... fuck's sake!' Klein tugged on the steering wheel and the van jerked left, then right as a honking horn blasted past. In the movement Haan's arm came away from Barton's neck and he growled in effort as he tried to wrestle his gun hand free.

The barrel edged closer and closer to Haan's face.

Three inches.

Two inches.

She let go of Barton's wrist and flung her head into his lap. Momentum sent his arm spinning past her. Boom. A single shot.

The dull, wet thwack told Haan exactly where the bullet ended up.

She didn't need to look to see that Klein was now dead. She could already feel the shift as the van, no control over its steering, tilted to the left. Straight for the verge and the drop down into the forest.

Haan, face in Barton's groin, had already reached into her jacket and wormed her hand around the grip of the gun. She fired without even taking it out. The bullet tore through her jacket, through Barton's jeans, and into the flesh of his thigh. He roared.

Haan jumped back. Pulled the gun out as she moved.

She pointed the barrel to Barton's chest. He mirrored her pose. Except she was calm and breathing lightly, whereas his face was creased in pain and anger. He went to lift up his gun. Haan's finger twitched on the trigger.

'You stupid—'

He never finished the sentence. The runaway van jolted viciously, bouncing up as it hit a fallen branch or a mound or whatever. Barton, Haan and Wheeler were all sent into the air.

Haan had just enough focus to dip her body right, and pull on the trigger. Splat. Centre mass. She fired again as the van crashed down. Haan smacked into the bench and her gun flew loose. She grabbed hold of the metal seat with both hands to keep her rooted.

In front of her Barton's body slumped down, the gun still in his hand. He was dead.

Haan looked to her right. Past the bloodied head of Klein. The runaway van raced onward, through the dense forest. Beyond the mess of blood and brain and skull that was dripping down the inside of the windscreen, Haan spotted it. A thick pine tree, right in their path.

No time. Haan could do nothing but brace herself and hold on for the horrific head-on smash.

30

She was in the jungle. South America. The call of the exotic animals – monkeys, birds – filled her ears. And the rustle of the leaves and branches in the impossibly humid air, which filled her with dread. They were closing in. Their guns at the ready. The enemy – her – in their sights.

A sound behind her. A voice? She spun, went to throw her gun up.

Too late. She was staring into a barrel, a white-toothed grin just out of focus beyond.

Bang.

Haan's eyes jolted open. A dream. No, a memory. More like a premonition.

Because she really was staring into a barrel.

Her head pounded, her vision blurred red from the blood dripping down her face. Her bleary eyes moved from beyond the barrel to the face of the man behind it.

Wheeler.

He opened his mouth to deliver the threat. 'Don't m–'

Lightning speed. Haan thrust both hands forward. Whipped

her left to the right, her right to the left. One hand knocked Wheeler's aim off, the other snatched the gun from his grasp. Gripping the barrel, she hauled the weapon up and the butt smacked into Wheeler's chin sending his eyes rolling.

'Idiot,' she muttered, her annoyance exactly what she needed to get her battered brain to focus.

She looked across the carnage as Wheeler reeled back. The van was wedged into a thick tree trunk, the whole back end suspended in the air. Klein's body was pressed forward up against the broken windscreen. Barton's was sprawled halfway across the front seat. Haan could tell from the angle of his head that the impact would have killed him even if he'd somehow survived the gunshots.

She went to move. Groaned in pain.

'So what now?' Wheeler asked.

Good question.

What the hell was she supposed to do? Call Chester and explain why two of the team were now dead? Or should she just drop everything and get the hell out of Dodge once and for all.

Haan leaned over and pulled on the side door handle. It took three tugs before the door finally came open, but it only moved a foot before it got wedged in position.

'Get out.' She waved the gun toward the door. She doubled her grip on the gun and glared at Wheeler.

The cuffs were still attached to his wrist though had come loose from the railing that had previously locked him to the bench. Like Haan, blood streaked his face and there was a tear in his jeans where something had slashed him. Despite the obvious injuries, he looked alert.

'I said get out,' Haan snapped. 'Make any attempt to tackle me and I'll unload every bullet I have left into your groin.'

She could tell by the look on his face that he knew she wasn't bluffing. Wheeler shuffled along. He pulled himself to the door and jumped down outside. Haan followed suit, though as she dropped to the piny needled-covered ground a shot of pain rose up through her left ankle.

'You okay?' Wheeler said.

Haan ignored him. She pointed the gun at him again, while taking her phone out with her other hand. The screen was cracked but it was still working. She opened up the map app. It took a while but eventually the screen loaded and she was able to get a sense of place and direction.

Over four miles from Fischer's home.

'Move,' she said, pointing the way with the gun.

They began a silent walk through the thick and undulating forest. With only whispers of sunlight above them, and the toil on her body from the crash, Haan was soon shivering.

'You're not calling for backup?' Wheeler was one step ahead of her, the gun pointed to his back.

'Just walk,' she grumbled.

But why wasn't she making the call?

They'd been going for ten minutes when Wheeler stopped and turned around. 'Can we at least walk side by side?'

'Whatever.'

So they did. The gun remained in Haan's grip, the barrel pointed to the ground.

'I like your new name,' Wheeler said.

Haan resisted looking over at him.

'When did that happen?'

'Shut up, Adam.'

'I don't get why it's you that's so sullen. I'm the one being marched off to face god knows what.'

'Because you stole two hundred million dollars from Bastian Fischer!'

Wheeler snorted. 'I did, didn't I. Did you ever stop to ask yourself why?'

'Did *you*? What did you expect would happen?'

'Well, I hadn't quite expected to get caught, had I.'

'Obviously you're not as clever as you think you are then.'

They carried on in silence. But Haan could tell Wheeler wasn't finished.

'I'm sorry,' he said.

'For Fischer?'

'No. For lying to you. Ten years ago.'

Haan glanced at him. She could sense his sincerity, even if the timing of his apology was a little too convenient. Wheeler just wanted to save his own skin.

'I was wrong to do that,' he added. 'But you weren't exactly straight either, were you. Just like I'm guessing you're not being straight with your new boss now. Right?'

Haan spun and grabbed Wheeler's neck. She pushed the gun barrel into his eye. He squirmed.

'You know nothing about me.'

She shoved him away and he shook his head in disgust.

'Apparently not. I thought you were better than this. Better than working for scum like him. Do you really not want to know why we robbed him?'

Haan said nothing.

'Do you even know how he got all that crypto in the first place?'

Still she didn't respond, though her brain was now whirring.

'Same as he got most of his money. I'm not the bad guy here.'

'What, you're going tell me you're Robin Hood?'

'Not a bad analogy actually.' He smiled wryly.

'Then who am I in your fairy tale?'

'A good question. And maybe it's me who's mistaken, but I think you're on the wrong side here. You're a good person. Too good to be willing to stand by while a man's young daughter is threatened. To be marching me through these woods to what I can only imagine is going to be a barbaric fate.'

The knot in Haan's stomach tightened.

'Move,' she said, waving the gun. They both set off again. 'The only thing that's going to make this better, is if you give the money back. All of it.'

'And then what? I get a bullet in the head rather than my skin pulled off?'

Haan said nothing to that.

'If I give you everything you need. Here. Now...'

Haan's brain was firing. If he did that, what would she do? Let him run free? Shoot him on the spot so that he was at least spared the fate of Fischer's basement?

'You had your chance back in that café. Whatever happens from now, it's on you.'

'No.' He reached out, grabbed her arm and spun her around. For some reason she didn't fight him off, even though the gun remained in her hand. They locked eyes. Haan felt a strange sensation.

'Whatever happens from here,' Wheeler said, 'the blood is on you.'

Haan opened her mouth to speak.

Crack.

Wheeler's body jolted. A spray of liquid spattered into Haan's face. Wheeler's eyes went wide. Haan looked to the spot above his ear. A hole half an inch wide.

Wheeler's body crumpled.

31

Of course, on realising Moreno was missing, Ryker expected the worst. He'd been through enough in his time to know when something didn't smell right. This stank. Even though, based on the evidence, there could be a perfectly good explanation for Moreno not being in her room. Perhaps she'd gone out for dinner. Maybe in someone else's room along this very corridor. Perhaps a late-night rehab session, or she'd gone to the shop or the café or whatever.

No. Ryker didn't buy any of that.

He grabbed her key from the side and headed out, locking the door behind him. He strode down the corridor. Poked his head into the vending area, just to be sure. No one there.

He headed down the stairs, along another corridor, up a flight of stairs, around a corner, down the stairs until he came to the main reception for the residential rehab wing. At this time of night the reception area was locked up from the outside, shutters drawn down over the outer doors. The main desk was empty, the only light in the area from dull wall lights. Ryker headed over to the desk, searched around. Couldn't find what he was looking for.

He was turning around to head back the other way when a hefty security guard, torch in hand, came bustling around a corner.

'Can I help you?' he asked.

'You'd better,' Ryker grimly replied.

Ten minutes later they were in the main security room for the hospital. A bank of CCTV monitors took up one whole corner of the space, with sixteen screens scrolling through the more than fifty live feeds covering every corner of the premises. It hadn't taken much to convince the guard who'd found Ryker – Soubani – that there was a problem, and that it wasn't Ryker. A missing patient was a big deal. Soubani had initially been intent on calling his superiors straight away. Ryker had just about managed to persuade him otherwise. They could call whoever after. Ryker needed to understand what had happened first.

'C-wing, you said?' asked Soubani, the guard sitting in front of the monitors.

'That's it.'

Beside him, his colleague Hogan folded his arms, flitting his eyes between Ryker and the screens. Hogan was suspicious, it seemed. Still somewhat agitated that Ryker was calling the shots.

That was fine by Ryker. He could understand the wariness. The guards in here were all well versed on the types of clientele that the hospital served – as a result, they were far more highly trained than a regular security guard. The only reason Ryker was now standing here, was because he'd spoken to Soubani countless times over the past year. Hogan was new to C-wing, and Ryker only knew him fleetingly. If there was to be a problem here tonight, it would be him.

'What time frame are you looking for?' Soubani asked.

'Work back from now,' Ryker said. 'I was here last night, so it's sometime between then and now.'

Soubani tapped away on his keyboard then brought up the camera feed from the corridor outside Moreno's room on the central screen. A press of a button later and the screen flickered as time wound backward, minute by minute. For more than half an hour there was no sign of anyone. The timestamp had wound to just before 9pm when the screen went black.

Soubani tutted and hit pause. 'Stupid thing.'

He exited the window, then tapped away and brought the live feed back up, before manually re-entering the time as 8.58pm. He hit play. The screen went black.

'It's–'

'Keep winding back,' Ryker said, his discomfort growing with each second.

Soubani shook his head but did so. The screen stayed black as the timestamp continued to trace back. At 8.03pm the feed came back to life. Outside Moreno's room, at that time, all was quiet.

'I don't under–'

'Check the other feeds over that period,' Ryker instructed. 'Work out from C-Wing toward the exits.'

Soubani did so. The room fell awkwardly silent as reality closed in.

'They're all the same,' Soubani said, after the fourth feed in a row showed the exact same black spot.

'Keep going.'

Soubani shook his head in disbelief. Ryker looked over to Hogan. His arms were still folded, though he was looking more and more concerned.

'This is impossible,' Soubani exclaimed. 'It looks like the

entire system was down. But... but I was here. I would have seen this.'

Which only made the scheme all the more brilliant. No one had suspected a thing.

'The screens looked normal to you?' Ryker asked.

'Absolutely,' Soubani answered, defiant.

'So you would have been watching exactly what happened. In real time. It's only the record that's been erased.'

Soubani turned to Ryker, his face full of angst. Concern for his own career prospects probably.

'Nothing happened. Nothing that looked unusual. Honestly.'

'Except it did happen,' Ryker stated.

Soubani looked at his colleague but Hogan had nothing to say.

'We need to call this in.' Soubani was anxious.

'No,' Ryker insisted.

Both men turned to him. Both clearly uncertain.

'Once I've gone you can call whoever, and I'm sorry I can't explain everything to you, but can we try one more thing?'

Soubani nodded. He looked at Hogan, who eventually nodded too.

Ryker explained what he wanted to check. The feed from the previous night. When he'd arrived to find Moreno with her mystery visitor. Her disappearance had to be linked, didn't it?

'No... it's exactly the same,' Soubani said five minutes later. 'Blank.'

He now looked perplexed.

Ryker shook his head. The negative result wasn't entirely unexpected, but it was unwelcome. He'd had the idea that he could get a screen grab of the man and woman who'd paid Moreno a visit before she'd gone missing, so he could try and ID them. But a good forty-five minutes of footage, immediately before and after their visit, was also missing.

Didn't that directly point to them being the likely culprits behind Moreno's disappearance? Or was that too obvious?

'I'm sorry, but... I'm not sure what else we can do to help you,' Soubani remarked. 'We need to report this.'

Ryker knew they had no other choice. But then Hogan spoke up.

'Wait,' he exclaimed. 'I do have one idea.'

Ryker was pleasantly surprised by Hogan's idea.

'You know the guy over here?' Ryker asked as he and Hogan headed across the road from the hospital to the building site on the other side.

'Not really. We've shared a smoke every now and then. From what I know Lake's been over here every night for a couple of months. We used to see each other lighting up from across the street. Then one night we just got chatting.'

He shrugged.

A few minutes later and they were gathered over Lake's monitor in his Portakabin. The building site had four cameras and one of those covered the main road and offered a good view of the entrance to the hospital. The first check had been on the recording for that evening, but there was nothing to see. No sign of Moreno or anyone else leaving the hospital to catch Ryker's eye.

But the previous evening...

'This them?' Lake asked.

'Yeah, that's them.' Ryker stared at the man and woman, walking away from the hospital. At that exact moment, Ryker had been inside Moreno's room, watching them from the other side of the glass.

'You know them?' Ryker asked Hogan.

He shook his head. No hint of deceit. 'Never seen them before.'

'Can you send me an image of that frame?' Ryker asked Lake.

'Send it?' Lake sounded confused.

'Here, let me.'

It took Ryker a couple of minutes, but a picture of the man and woman was soon in the ether for him to collect at his whim.

'That it?'

'Yeah,' Ryker said.

He was done there. Though he was a long way from being done for the night.

32

Life had taught Ryker to always take precautions, which was why he'd uploaded the data pulled together over the last few days to a secure cloud account. So there was nothing in his apartment that he absolutely needed. Still, that was where he headed next. He had clothes there, money, IDs, weapons. Yes, he also had a stash of each of those in a safe deposit box in a private bank near Hyde Park, but going back to the apartment was a better move. It would give him a glimpse of how much shit he was in following events earlier in the day in Shoreditch.

Quite a lot, apparently.

He spotted the two vehicles – a van and car – from a hundred yards away. He'd seen enough over the last few days to understand now that someone – MI5, most likely – had been keeping tabs on him. But was it just tabs on him, or on Tufan, Akkan too?

The street surveillance hadn't particularly been a problem before, at least before Ryker's actions had led to Akkan's death. Before Ryker had refused to co-operate with Kaspovich and had instead tackled him and run. And before he'd found Moreno missing and strongly suspected that the UK government was somehow behind her disappearance. He was sure MI5 would now seriously step up their efforts; not just watch him now, but try to bring him in.

If they found him.

As he walked along, edging closer to the watchers, he missed his phone. If he'd still had it on him he could have used the app for the security camera in his apartment to check for intruders. He had checked before turning the phone off and dumping it, and everything had been fine then, several hours ago. What about now? Was Kaspovich or someone else waiting for him inside? Had they simply trashed the place and taken everything they thought was of use?

Ryker was only twenty yards from the white van, which was parked in a dark spot just out of reach of the nearest two lamp posts. He was approaching from the back so could see nothing of the occupants inside, except for the faint shadow of a face in the passenger side mirror.

Ryker balled his fists in his pockets. He could open the door, grab the guy, pull him out and turn the tables. Figure out who'd sent them, what they'd been told, find the answer as to who – if anyone – had been inside his home and what they'd taken.

No. There was simply no point. The very fact they were here told Ryker all he needed to know. If he wanted to keep going with this investigation, the only way forward was to slink away into the darkness.

Head down, he crossed over the road and walked into the convenience store that took up the bottom corner unit of his apartment building. He bought a pack of mints, eyes busy on the street outside. Nothing. No indication anyone was coming from the vehicles to intercept him.

He headed back out, glanced to the van and the car parked further along. He was in the clear. Ryker turned and casually walked away. He looked over his shoulder several times as he moved, but there was no one following him. Even so, ominous thoughts burrowed into his mind as he walked.

Was he kissing goodbye to James Ryker for good? Not that James Ryker was even his real name, but it was an identity that meant something to him. An identity he'd taken after he'd come through the other side of a dark life with the JIA. Before that, he'd been Carl Logan. James Ryker was a name that had marked hope and a new beginning.

But just like Logan's existence, perhaps now James Ryker and the life that name represented was coming to an end.

The time was edging past 1am when Ryker emerged on a street in Islington that was lined with handsome five-storey Georgian terraces. He'd been here before, though not for some time, and he wasn't sure he'd be overly welcome tonight. At this hour the street was quiet, no one in sight, even though the ever-bustling Islington High Street, with its bars and restaurants, was only a hundred yards away.

Ryker arrived at the steps to number twenty-six and headed up to the magnetically-locked doors. The vast majority of the houses on this street, and those around, had been broken up into multiple apartments over recent decades. This building was slightly unusual in that it contained only two apartments; the first two storeys and basement belonging to one, and the top three storeys to another.

Ryker didn't head up the steps to the front door, instead moved around to the arched alleyway that led to the modest back gardens of twenty-six and its neighbour. Ryker scaled the gate, ignored the security light that clicked on, and confidently moved over to the fire escape at the back of the building. The security light soon turned off again without so much as a glimpse out of a window from anyone inside the nearby properties.

In the clear, Ryker continued up the metal staircase until he was pressed against the window – a restored wooden sash – for what he knew was the kitchen for 26b. On the inside of the window frame were two jammers to make it harder to jimmy the unit open, as well as a contact sensor linked to the home security system.

Not to worry, Ryker wasn't going to open the window, as such.

He took the knife from his pocket and carefully drew it along the edges of the bottom pane of the window, all the way around, cutting underneath the outer wooden beading which he was then able to prise off. He next cut through the silicone sealant, the only thing still holding the glass unit in place before digging the blade in, beyond the wood frame and the glass, until the tip of the metal poked through on the inside. A gentle leverage was all that was then required to pop the sealed double-glazed unit from the window casing. Ryker carefully took the glass in his hands and laid it onto the metal gangway he was standing on.

Job done, he climbed inside.

The kitchen was quiet, and dark. Up in the corner of the room a little red light blinked away – an infra-red motion sensor detecting his every movement. That was fine. Ryker had foreseen this and planned ahead. A basic radio-signal jammer he'd bought earlier, tuned to the right frequency, was enough to ensure the wireless sensor could no longer communicate with its base station. Not that the system in this house wasn't up to standard, it was simply that Ryker knew this place inside out, and how to exploit every weakness.

Ryker carried on through into the entrance hallway. The only other room on this floor was a grand living and eating area.

He wasn't going in there. On the middle floor were three bedrooms, and on the top floor another bedroom plus home office plus some other room which didn't really have much of a function.

Moving as deftly as he could, Ryker headed up the stairs to the office. He left the lights off as he entered. There was no covering over the two skylights in here and the light of the moon was enough to show the basic layout, even if Ryker hadn't known already.

A computer hummed away under a desk. Ryker headed for it and quietly eased himself into the sturdy leather chair. He fired up the computer, the desktop whirred and the screen flickered to life.

After a few seconds he was prompted for a password. Not a problem. He put in the password, and after setting up some basic security to mask his online presence here and on this machine, he was soon inputting his own credentials to gain entry to the government servers he had access to.

The government servers he *used* to have access to, at least. Because every single one of them was now locked.

Ryker angrily grit his teeth. This wasn't exactly unexpected, yet it still riled to know that someone had actually taken the decision to make it happen. Kaspovich?

Ryker wondered whether his attempt at access had sent out an alert. Most likely yes. That was fine. Whoever was receiving that alert wouldn't be able to pinpoint Ryker's location. At least not until they'd done a lot of investigative work to peel back the layers he'd put in place to disguise the IP address he was using. He'd be long gone from here before then.

One more thing to try. Not his access details, but someone else's.

Bingo. Ryker was in.

First things first. The picture from the building site. He

found it in his cloud data and uploaded it to the facial recognition search facilities of over a dozen government organisations. The desktop chugged away and within minutes was spitting out results. Negative results mostly. But one database did have a hit on the man, although not the woman. An SIS database. SIS, the official title for what was more commonly known as MI6. The only problem was Ryker – or at least his host – didn't have the right privileges to view the results.

Which was odd to say the least.

A dead end, though one that had given Ryker a lot to think about.

Next up was the information Ryker had gathered earlier in the day at Akkan's warehouse or office or whatever that place was; the names of the people and various companies he'd seen paperwork and goods for.

His searches soon turned into something of a minefield, with vast networks of inter-linked companies and shell corporations. It was hard to fathom what many of them did and where ultimate ownership lay. Still, bit by bit, Ryker was able to hone the search until his area of focus was much narrower indeed. Although he wasn't yet at the top of the chain, in many cases the data pointed to a group of companies in the Cayman Islands. One in particular cropped up multiple times, the cryptically named B56L.

The Cayman Islands, a tax haven, is a country notorious for its lack of publicly available data on companies incorporated there. Which was often the sole reason why so many millionaires and billionaires had dealings there. For the most part it was nearly impossible to identify the beneficial owners of Cayman Island entities. But Ryker wasn't most people, and after some more searching and cross-referring he was staring at a recognisable, though entirely unexpected name.

Footsteps on the stairs. Quiet, someone treading carefully. No, not on the stairs, closer than that.

The door sprang open, the lights flicked on.

'Ryker!' Winter bellowed.

Ryker closed the browser screen, the name Bastian Fischer swimming in his mind.

33

'What the fuck are you doing in my house?' Winter blasted.

Ryker was a little taken aback. Not by the seething anger, but by the swearing. He wasn't sure he'd ever heard Winter curse, ever, and there'd certainly been plenty of times that warranted his doing so.

'I asked you a question,' Winter said.

'There were MI5 agents outside my apartment,' Ryker said. 'And all my accounts are blocked. Seemed like a good place to come to find some answers.'

Winter stepped in and gently pushed the door to, then moved a little closer. He was being quiet, despite his initial outburst.

'Mrs W in?'

'Of course she is. It's one in the morning. How dare you come here like this.'

'What choice did you leave me?'

'Choice? Don't you try to put any of this on me!'

Ryker glared at Winter who stared right back.

'Moreno's gone,' Ryker said. He looked for a tell in Winter's face. Any reaction at all that would give away that this wasn't news to the Commander. He saw nothing. Other than the anger which remained.

'What do you mean gone?'

'As in she's not at the hospital anymore. And I think someone took her.'

Ryker briefly explained the situation. Moreno's mystery visitors. What he'd seen on the CCTV. Winter's anger slowly subsided, though he didn't say a word.

'A cool head, Ryker, that's the most important thing right now,' Winter eventually spoke after a tense few moments of silence.

'No,' Ryker said. 'The most important thing now is to find who took her and make them pay.'

'Is it? Or is the most important thing to find Moreno and make sure she's okay?'

Surely that didn't even need to be said, Ryker thought. But then again, why hadn't those words come from his lips? Why was it the thought of revenge that dominated his mind?

Perhaps because he'd been here before. Too many times in the past those closest to Ryker had wound up missing and dead, so it wasn't a leap to think it was already too late for Moreno. He would always blame himself for the mistakes he'd made, for those who'd lost their lives in the past because of him, and while he couldn't bear the thought that Moreno was now another life gone too soon because of him, he was damn sure that he'd avenge her if it came to that.

But Winter was right. Finding Moreno alive, was the priority.

'How on earth did they manage to hack into the CCTV system like that?' Winter said.

It was a good question. Not that Ryker felt it was that impressive a feat – he was sure he could have done the same. The point was he wasn't most people. This wasn't random, this wasn't some bunch of idiots. Whoever had taken Moreno was clever, conniving.

'This has to be related to Parker.' Ryker saw no other explanation.

Winter raised an eyebrow. 'Just because that's the obvious explanation, doesn't mean it's the only one. Or the right one.'

'I've been under surveillance ever since the Parker meet went tits-up on Monday.'

'By who?'

Now it was Ryker's turn to give Winter a scathing look. 'Well there's a good question.'

'You're blaming me?' Winter looked genuinely offended.

'JIA. MI5. The list of people who do this sort of thing isn't long.'

Winter seemed to mull it over, and didn't bite back. Did he know something?

'Honestly, I think you're reaching,' he said eventually.

'Plus there're the two spooks I saw Moreno with last night.'

'Two spooks? You know that how?'

Ryker huffed but didn't say anything to that.

'Moreno is still officially on the payroll of MI6, you know,' Winter said. 'There's nothing suspicious about her getting visits from colleagues.'

'That's not what this was. She would have told me.'

Now Winter looked really dubious.

'Ryker, she's a spy. I know you two are close, in many ways I think you two were made for each other, like bloody peas in a pod or something, but do you really think she's always going to tell you everything?'

Ryker still said nothing.

'Anyway, this is beside the point,' Winter continued. 'The point is, she's gone, and–'

'And I'm going to find out who took her. My way.'

Winter sighed and looked away. 'Ryker, you can't go on like this. The world has moved on from twenty years ago.'

'I've no idea what you mean by that.'

'Then listen. This case. Parker, Yedlin, Akkan, Moreno, if she's even linked to this at all. I'll admit I don't know everything, and I'll admit that MI5 and others aren't being entirely forthcoming, but you have to see how badly this is playing out. The media are all over what's going on. The three dead guys in the Range Rover, the dead guys in that garage, there's footage of it all over the internet, and the conspiracy nuts are jumping on it big time. But conspiracy nuts aren't what they used to be. Many of them are now legitimate commentators. The mainstream press are even starting to question what the hell is going on in the nation's intelligence services, and why everything related to these deaths is being kept so hush-hush.'

'Then why isn't it being buried? Some smokescreen story so it all goes away.'

'It's not that simple anymore. I hate to say it, Ryker... you're putting a lot of people in jeopardy. MI5 made this happen, but *everyone* has been told to disassociate from you because–'

'I'm a liability?'

Winter didn't need to reply. Perhaps he was right. The world was moving on. The actions of governments, police, armed forces, intelligence services were so much more in the public spotlight than at any point in history. But that didn't mean that Ryker should or would just slink away.

'I'm sorry, but I'm not done. I will figure this out, and I will get Moreno back.'

Winter looked exasperated. 'Have you processed a single word I've said?'

Ryker looked back to the computer screen. 'The pair who visited Moreno–'

'Ryker, haven't we done this one already?'

'Have we? The CCTV footage the night Moreno vanished is gone. But so is the footage from when those two showed up.'

'So you're saying they're the ones who took Moreno?'

'That's more plausible than there being two sets of people who could gain access to the hospital's security system and doctor footage in exactly the same way.'

Winter didn't say anything, which confirmed Ryker's point.

'Then–'

'Are you seriously suggesting that MI6 have kidnapped Moreno?'

'No,' he said after a few moments. 'But I am saying someone in MI6, or maybe MI5, can give us answers. The thing is, I found their faces.'

'Who?'

'The man and the woman. The CCTV footage was erased, but I still got them.'

'How?'

'Doesn't matter. The man, he shows up in SIS's–'

'Ryker, what are you doing?' His exasperation was clear.

'Why would his profile be locked? To you?'

'Because this is nothing to do with me! Or you!'

Ryker shook his head.

'Tell me about Bastian Fischer.'

Silence.

Not good.

'You know who Fischer is, right?'

'Of course I know the name,' Winter retorted. 'He's not exactly a recluse.'

'No. He's not. And he's a multi-billionaire. One of the richest men in Europe, probably in the world. How is he involved in all this?'

'Who says he's involved?'

'I do.'

Winter shook his head. 'I'm sorry, Ryker, I can't help you with this.'

'No, you *could* help me. The problem is that you won't.'

'And it's not because I doubt that you'd do what needs to be done. But at what cost?'

A very strange answer indeed. Winter wasn't even trying to hide he knew more than he was telling.

There was a faint thud downstairs. Both men paused. Ryker got to his feet.

'Peter?' came the questioning voice, drifting up the stairs.

Winter relaxed a little. 'Coming, honey. Sorry, just replying to a message.'

'At 1am?' she shouted. 'Idiot!'

Ryker stifled a laugh. Winter took the reprimand on the chin. Clearly it was a common enough occurrence.

The upbeat moment didn't last for Ryker. He checked his watch. He'd been here too long. Given the way this conversation had gone, there was a good chance Winter had already somehow sent out an alert and Ryker didn't fancy another confrontation tonight.

'Last chance. What do you know that you're not telling me?' Ryker demanded.

Winter paused, as if trying to decide if he would open up or not.

'All I know is that sometimes it's best to walk away.'

Ryker shook his head, disappointed. 'That's not good enough for me.'

'You're not the guardian of the world, Ryker, and one way or another, everything you think you're stumbling across will get figured out. The right way. But I'm asking you, as a friend, to stop. Before you go so far that even I can't pull you out.'

'You know I can't do that.'

'Then I think this is it between us. And I truly do mean that. I can't have you put not just my job, but my whole life at risk.'

'Your whole life has been at risk every damn day you've worked for the JIA. I don't see why this is any different.'

Winter said nothing as he stepped aside from the doorway.

Ryker moved forward, eyes locked with Winter's. He paused. There was so much left to say, but he couldn't find the words.

He said nothing, just walked away.

34

At least she wasn't in the basement. Not yet. She was in room ten. A formal and functional room that wouldn't have looked out of place as a conference room in a modern office block, with a large, oval glass table, black leather chairs and grey walls and carpets. Except this wasn't a conference. Haan was seated on a chair by the window, pulled away from the table. She wasn't cuffed or tied down or anything like that, but this certainly felt more like an interrogation than a friendly discussion, even more so than the last time.

Chester was sitting opposite her with her camera phone recording on a tripod. She was glaring at Haan, elbows on the glass table. Fischer was in the room too, on his feet, leaning against the wall, arms folded. Haan knew there were two of the security team outside the door. Not her team anymore, it seemed.

'No.' Fischer shook his head, as if he was talking to an idiotic child. 'You're going to have to explain it to me again.'

'Barton fucked up,' Haan said. 'I tried to control him, but the man was a fool.'

Haan looked from Chester to Fischer as she spoke, her agitation clear, and well justified as far as she was concerned, even if she wasn't being entirely truthful. What kind of torture would she endure before she came clean? Should she just save herself the pain and spill all now? Wasn't protecting herself the most important thing?

No. Stay strong.

'To be honest, Mr Fischer, I'm a bit surprised a man like that ever got through the recruitment process,' Haan added.

Fischer glanced over to Chester now as though himself questioning that point.

'I can assure you he was perfectly qualified,' Chester said coolly. 'So please try and explain the situation again, as Mr Fischer asked.'

Haan sighed and folded her arms. 'As you know, we learned that Adam Wheeler is a British national and a convicted computer hacker who used to work for the UK's GCHQ. Before his conviction, that is. He's a guy who had the smarts to perform a heist like this, though it is a little surprising a man like him was involved in something so elaborate. Anyway, we tracked Wheeler to Frichebois, but we didn't know where he was staying, so we employed some basic surveillance to fish him out–'

'I heard you took him for coffee,' Fischer said.

Well there wasn't a torture chamber nearby, Haan felt like responding. She turned her full attention to the big boss now, giving him a scathing look that was at odds with the curdling of her insides.

'The priority was getting back your crypto,' she offered as calmly as she could. 'It was my call that it was better to keep Wheeler in town, and quietly, until we got what we needed from him. We did have leverage though. I sent a man to England to watch his young daughter, so it's not as if it was an enjoyable coffee break for our guy.'

Fischer shook his head as if disgusted at the step of involving Wheeler's daughter. Like he was a man of high morals.

'I admit it didn't work out how I intended. I didn't anticipate Wheeler to be stupid enough to run and for all he knew, put his own daughter at risk. But it was Barton who screwed this up. When I realised there was heat on us, I ordered Barton and Klein to clear out. Barton instead shot at a Gendarme on a crowded street in broad daylight. From there it was simply damage limitation. Get Wheeler. Get out of town.'

'Which you did,' Chester said. 'But only after leaving a heck of a mess for me to clear up with the French authorities.'

'And I still don't understand how that resulted in a blood-bath in the van,' Fischer added.

Haan sighed. 'It's as I already explained. Once again, Barton was a moron.'

Fischer gave Chester another unimpressed look. Did that mean he was coming around to Haan's side?

'Barton caused that mess in Frichebois,' Haan continued. 'I was pissed off. We got into an argument. He wanted to torture Wheeler there and then in the van. He shot at Wheeler. I wasn't having any of it.'

'Why not?' Fischer said. 'Getting my money back was the priority. Why care about Wheeler?'

'Actually, at that moment getting us all back here, without a trail of police behind us, was the most important thing. That was the call I made. Barton didn't listen.'

'So you shot him?' Fischer said, in such a way as to suggest he still couldn't see the logical jump.

'He turned his gun on me first. I tackled him. Unfortunately, Klein got hit when Barton tried to unload on me.'

The room went silent now, all eyes on Haan. Did they believe this part? She didn't know for sure but she wouldn't put it past Fischer and Chester to have some crime-scene investigators up their sleeves who'd already been over that van, and the bodies of Klein and Barton, and decided exactly which guns the bullets that killed them both came from. That would be fine. It would at least confirm *this* part of the story as the truth.

'Klein was dead at the wheel,' Haan continued. 'We were heading downhill in the forest. The crash was inevitable. I took Barton out before he got to me. Simple as that.'

'And then both you and Wheeler decided to go for a nice walk through the forest,' Fischer stated matter-of-factly.

'A walk back to here, yes.'

'You didn't call for help,' Chester said. 'Why?'

The toughest question so far. Was there a logical answer that wouldn't get her strung up?

Haan paused and sighed, as though building up to say something that was hard to admit. 'Honestly? I was a little worried. For my own safety. I had just killed Barton, and it would make sense for Klein's death to be pinned on me too. I didn't want to make the call and then find I had their chums out after me. I thought it best to get back here with Wheeler and speak to you both, as quickly as possible.'

That seemed to give both Fischer and Chester food for thought.

'Perhaps *you* could explain something to *me*,' Haan said. Fischer raised an eyebrow. 'Why is Wheeler dead?'

It was several hours since he'd been shot in the forest. Seconds afterward, Haan had been surrounded by a fully geared and tooled assault team of four, dressed head to toe in camouflage and carrying heavy-duty weaponry. The way they moved and acted, they were definitely elite military. How on earth did Fischer even find these people, and get them working for him?

Chester sighed. 'I think we can answer that,' she said. 'We're asking you to be straight with us, so it's only fair.'

Fischer didn't agree or disagree.

'We heard about the incident in Frichebois even before you called me from the van to say you had Wheeler. I sent a team there to try to clear up the mess. We found where Wheeler was staying–'

'What? How?'

'That's not important. What's important is that we got the digital keys. We've since been able to trace all of the crypto transactions, and very soon Mr Fischer will have every cent of his money back.'

Haan shook her head in disbelief at just how little she knew, and how much had been achieved by others. She was also more than a little sad that Wheeler was dead. Whatever the reason he'd got himself mixed up in the heist, Haan believed he was a good guy. At least compared to many others she knew.

'But Wheeler could still have been useful,' Haan said, confused. 'We still don't know the identities of the other members of his team, nor if there was anyone else who'd helped them or even put them up to this.'

'No,' Chester said. 'We don't.' Though the ever so brief look that she and Fischer shared suggested otherwise. Possibly.

'So why is he dead?'

A pause from Chester. 'The retrieval team weren't given specific orders to shoot and kill Wheeler on sight. But when he grabbed you... it wasn't the perfect outcome, I'll admit.'

Fischer looked pissed off now. He wouldn't look at Chester, as though some of the blame was on her. It made Haan feel a lot better to know that she wasn't the only one under the spotlight. The whole security team operated under Chester, so any failings ultimately reflected on her.

What had happened to the poor guy who'd pulled the trigger? Haan wondered. Perhaps they hadn't been so elite after all.

The room fell silent.

'That's everything I can think of,' Haan said.

Fischer and Chester didn't say anything more. At least not to Haan. Fischer moved over to Chester and leaned toward her and the two of them had a brief and ultra-quiet conversation. When they were finished Fischer walked to the door, opened it and stepped out without so much of a glance to Haan.

The door closed behind him. Haan fixed her gaze on Chester as her heart rattled away in her chest.

'So what now?' Haan asked.

Worst case was Chester would say nothing, and the goons would descend to tackle Haan and drag her away. Best case was for Chester to say something along the lines of 'take a few days off.' Or 'you're not to leave this house until further notice.'

Instead she commanded, 'get back to work.'

Then she got to her feet, grabbed the phone and the tripod, and headed for the door. Seconds later, Haan was alone in the room.

She waited for several minutes, barely moving, still expecting the door to burst open any second with a hit squad.

It didn't.

She wanted to heave a sigh of relief. She wanted to sob and shout and scream, anything to channel away the tension that was consuming her. She didn't do any of that. Her eyes fell upon the tiny lens of the CCTV camera up in the corner of the room.

Was someone watching her right now? Fischer? Chester?

Haan didn't know what to think. Had she really been let off, or was she simply under extra scrutiny now, both Fischer and Chester waiting for her to make one final and fatal mistake?

Did they already know the truth, and were simply toying with her to prolong her suffering?

Only time would tell.

35

Ryker was left with few options after leaving Winter's home. He'd already spent much of the cash he had on the jammer and other basic equipment to get inside the JIA Commander's plush apartment, so not long after leaving Winter's he'd used a cashpoint to take out as much hard currency as he could on his debit and credit cards. He wouldn't be using those electronic means – easily traceable, and easily blocked – again for the foreseeable future.

The cash he now had would see him through the night, possibly a few days if he was careful, but to stay on the move he'd need to either go back to his apartment or to the safe deposit box. Even then, his reserves would soon dwindle.

His apartment was a no, he decided. The surveillance team outside his building hadn't seen him last time, but only because he'd scarpered without trying to get inside, and there was no point in giving MI5 a head start on his whereabouts if they really were intent on snaring him. He couldn't retrieve what he needed from the safe deposit box until the morning, so the only other option for shelter was to pay cash for a room at a poxy hotel in the West End.

Sad really, that other than Moreno – who'd disappeared – and Winter – who'd pretty much disowned him – he had no one else to turn to.

The next morning, he arrived at Carter & Blake's, located in a handsome sandstone building on a plush street on the edge of Hyde Park, three minutes after opening. After making it through the protracted security procedure, he soon emerged with his swag bag full. He hadn't taken everything, not in one swoop, and he hadn't taken any weapons. Whatever he did next, wherever he travelled, arming himself was a potentially big problem. He couldn't afford to be caught with an unlicensed firearm, not when he no longer had an ally to pull some strings. It was back to basics for him.

Well, almost. Because he did have one mod con that he'd already put to good use since he'd checked into the hotel the previous night. A tablet computer. Not just any tablet computer, but Peter Winter's.

Had the Commander even realised it was missing?

It didn't matter to Ryker either way. After uploading all of the stored data from the device to the cloud for later perusal, he'd run a cleansing software to overwrite the hard drive several times, before performing a hard factory reset. He'd also taken the device apart and run a series of tests over the hardware to make sure there was no tracking or bugging equipment. There was nothing. Aside from a few scuffs and scratches, the tablet was now as good as new, and exactly what Ryker needed to figure out his next step.

Which he had managed to do the previous night before he'd got some paltry sleep. And so, after leaving the bank, he headed straight for the nearest Tube station, his next destination London St Pancras and the Eurostar terminal.

～

It had been years since Ryker had last been to Paris. For all its obvious charm, it wasn't a city he'd ever wanted to go back to. In Paris, there were far too many painful memories better left somewhere deep in the recesses of his mind. Much like the majority of his life.

Yet he wasn't going to pass up on this opportunity.

There was only one moment of tension for Ryker on the journey to the French capital, and that came right at the start as he showed his passport at the Eurostar terminal in St Pancras. His fake Irish passport in the name of Eoin Grigg. It was a basic identity that he'd set up himself and he had never used it before, so it was clean as a whistle – but also paper thin. The good thing, though, was that it was an identity Winter and MI5 and the like knew nothing about.

Once successfully through the border check it was time to relax. Ryker would soon be in mainland Europe, and within one of the twenty-six European states signed up to the Schengen Agreement. It essentially meant borderless travel from there on, as long as he remained in those countries.

He hoped it would be sufficient given his intention on tracking down Bastian Fischer – a German national whose vast business empire was spread throughout his home continent.

Ryker had been aware of the multi-billionaire before last night – how could he not be? Fischer wasn't just rich, he had a megalomaniac persona and kept his profile extremely public. Ryker's basic research into the man's past had highlighted that Fischer was anything but a rags-to-riches story. Still, his was a classic, more common than most of the mega-rich would care to admit: Fischer had acquired his wealth through good fortune and a huge leg-up early on in his adult life.

Fischer's grandfather – a dual German and Swiss national – had been a shipping magnate at the start of the twentieth century, and despite never officially serving the Nazi party, had come out of the Second World War as one of the richest men on the continent. Upon his death in the 1950s, his fortune was split between three sons. One of those sons had survived little more than twelve months before dying in a freak helicopter accident in the Alps. The two other sons had fought for control of the original business, until eventually Bastian's father won when his brother was convicted of tax fraud.

By that point, the family fortune was on a slow decline through various circumstances, but particularly the in-family squabbles, and it was only in the early 1990s when Bastian graduated from university with an MBA, and immediately took a position on the board of his father's company, that the family's fortunes once again took an upward turn.

Bastian wasn't interested in shipping – buying, dismantling and selling were his forte. With an ever-present tap of cheap debt from various banks, Fischer bought struggling companies in any field of industry, stripped them down, and either made them viable again before selling them on, or just wound them down completely. Most of the time this made him a lot of money, even if on numerous occasions the businesses he was stripping had no future option but bankruptcy. An easy way to avoid paying off those bank debts, and a sure way to lead to countless job losses.

For Fischer, though, it was always onward and upward, despite the destruction he left in his wake. Over the years his bullish philosophy had seen his empire grow to include companies in all major industries across the globe: oil and gas, pharma, tech, automotive. He even owned a large press company with the second largest readership in Germany, the highest in Poland, and the top ten in virtually every other European country.

Which was particularly handy for a man like Fischer who seemed to thrive off attention. Taking a firm hand with his home nation's press, he'd been able to paint a picture of himself as a national hero – and from what Ryker could see, many people bought into it.

Fischer's life in the spotlight had been far from plain sailing though, particularly outside of Germany. Allegations of fraud and tax evasion had dogged him for years, and more than once hefty criticism from trade unions and the like had been levied against him when the livelihoods of the thousands of employees were put out of work by his shark-like corporate tactics.

No allegations had ever stuck though, nor did it even seem to tarnish his reputation, perhaps in large part due to his excellent manipulation of the media.

Ryker was surprised he hadn't been able to find out more about Fischer's personal life. Fischer was rumoured to be behind some of the world's largest art purchases, though had never admitted to this, but was open about his love for sport – which included part ownership of both a Bundesliga football team, and a fledgling F1 team. Otherwise, Fischer was a very private man. He'd been married once, but his wife had succumbed to cancer before they'd ever had children, and he'd never remarried or even been in another relationship from what Ryker could tell.

The other element of the story that Ryker continued to struggle with was why Fischer was on *his* radar at all. Other than Fischer's businesses selling car parts to Akkan, what on earth did Fischer have to do with Parker, Yedlin, Moreno?

Was Ryker reaching too far?

Time to find out the answers from the man himself.

36

The Hotel Le Grande was two streets away from the Champs-Élysées. Ryker could see the majestic Arc de Triomphe as he headed along the wide avenue toward the neo-classical hotel. A sprawling stone structure, the hotel had a wide elevated facade with twelve steps leading up to the columned entrance. The bottom of the steps was where Ryker chose to hang out.

The time was nearing 4pm and the sun was slowly moving down in the deep blue sky off to Ryker's left. Being central, and so close to key tourist sights, the pavements here were busy and there was a constant flow of people coming into and out of the posh hotel which not only had over 300 bedrooms, but extensive conference facilities too.

The latter being why Ryker was here. And Fischer.

Ryker had had time to check into a hotel before coming here, in the not-too-far-away district of Montparnasse – an arty enclave south of the Seine. Which was also close to where Fischer was staying, at a swanky apartment he owned, just north of the glorious Luxembourg Gardens.

Before coming to the Hotel Le Grande, Ryker had performed

a walk-by past Fischer's building. In the daytime he couldn't hang around for long, given the plethora of security-conscious rich folk who were there. Come night-time, though, perhaps...

For now, he would remain outside the Hotel Le Grande, where Fischer along with over fifty other guests were attending a summit on carbon emissions in the automotive industry. A grand public gesture, more than anything, Ryker had decided, as had a small group of climate-change activists who had been shepherded behind a metal fence, and were being closely watched by a gaggle of policemen who nearly outnumbered the protesters. There were also a gathering of news crews sitting in wait, though relatively low key, and a passer-by probably wouldn't have paid much attention to the scene.

Which suited Ryker.

He remained rooted for nearly thirty minutes, just waiting and observing. He checked his watch. The conference was supposed to have finished by 4pm, and he could tell some of the onlookers, including the protesters, were getting bored with the wait.

Then, finally, some action. A rush of noise came from the top of the stairs. Ryker looked up to see the hotel doors swinging open and four burly security guards – black suits and ties, sunglasses on, cords dangling from their earpieces – came out. Ryker stifled a smile. The guys were so over the top it was almost beyond parody. A visual deterrent, nothing more. Clearly the men were just basic hired help, perhaps put on by the conference organisers.

The security guards stood watch across the steps as a stream of smartly dressed men and women emerged, some with more overt security, others with none at all. Some of the guests climbed into waiting taxis and chauffeur-driven cars at the roadside near where Ryker was standing. Others – perhaps the more environmentally conscious of those at the low-carbon event – headed away on foot.

After some initial frantic heckling, the protesters looked like they'd had enough, and were getting no attention from anyone other than the bored-looking police officers. They also started to disperse. But not Ryker: he remained waiting for Fischer.

Some ten minutes after the doors had opened, a Tesla pulled up on the street a few yards from Ryker. Moments later, Fischer finally showed his face, walking confidently out of the hotel. He was smaller than Ryker had imagined, both in height and stature, though he moved with an untroubled arrogance. Striding along at either side of him was a smartly dressed woman in a skirt-suit, light hair pulled back so tightly it made the skin on her face look pinched, and a young suited man. The three were busy chatting away among themselves.

Ryker glanced across to the press. Overly polite, they remained patiently waiting at the bottom of the steps. This wasn't some frenzied free-for-all. Well, he figured, when you own the companies they work for...

Ryker was about to set off up the steps when something about the woman made him pause for a few seconds. The way she moved, the way she looked at the world around her...

He shrugged it off and started up the steps. The woman clocked him first, but before she could make a move to intercept, he thrust out the cobbled together ID card, which he whipped away just as quickly.

'Greg Matthews, BBC,' Ryker said.

He had the attention of all three. The two chaperones looked particularly unimpressed. Fischer gave a cursory smile, though he wasn't about to stop moving until Ryker darted right in front of them.

'I wanted to ask you a question about events in London,' Ryker said in his best journo style.

Now he had Fischer's attention.

'What events?' the woman asked.

The fact she had spoken up for the boss was telling.

Ryker dug in his pocket and pulled out the recently acquired burner phone which he'd downloaded the photo to. He held the device out, screen facing Fischer.

'This man, Yunus Akkan, part of a Turkish organised crime ring, was found dead yesterday. I believe you knew him.'

Fischer looked genuinely baffled, as did the young man next to him. The woman... she looked about ready to explode.

'Sorry, I've no idea who that man is,' Fischer answered, 'but I do need to go.'

Fischer sidestepped and went to move past Ryker.

Not so quickly.

Ryker reached out and grabbed Fischer by the shoulder.

'Are you sure, because–'

'That's enough.' The woman seized Ryker's arm, pulling him off. 'How dare you. What did you say your name was?'

Ryker stepped back. The woman was standing right in front of him as Fischer and the other man rushed down the steps to the waiting car. The other journalists were looking sheepish now, not sure whether they wanted to even bother trying to get some precious seconds from Fischer anymore.

'I asked you what your name is?'

'Greg Matthews,' Ryker said. 'And yours?'

She seemed to think about that for a few seconds, but then turned and headed after Fischer who was already at the car.

All in all a revealing few seconds. Not least because Ryker was now intrigued as to exactly who Fischer's sidekick was, but also because of the other plants he'd spotted. First when he'd moved to speak to Fischer, but most pronounced at the moment he'd grabbed hold of Fischer. The woman had been quick to react. Far quicker than the four hired lumps who remained at the top of the steps. But not nearly as quick as the other two men; one in among the remaining protesters, and another at the top of the steps, standing casually by a thick stone column, pretending to play on his phone.

Very subtle indeed. Ryker hadn't thought anything of the two men until they'd flinched.

So who were they? Fischer's real security? Or intelligence operatives of some sort?

Fischer was in his car. The Tesla's electric engine whined as it pulled away. Ryker looked across. The quick-acting protester had disappeared from sight, but he couldn't have gone far. The man with the phone was heading for the hotel entrance.

He was the one Ryker decided to follow.

Ryker slipped a cap over his head as he strode up the steps. There was likely to be a whole host of CCTV cameras inside the hotel and he wanted to remain hard to identify for this next move.

The man he followed into the hotel looked innocuous enough. Around six feet tall, he was thick-framed but not so much to catch attention. He was casually dressed though his clothes expressed a certain level of wealth – or at least a taste for the expensive. His phone was now away, his empty hands by his sides as he stepped across the shining marble floor of the hotel's inner atrium that was crowded with business people and more casually dressed tourists.

More than once the man glanced over his shoulder as he moved, and Ryker held back as much as he could. The man moved over to the bank of three elevators beyond the reception desk, where other people were already waiting. He pressed on the down button. Interesting.

His lift came first. The doors opened and several people emerged. He was the only person to get in.

Ryker rushed forward.

'Hold the door!'

The man didn't. But one of the other hotel guests shoved his foot in the way of the closing doors which bounced off his toes and slid back open.

'Thank you!' Ryker said as he darted inside.

He let out a breath and looked down to the floor numbers. Minus two was lit up. Parking level. So this guy wasn't staying.

The lift set off. Both Ryker and the man were facing the doors, both of them stood right up against the mirrored back wall. Ryker glanced over.

'So how do you know Bastian Fischer?' Ryker asked.

'Comment?' The man looked confused.

'Bastian Fischer. You work for him?'

'I'm sorry,' the man said in what Ryker took to be deliberately terrible English. 'I no understand you.'

Ryker reached forward and thumped the emergency button and the lift jolted to a halt.

'You sure about that–'

Ryker ducked when he saw the fist flying toward him. The knuckles grazed his shoulder. He sprang back up, grabbed the man by his neck and took him off his feet, slamming his head against the mirror, causing the glass to crack. The guy winced.

His hand went somewhere behind him. Out came the gun.

Ryker was ready. He grabbed the guy's wrist and thrust his arm up against the wall too. He bashed the guy's head another time, squeezed his neck a little harder, then bashed the wrist.

'Drop it,' Ryker commanded.

The man did. He let go of the wrist and fished in the guy's trouser pocket. He took out a phone and a wallet, which he flipped open.

'Eric Hastings. Very French that.' Ryker put the wallet and phone in his own pocket.

'Fuck you,' Hastings choked out.

That got his head another slam.

'Who was the woman with Fischer?' Ryker asked.

Hastings glared down. His face was bright red. He was about to pass out from lack of oxygen. Ryker released his grip ever so slightly.

'Who is she?'

The lift clunked into life. Still heading down. Ryker looked up to the top corner. A camera. Most likely someone in the hotel's security team had seen the ruckus. If so, a security team would be standing there at parking level when the doors opened.

Ryker let go of Hastings's neck and grabbed his shoulders to thrust him toward the door. He only then realised that Hastings was now clutching a tiny can of pepper spray. Ryker squeezed his eyes shut and threw his head down as the noxious spray blasted toward him.

The lift came to a stop and the doors shuddered open. Ryker, still grasping Hastings, flung him forward. There was a thump as he collided with whoever was waiting there. Then shouting. Banging.

Head still down, Ryker barrelled forward. He only opened his eyes when he was sure he was clear from the toxic mist.

When he did, he saw Hastings hobbling away. Ryker was about to give chase when his ankle was caught. He plummeted to the ground.

Behind him was the security guard, sprawled out on the floor, head streaming blood, his hand wrapped around the bottom of Ryker's leg. Ryker kicked him off. The guy was in no fit state, already losing consciousness from whatever Hastings had done to him, and his head slumped.

A car engine fired into life. Its revs pulsed around the enclosed car park and all through Ryker. A moment later a BMW blasted out of its spot and raced toward the exit ramp.

Hastings, no doubt.

Ryker could do nothing.

Not ideal, but Ryker had plenty of food for thought. He pulled himself up, took one last look at the poor sod on the ground, then jogged toward the exit.

37

There were several problems for Ryker to tackle once back at his hotel room. Firstly, when he fired up his tablet computer and attempted to log in to Winter's JIA account, he was rebuffed. Winter had changed his credentials. Sensible, under the circumstances, but frustrating because it blocked yet another avenue to results, as Ryker had been set on trying to find out more, both on Fischer's two sidekicks and Eric Hastings.

Still, he did his best, and at least was able find that Eric Hastings seemed to be a genuine identity, and that at age fifteen, hailing from Yorkshire, he'd won a national kickboxing competition. Nothing on his adult career path, though, no apparent military or criminal history or anything like that to be found.

Another problem for Ryker was the news. As Ryker searched on the tablet, he had the hotel room's boxy TV on in the background. A dedicated Parisian news station. The problem was, his face was on the TV.

Greg Matthews. Wanted for assault with a deadly weapon. There were two separate shots displayed in the coverage. The one of him on the steps, as he'd approached Fischer, must have been taken from among the protesters. It wasn't particularly clear, and not at all clear for anyone who'd not seen Ryker before. The other was CCTV footage from the lift, a freeze frame showing him smashing Hastings's head against the mirror. In that one Ryker's face was obscured by his cap.

Ryker had known the risk of confronting Fischer in public, and in tackling Hastings in semi-public, so it didn't come as a surprise that his actions had been captured. What was more of a surprise was how quickly the news had come to the fore and had been given such prominent placing, and how it had been spun to be more than it was: assault with a deadly weapon. What? A lift mirror?

It all came back to the issue of Fischer having direct and influential control over certain key elements of the press.

Not an insurmountable problem, but Ryker would need to be more cautious if he was to get through the remaining time in Paris unscathed.

And at least it seemed that no one knew his real name.

He switched the station to BBC World News.

And that was when the biggest problem of all hit home.

'Who is this?' came the voice through the tablet's speaker – an audio call.

'Surprise,' Ryker said.

'Not really actually.' Winter sighed. 'Though how are you...'

He trailed off. Ryker waited for the rest of the question. It didn't come. Was that because Winter had realised he was about to put his foot in it? Why? What was the question? *Why is the number calling me showing as from Morocco when I know you're in France?*

'You have seen the news then,' Winter said.

Ryker turned his eyes back to the BBC news report.

'Yeah. What do you know?'

A pause. To be honest he was a little surprised Winter hadn't already ended the call. Why hadn't he?

'Winter, this affects me more than you. I'm really not asking for much.'

'Affects you more? Ryker, you have no idea.'

'I think I do. I was working on the Parker and Yedlin investigation for months.'

'Yes, I know. And you were close to breaking the case open.'

Namely finding the smoking gun to prove that Parker, a high-profile banker, had been secretly funding Yedlin, a right-wing extremist who many believed was responsible for attacks against Palestinians in the Middle East, as well as stoking violence and hatred on both sides of the uneasy Israeli political divide.

'The issue is, Ryker, what you're seeing on the news isn't the whole story.'

'No?'

'It's true that Yedlin's body was found yesterday, dredged up from a man-made lake in the Cotswolds. ID was confirmed this morning.'

Apparently a dog walker had alerted the authorities after their mutt came out of the water with a finger in its mouth. Which was pretty much all that was being said on the news, together with Yedlin's obvious background and therefore the theories about why he was dead.

Ryker's mind took him back to the warehouse in London and Yedlin's henchman, Benado. Was he still alive? He and the others had been protecting the boss. So what had gone wrong?

'What am I not seeing?' Ryker asked.

'Yedlin was executed. Same as Pa–'

'But no others?'

'No other whats?'

Ryker didn't answer. His brain whirred.

'This doesn't change what I said to you days ago. We were rumbled. Whatever Parker and Yedlin were doing together, they weren't the top of the chain. When it was known that one or both Parker and Yedlin were about to fall into MI5 hands, they were taken out.'

'I'm not going to dispute that, but Yedlin isn't even my biggest concern right now.'

Another sigh from Winter. 'I've had word on an exclusive that's running first thing tomorrow. Both *The Guardian* and *The Telegraph* are running the same piece concurrently.'

Odd, given they were huge political rivals.

'The link back to us is already known.'

Winter let that one sit. Ryker played it over in his mind.

'As in–'

'As in they know everything we knew about Parker and Yedlin's dirty deals. But that's not all. They also know that MI5 were leading an investigation into the pair. An investigation that they're going to say was botched through shady practices and incompetence, and has so far led to blood and bodies across London and the south, including the death of an innocent man taken out by a runaway Range Rover.'

Ryker was tense as Winter's rant came to an end.

'The only way the press could know all that–'

'Most likely it's come from the inside,' Winter said. 'Yes, I know. But even that isn't my biggest headache. This is just another in a long line of recent hatchet jobs aimed at us.'

Ryker wasn't sure Winter was including him in *us* or not.

'MI5, MI6, the JIA, have never been under this much scrutiny. Have never received such detailed negative press before.'

'The public know nothing about the JIA.'

'It's only a matter of time, Ryker.' Winter sounded dismayed. 'I don't want to sound overly dramatic, but the whole intelligence landscape in this country could be upturned.'

'There's a mole,' Ryker insisted. 'You have to find who it is.'

Winter was silent now.

'I can help.'

'No, Ryker,' Winter said. 'I'm really not sure a man like you could. And perhaps I'm jumping the gun a bit here, but it might be time to start seriously considering your own position, given your role in that crash.'

Ryker squeezed his fists tightly, his nails digging into his skin. Was Winter threatening him that he was about to be thrown under the bus, or was it just friendly advice?

'Who's the journalist?' Ryker said.

'Ryker, you even attempt to–'

'Who?'

'I honestly don't know. The story will be published under a pseudonym – Judy Jones. The papers aren't exactly going to make it that easy for us, are they?'

Ryker was about to reaffirm his position, but there was knock on the door. He paused and looked over, as though if he stared at the scratched-up wood hard enough he'd eke a clue as to who was on the other side.

Another knock.

'*Housekeeping.*'

Except Ryker didn't buy that for a second. Which was why, rather than attempting to answer the door, he ended the call, grabbed the tablet and threw it, and himself, across the bed and to the floor.

38

There was no explosion. The door didn't suddenly crash open. Whoever was out there, they weren't so overt as that. Yet Ryker's decision to dive for cover, out of view of the door, proved sensible moments later when he heard the click-click as the lock on the door was released.

Ryker held his breath and listened as the screen of the tablet, a few inches from his face, went black. A whoosh as the door was pushed open. Footsteps, as soft as could be. But not quite soft enough on the old floor. At least two people, Ryker decided.

He silently rolled into position, his front on the floor, his neck craned so he could see just beyond the edge of the bed. He spread his hands onto the mottled carpet. Pushed his toes down. His body stretched out to keep him low, he was almost in the bottom position of a push-up, ready and waiting to spring upright.

The bedroom door closed softly.

The edge of a shoe poked around the end of the bed.

Ryker burst upward.

Two other men in the room. Unarmed. Or at least no weapons were in their hands.

Ryker barrelled into the first one and crashed him against the wall. An uppercut to the edge of his jaw sent his eyes rolling. Ryker tossed him to the floor and spun around.

Hastings. Two yards away. An angry sneer on his face.

Now with a suppressed pistol in his hand.

Ryker lifted his arm and ducked his head behind it as he charged forward. He grabbed a lamp from the desk and flung it without looking. There was a muffled pop a split second before Ryker barged into Hastings and the two men fell to the floor.

At once, Ryker pinned Hastings's gun hand to the carpet, amidst the broken glass from the lampshade, and thrust his other elbow down into Hastings's nose. Blood erupted. Hastings's grip on the gun loosened, and Ryker could prise the gun from his grip.

He whipped his head around. No, there was no attack from behind. The uppercut had left the second man sprawled on the floor.

Ryker turned his attention back to Hastings. He shoved the gun's barrel up against the man's temple.

'What are you doing here?' Ryker snarled.

Hastings's eyes were fixed on Ryker, but he said nothing. Gave nothing away. No fear, not even anger.

'How did you find me?' Ryker was worried. He'd had no indication that Hastings or anyone else from Fischer's posse had followed him here earlier. So how had they tracked him so quickly?

'You ever been shot before?' Ryker asked when he got no answer to his first question.

Still nothing from Hastings. Ryker pulled the gun from Hastings's head and pushed the barrel of the suppressor against his shoulder. He didn't flinch.

Ryker didn't really want to shoot him and Hastings probably knew. They were in a hotel in central Paris. Yes, the gun had a suppressor, but that didn't make the shots silent – not like in the movies. One shot had already gone off. If that hadn't raised suspicion, another surely would, and Ryker was already a wanted man.

But he also wanted answers.

His finger twitched on the trigger. Then the sound of not-too-distant sirens caught his attention. Ryker's eyes remained on Hastings. Finally something. A look of confidence. A look of someone who believed to be fully in control. His mouth turned up ever so slightly.

Then he bucked and his hand flashed in front of Ryker, who was able to twist sideways, but not quite far enough as the glass shard in Hastings's hand slashed through the air. There was a jolt of pain as the improvised tool cut into Ryker's side.

Hastings bucked again, trying to throw Ryker off. Not going to happen. Ryker tossed the gun a few inches in the air, caught the barrel, then used all the power and weight in his upper body to smash the butt of the gun down onto Hastings's head. Once. Twice.

Hastings's arm flopped. The glass bounced away. His body sank onto the carpet as a gash on the side of his head oozed thick red blood.

Ryker checked the cut on his side, just above his waist. Two inches long, the wound was deep enough for the dark red of muscle below to be visible. Anger taking over, Ryker jumped up off Hastings and grabbed a spare T-shirt and used another of the shards from the floor to cut a swathe of fabric off. He hastily tied the fabric into place, to at least stop the blood flow, and to offer some basic protection to the gaping wound.

Stitches were needed, but not just yet. The sound of sirens were getting louder all the time. So too was a muffled commotion outside the door to Ryker's room. Were the police already out there? Or was it the hotel's security team clearing unsuspecting guests out of the way?

Did Hastings have more people out there?

Ryker moved over to the window and peered out down below. Two police cars, lights flashing, were stationed on the street outside the hotel. Were more on the way? Ryker's brain crashed with conflicting thoughts. Yes, there'd been a racket in the room – pushing the man up against the wall, the broken lamp, the muffled gunshot – probably enough for someone to have called the police. But was it enough for them to have sent such a swift and hefty response?

Ryker didn't believe so. Particularly not when put together with that knowing look on Hastings's face. He'd known the police were coming, and he'd not been in the least bit concerned.

It was time to go.

39

Ryker collected the few things he needed into a rucksack and quickly felt around the two men for anything of significance or use. No wallets, no IDs. A phone each. A gun each. Ryker took the phones, and left the guns. If the police caught him, carrying a weapon would only make his position more serious, and gone were the days when he could rely on his boss to get him out of hot water.

He darted over to the door. Pushed his ear up against it.

He could hear nothing from out in the corridor now.

He carefully opened the door and stuck his head out a few inches. No one there. No sounds of anyone even.

Ryker edged out, closing the door silently behind him. Looked left and right again. Still nothing.

At the far end of the corridor was a fire escape. From his earlier recce of the hotel, Ryker knew the door opened onto a staircase leading down to a quiet side street. But the police, if they were even a little intelligent, would already be stationed at the bottom of the steps. And the door was alarmed.

Instead, Ryker rushed quickly but quietly along the corridor in the other direction, toward the main stairwell. Perhaps at first glance not the most sensible idea, given the police would most likely come in looking for him through the main foyer. But he wasn't going down.

He reached the double doors. Pushed through them. Raced to the bannister and looked down. He couldn't see anyone, but could hear the rush of footsteps heading up.

Ryker spun and darted to the wall, balled his fist and smashed the little glass panel on the fire alarm.

The distraction would surely help. It might even be enough to get the police to wrongly focus all their attention on that fire escape.

Ryker bounded up the stairs, taking them two at a time. Two storeys later he reached the top and he raced along the corridor of the top floor, his sights set on a door about halfway along. By now there were a good half-dozen guests confusedly roaming around him, seemingly unsure whether they should be scared or not, and how to get out quickly and safely. Ryker paid them little attention, even if he received a few questioning glances himself.

He tried the handle of the door. Something of a reactionary move, as he was already prepared to pick the lock. But it wasn't locked. Odd.

He opened the door. Looked up the short set of stairs that led to another closed door. Ryker headed up. A little more cautiously than before. He pulled down the handle of the top door. Unlocked too.

He swung it open with force as he burst out, not quite sure what he was expecting to see as he moved out onto the hotel's roof.

Nothing. No one.

Ryker moved forward.

No. Not no one.

It was the shadow that gave the guy away. A looming shadow

that flicked in front of Ryker just a few inches, cast by the lowering afternoon sun behind him as the man moved.

Ryker darted left as he spun to see the man jump down from the roof of the stairs which Ryker had emerged from. Ryker very nearly caught him as he flew through the air, but could do nothing to stop the downward momentum and both men clattered to the floor. Much like when Ryker had felled Hastings in the hotel room, except this time Ryker wasn't in prime position, and soon found himself pinned and staring into the barrel of a gun.

He recognised the man on top of him. The other one from Fischer's conference. The one who'd been hiding among the protesters.

'Now what?' Ryker said, sounding calm despite his predicament.

The man didn't say anything. At least not to Ryker. Though he did duck his head ever so slightly to speak into the tiny mic attached to the lapel of his shirt.

So who was he speaking to?

'I have him. Rooftop.'

English.

Regardless, the man's decision to speak to his friends was enough of a distraction.

Ryker's arms were useless, but the guy had left his own limbs too exposed, his wrists only inches from Ryker's face. Ryker jerked and pulled his head up as far and fast as he could, opened his mouth and sunk his teeth into the flesh just above the guy's wrist.

He opened fire with the gun, but the barrel was now pointing over Ryker's head. The man yelled in surprise and pain and Ryker winced as he took a blow to the head from a flying fist. He held on, trying to block out the grim thoughts as his mouth filled with blood. He took another blow to the head, which only caused him to clamp down even harder. He was sure he hit bone. But Ryker was desperate. This was fight or die. He ground his jaw from side to side and the man screamed. Ryker took his chance. He let go and heaved upward. Suddenly, he had the momentum.

By the time he was on his feet, he had the man off the ground and he tossed him down. The man's head clattered against the edge of the door frame. His head rolled. He wasn't unconscious, but he was out of it for now.

Spitting out blood and wiping his mouth, Ryker thought about going to him. Checking his pockets. Tossing the gun.

The voices and the thudding footsteps from inside the hotel told him he didn't have time.

He turned and ran.

Ryker didn't break stride as he hurtled along toward the edge of the nine-storey building. He bounded up onto the top of the two-foot ledge, and thrust his arms forward as he leaped through the air. He didn't look down to the gaping empty space beneath him. Kept his gaze focused on the rooftop of the slightly lower building next along.

He made it with almost a yard to spare, and rolled into the fall to save his knees and ankles from the shock of the impact. Which worked, though the knock his arm took in the process sent a rush of pain up his shoulder and into his neck.

Ryker shook it off and was soon on his feet. He risked a look behind him. Wished he hadn't, because he could now see the armed man, back on his feet, racing forward.

Ryker turned and got moving again. This time he took a hard right. He knew he'd never make the jump straight ahead, and in this direction was a grotty apartment block that had little security. From there, Ryker could make a quick escape back onto the streets of Paris.

In theory. But in Ryker's calculations he hadn't reckoned on what happened next.

He reached the edge. Just like before he didn't break stride as he broke over the top. Except this time his leap of faith was accompanied by a bang from behind. The bang of a gun.

The bullet grazed Ryker's arm and splatted into the stonework of the building he was heading for. Probably not a particularly bad wound, all told. But it knocked Ryker off course.

His front foot made it over the lip of the building, but his trailing leg smacked into the edge. He pushed his hands forward but there was nothing to grip on the flat surface. Ryker's whole body swayed backward, and he imagined himself tumbling down into the abyss.

His body slipped over the edge. His fingertips somehow managed to get just enough purchase on the edge of the roof, and Ryker was left dangling.

He wouldn't be able to hold on for long, and with nothing but the ends of his fingers holding his entire body weight, there was no way of gaining enough traction to pull himself up.

He glanced left, right, below. Then to his hands as the fingers of his left hand slipped free.

He was going down.

Ryker tried his best to swing as his right hand inevitably gave way too.

Ryker plummeted, but that final push meant he was at least plummeting sideways. He reached out. Grasped hold of the metal railings of a balcony. His hands slipped all the way down the metal poles until they hit the bottom and his arms smacked against the concrete floor of the balcony. The jolt to his body very nearly caused him to lose his grip straight away. He winced in pain.

Somehow he held on.

At least this time, gripping onto the metal, he was able to

push his forearms down into the concrete. He hauled himself up, grimacing and groaning from effort. He straddled the metal railing before collapsing against the wall of the apartment, chest heaving, the muscles on his fingers, hands and arms on fire. He looked back up to the edge he'd jumped from. Half expecting to see the armed man, ready to take a pot-shot at him.

He wasn't there. So where was he? Had he not been brave enough to make the first jump? Or was he already corralling the troops to cut Ryker off down below?

Ryker would soon find out. His battered body near spent, he pulled himself back up and glanced through the balcony doors of the apartment. Definitely occupied, though he could see no one inside. He lifted his foot and crashed his heel into the glass. It cracked. Two more blows and the double-glazed unit was in pieces. Ryker reached in to unlock the door and stepped inside.

He listened for a second. Anyone home would have been alerted by the sound. Obviously, the place was empty right now. Which was a good thing. Nor was there an alarm. Even better.

Ryker rushed through the cluttered space and to the door. He opened it and glanced along the dingy corridor. No one there either. Ryker headed out, to the stairs, raced down and came to an open foyer.

People here. Two just coming in through the double doors. Two others standing chatting. Ryker slowed. Tried to look casual. Despite the sweat pouring from his brow and the blood seeping through his jacket on his arm and side.

He pulled on a cap. No one paid him any attention. The people here weren't on high alert.

Ryker pushed open the doors and stepped out onto the narrow street. Not heaving here, but there were plenty of people about.

He looked up and down. In the distance he could see flashes

of blue up where the hotel was, but there was no onrush of police coming his way.

He shook his head. He wasn't quite sure why. Anger? Disgust? Confusion?

His head filled with fractious thoughts, he turned and walked away.

First up was tending to his wounds. After that, he had a clear destination in mind.

40

Three days. That's how long it took Haan to build up the courage for the meeting.

The most off-putting aspect of the whole episode was how ordinary everything seemed in the days after Wheeler had been shot. After Barton and Klein had been shot. Haan had barely heard another word about it.

The last member of the heist team, the guy in the basement, hadn't made it, although he had still been alive when his and the identities of the other men were finally confirmed. A German national, a Belgium and another Brit. Quite an international team, and Haan and Chester felt they still didn't have the full picture how and why that team had been put together.

That said, the fact Fischer now had his money back, and that the four heist team members were all dead, had brought some closure. At least to the immediate manhunt. More work was carrying on in the background to identify co-conspirators, though so far Haan had only had a cursory role in that.

She'd been left to get on with her everyday duties, making sure the house was secure, and helping to arrange and organise security for Fischer's transcontinental movements. Not exactly utilising her skill set and experience to the fullest, but certainly better than many of the alternatives given the position she was now in.

Still, the three days up to this point had been among the slowest of her life. Every moment spent second-guessing, wondering whether there was an ulterior motive to each word spoken to her, each action taken by others.

She couldn't go on like this.

She'd chosen Baden-Baden for the meeting. It was local enough, yet not so small that her presence would be obvious. She parked the Mercedes A-Class – one of many pool cars that Chester's team had access to – in the car park for a large convenience store. She did need to go to the shop, but that wasn't the reason she'd come to town.

As had been the case for the last few days – no, scratch that, it had been like this for months – Haan couldn't shake the feeling that she was being watched. No one had followed her here from Fischer's home, she was sure of that, though she also knew that Chester's team had the means to track all of the vehicles in real time. They'd know where Haan was. It wouldn't have been unthinkable to have bugged her phone and other equipment too, which was why she'd left most of her belongings, except her credit card and some cash, in the car.

Were there eyes on her now?

She would never rule it out, yet she had to do this.

Being as careful as she could, Haan made her way around the town on foot, something of a circuitous route that took her in and out of three different shops on the way. Definitely no one following her, she decided.

It was early afternoon, and when she finally arrived at the plain-looking bar-cum-restaurant it was near empty inside. With low ceilings and wood panelling everywhere, the inside looked like a cross between an English country pub and a Swiss ski chalet.

The few other punters paid Haan no attention as she ordered a sparkling water and took a seat in a quiet corner. Six minutes early.

A few minutes later, casual as ever, both in his clothes and his manner, Kyle Schiffler strode over to her table and took a seat.

'You're not thirsty?' Haan asked, indicating to the bar.

'I'm fine,' Schiffler responded. He held her eye for a moment before shaking his head. 'Go on then, give me the snapshot.'

She did. Everything he needed to know – albeit in short form – about what had happened since the heist had gone wrong. Some of this, such as Wheeler's identity, Schiffler already knew from the highly secure and encrypted messages Haan had been able to send out, but it was good to finally let loose and explain things properly.

'Shit,' was Schiffler's uninspired response when Haan had finished.

She said nothing but watched him for a few moments as he sat there, deep in thought. Schiffler was probably only a few years older than she was, with just the smallest hints of grey in his wavy, mousy-brown hair. He had a straight-laced look and a gentle face that fit the man and his role perfectly. Schiffler was a good guy, but he was a behind-the-scenes guy. Life hadn't worn him down like it did to people out doing the dirty work.

'What are you asking for?' he said.

'I think they know.' Haan tried to sound in control.

Schiffler shook his head. 'About you and Wheeler?'

'About everything.'

'You weren't even working for us back then, when you and Wheeler first met.'

'No, but I also wasn't called Daisy Haan back then. If they've found out about my and Wheeler's past, they've found everything else too.'

'Then why are you still alive?' He looked embarrassed by his clumsy and heartless question. 'Sorry, I didn't mean... I mean, why are they letting you carry on as normal if they know? It makes no sense.'

Haan went silent as she thought. It was a question that had bugged her incessantly.

'I'm a government agent,' she finally offered. 'They won't execute me, just like that. They can't afford the fallout right now.' Although she certainly wouldn't rule that out as her fate. 'I think they're trying to find out *why*. Which would explain why they're keeping me close. They want to figure out who I work for, who sent me, and what we know.'

Schiffler looked around him nervously now.

'I'm sorry about Wheeler,' he said. 'I know you two had something of a past.'

Haan resisted rolling her eyes. 'You say it like we were married or something. Yeah I knew Wheeler. We were both different people back then. The biggest issue for me isn't that he's dead, it's about trying to understand what made him target Fischer at all.'

A quizzical look from Schiffler. 'You think it was because of you?'

'No. Not directly at least.'

She didn't elaborate, even though she had plenty of her own theories. Wheeler had intimated that there was more to him stealing from Fischer than just the money. So what was the motivation?

'Jesus, this is a mess,' Schiffler said. 'We can pull you out.'

'No.' Haan shook her head solemnly. 'I'm not going on the run. I've seen Fischer's reach. I'd never be safe.'

'Then just quit,' Schiffler said. 'You're an employee. You said yourself they're just carrying on as normal now, so act normal.

Hand in your notice, say you're sorry for messing up, and leave that place for good.'

Haan gave him the look his ridiculous statement deserved. 'I can't believe you actually suggested that.'

'I–'

'Hand in my notice? Have you forgotten what I've been involved in the last few months? For fuck's sake, I gutted a man a few days ago–'

'A man who was about to attack you.'

'I was party to them torturing an–'

'I'm well aware of what you've been through,' he whispered, leaning in as though worried that her increasing agitation was going to get them rumbled.

'Are you?' she said. 'Because you haven't *lived* it. And I'm sorry, but they don't just let people leave, and even if they did say yes, and it looked and felt to me like I was free, they would still keep tabs on me. On Daisy Haan at least. They'd soon figure it out.'

'Then what are you proposing?'

'Well that's both the issue and the solution, isn't it?'

'What is?'

'I'm not Daisy Haan. But it's Daisy that needs to leave that place.'

Schiffler frowned, but the look soon dropped away. He got it.

'There must be a way,' Haan stated.

'You're right. I think there is.' He got up to leave. 'I'll be in touch.'

41

Was it a gamble? Yes. The Paris conference was over, so Fischer's official time in the city was done, it was the weekend and Fischer's home was only a few hours' drive away. Ryker figured, even with Fischer being a jet-setter who could be travelling around the world for all he knew, the odds were good enough to make his home in the German Black Forest Fischer's next destination.

If not, so be it. Ryker would have some time on his own to figure out how to get into the mansion and see if he could find the evidence to cement the link between Parker, Yedlin, Akkan, and most importantly Moreno's disappearance, back to the billionaire. Perhaps it was better if Fischer wasn't there anyway.

Ryker's journey from Paris in a cheap rental car took far more than the five hours his GPS had suggested, but only because he decided to stop and rest along the way, in a small town close to the German border. The night in the basic hotel gave him a chance to not only recover from the hotel fight the previous day, but to do some more research. Mostly frustrating research, as Fischer's life, however public, was a closed book once the celebrity-face-everywhere surface was wiped away.

The phones Ryker had taken from Hastings and his colleague also proved useless. The devices had been remotely blocked with software that Ryker simply didn't have the knowledge or the tools to break through – sophisticated software, which was an eye-opener. Most likely, the hard drives on the devices had been remotely overwritten too, so there really wasn't any point in spending time trying to access them. Ryker begrudgingly dumped the phones and moved on.

One of the few bright spots of his work was that Ryker managed to identify Fischer's female companion: a British woman named Kathy Chester. She was something of an enigma. Ryker discovered that she was a graduate of the London School of Economics, and in her early twenties had worked in the anti-corruption team of a global consulting firm. Yet her life over the last ten years had been almost entirely off the grid – except for the regular photo ops with Fischer at official events.

When Ryker awoke at 7am the next morning, he was feeling far more groggy than he'd hoped, despite the pleasantly warming rays of sunshine that seeped in through the threadbare curtains of his room.

He achingly got out of bed, clutching his side. He spent the next few minutes checking and redressing the two wounds from the previous day. No sign of infection, but he was definitely suffering from the toil of the last week, and he chucked a few too many pills down his throat to try to get himself feeling fighting fit again.

Not that he would be deterred from the task ahead, however bad he felt.

As he had done the previous evening, Ryker attempted to reach Winter via various modes of communication – payphone, regular mobile, VoIP, secure messenger – but he had zero bites, and as a result was becoming increasingly concerned – for himself.

Just as Winter had predicted when they'd last spoken, the UK press had run a heavily publicised exposé of the Parker/Yedlin mess, taking direct aim at the UK's intelligence community, in particular MI5, for its botched sting operation. The backlash had only just begun, and Ryker could well imagine it ramping up several notches over the coming days. Was that why Winter was now ignoring him? Was he under strict orders to do so? Had Winter been removed from the JIA altogether because of the furore?

No, if that was the case, he surely would have tried to reach out to tell Ryker. Wouldn't he?

Whatever the answer, there was no doubt that Ryker was feeling increasingly isolated as he made the short journey over the border into Germany, and into the rolling pine forests that dominated the region. The simple fact was that for years, as an agent with the JIA, Ryker had worked alone on investigations, often deep undercover, and he knew too well how that dark area of government operations worked. Back in those days if Ryker was caught behind enemy lines, there was a good chance that his own people would simply abandon him. He'd lived with that prospect over countless so called black-ops, and had pulled himself out of numerous life-threatening positions without the help of anyone else, knowing that if he didn't, his days were over.

So why did this situation feel different?

Perhaps it was because, if the likes of MI5 and the JIA were under full-on attack, then Ryker – having lived a life of clandestine violence at the behest of the UK government – was a legitimate target.

Would he soon find himself enemy number one?

And yet, despite that, rather than lying low and hoping the storm would pass, he was on a personal mission en route to the home of one of the world's wealthiest and most famous people.

There, no doubt, would be further confrontation, one way or another...

As the saying goes, live by the sword, die by the sword. Ryker grinned wryly.

He dumped the car two miles from Fischer's home, deep in a dense pine forest with sporadic narrow and twisting roads. To make sure the vehicle remained out of sight from anyone driving by, he left the car a couple of hundred yards off the tarmac.

He made his way through the trees on foot, the ground beneath him rising and falling, steeply at times, making the going slow and strenuous. He used a handheld GPS to help guide him, having left most of the electronic equipment he'd previously purchased in the safe of a newly rented hotel room in a small town not far from Fischer's home. Ryker was still unsure how Hastings and crew had tracked him to his Paris hotel. One obvious theory was that they'd somehow managed to hack his equipment. The GPS, however, was new, and far more difficult to hack than a phone or tablet which were particularly prone to malware through their wifi and cellular network connections.

Other than some small birds and squirrels, Ryker saw nothing and no one on his traipse toward Fischer's home. He'd been wondering how far out from the property the security would stretch. Sentries in the forest? CCTV in the trees? Booby traps? He wouldn't have put any of that past Fischer, but Ryker saw nothing.

Perhaps that was a problem. Was Fischer simply one step – or several steps – ahead of him?

Ryker wouldn't be deterred.

He carried on and when he was 500 yards out and satisfied

of direction, he stuffed the GPS into his backpack. Barely two minutes later, Ryker came over the top of a small rise in the forest, and down in the sprawling valley that opened out in front of him he caught a glimpse of the white paint of a rendered wall.

Ryker moved more cautiously, looking around him, and upward to the trees, for signs of anyone or anything registering his approach.

Despite the slow pace it wasn't long before he was fifty yards from the wall which stretched out to the left and right as far as he could see through the dense trees. At little more than seven feet high, the wall didn't have any barbed wire or other deterrents on top – after all, this was supposed to be a home, and not a fortress.

He could also see three CCTV cameras perched on the wall from where he was standing, but he was sure he remained in cover at this distance, with each of the cameras pointed down facing sides of the wall to capture as much of the area immediately along the perimeter as possible.

Ryker didn't have the means to try to interfere with cameras' signals. It was possible that he could devise such a means if he went away, gave it some thought and came back at a later point.

No. He was here now.

What was the worst that could happen?

He decided to move on, but he wouldn't head straight for the wall. Instead he'd move around it, keeping his distance, so he could properly scope the layout and the entrances.

He'd only moved a few more yards, however, when a sound behind him caused him to freeze. The snapping of a twig.

'Put your hands where I can see them,' came a voice.

English. Although not native.

Ryker moved his hands above his head and turned to face the man. Dressed in brown-and-green camouflage, carrying a semi-automatic weapon, he looked like an infantry soldier. Some home security. As Ryker stared, another two identically-dressed men emerged through the trees.

'Come on, this way,' said the man brandishing the gun, indicating toward the house.

'You lead the way,' Ryker said, just about managing to withhold his smile.

Had he really expected to be able to get to Fischer's property, in broad daylight, while the big man was home, without any real pre-planning and by simply walking up to the front door? He'd hoped it was possible, but his somewhat blasé approach had also been a research exercise. An interesting test, as it turned out, to see exactly what level of security Fischer was operating. Of course it was never ideal to be held at gunpoint, but the big question was what would come next?

The three armed men escorted Ryker along the perimeter wall to a wide metal gate. The main entrance, Ryker presumed, given the size of it.

One of the men stepped forward and placed his hand upon a scanner next to the gate, before inputting a code into a keypad which slid out from a tiny slit in the wall. Moments later the hefty gate silently and effortlessly glided out of view, disappearing into a crevice in the wall. Sleek, slick. Expensive.

'Move.'

Ryker took a prod in the back from a rifle barrel and edged forward. Dumbstruck wasn't quite the word to describe his reaction as he stared beyond the gates. He'd been to some impressive properties in his time, had brushed shoulders with the mega-rich over the years, but Fischer's home was a different prospect altogether.

The gargantuan gardens that greeted him were simply breathtaking. The backdrop of the Black Forest mountains that surrounded them provided a stark yet blissful contrast to the heavily-manicured lawns and shrubs and trees and water features. Yet it was the home itself which took centre stage. Two storeys tall, the mansion was cuboid in design, with squares jutting out left, right, up and down, everything either glistening glass or white render or grey powder-coated aluminium. The ultra-modern, almost space-age design wasn't to Ryker's taste, but it was an impressive statement of style with the wealth to match it.

A couple of hundred yards later and they were finally approaching the outer double doors to the house, which remained shut. Despite the large turning circle by the entrance, there were no vehicles in sight. What he had seen, on the walk over, was an empty helipad. Did that mean anything?

So was Fischer not here after all?

One of the armed men spoke into a mic on his lapel and thirty seconds later the entrance doors slid open. Ryker was a little disappointed that he hadn't seen the guards open the doors from the outside, which would have given away further detail about the house's security. Was that deliberate?

Ryker stared inside. And there she was. Kathy Chester. A little less formally dressed than in Paris, but still pristine from head to toe.

'Okay, thank you,' Chester said to the men surrounding Ryker. 'I'll take it from here.'

At first Ryker had thought Chester was alone inside the expansive marble-covered entrance hall, but out of the shadows stepped a man. Not Fischer, which was a shame, but Hastings.

At least Ryker now had a definitive answer to that one. Hastings's face looked like he'd been through twelve rounds with a heavyweight, all swollen and purple. His sneer today was extra deep.

'Come on then,' Chester said, catching Ryker's eye. 'Follow me, Mr Ryker.'

42

No one spoke as Chester and Hastings escorted Ryker on a frustratingly short journey through Fischer's home. He'd been hoping to get a better sense of the internal layout, but having moved across the foyer, dominated by a spectacular floating staircase, Ryker was taken down a more bland corridor into the first room they came to. Even though it was at least twenty feet by twenty feet, and decked out in tasteful modern furnishings, including two large and sumptuous sofas, a state-of-the-art TV and music system, the room felt a little unloved. Certainly not Fischer's main living space, Ryker decided. A restroom for the staff, perhaps?

A coffee machine lay untouched in the corner. Ryker wasn't going to be afforded any hospitality, apparently.

Ryker took one of the sofas. Chester took the one opposite. Hastings stood over by the window, arms folded. No one stood by the doorway, blocking Ryker's exit, as though Chester didn't think it remotely likely that Ryker would try to do anything stupid.

'It would have been preferable if you'd tried to approach us a little more openly,' Chester said. 'And a little less deceitfully.'

'You mean like Hastings over here,' Ryker said. 'Breaking into my hotel room and then trying to shoot me?'

Chester said nothing. She shook her head ever so slightly, as though disappointed in someone or something.

'What are you doing here, Mr Ryker?'

The second time she'd used his name. How on earth did they know his identity? Once again Ryker questioned their reach. He was sure Chester wanted him to ask – why else was she using his name so brazenly? – but he wouldn't. He'd play along with this game, and see where it was going.

'So where's Bastian?' Ryker asked.

Chester sighed. 'On business.'

'You didn't go with him?'

'I don't always. Only when he needs me. I'm not his chaperone.'

'It's a shame he's not here. I had quite a few questions for him.'

'Anything you had to say to Mr Fischer, you can say to me.'

'Fair enough.'

'So I'll ask you again, Mr Ryker, why are you here?'

'Given you've figured out who I am,' Ryker said, 'you probably also know who I work for.'

Chester turned up her hands, a look of confusion. 'You don't work for anybody, is my understanding.'

Ryker tried to show no reaction to that. 'Let's start with the basics then. Recently I was working *with* the UK government. Part of a covert investigation into two men. Clint Parker and Yuri Yedlin. You know them?'

'I understand they are both dead,' Chester replied. 'I do watch the news, you know.'

Watch the news? Fischer and his allies *created* the news.

'Yes, they're both dead,' Ryker said. 'And I'm trying to find out why.'

'Unfortunately you won't find any answers here.'

'No? So Fischer didn't know Parker and Yedlin? Neither did you?'

Chester shook her head.

'And you had nothing to do with their deaths?'

'Why on earth would you think that?'

Ryker didn't respond, but he stared hard at Chester, trying to read her face.

Nothing. Her expression was stone cold.

'You want me to tell you what I think?' Ryker said.

Chester sighed, before looking over to Hastings. Ryker glanced over to see the man had barely moved. His glare remained on Ryker.

'He really hates me, doesn't he?' Ryker remarked.

'You gave him quite a concussion. Technically he shouldn't be on duty after a day like that, but he insisted, though I had a different team travel with Mr Fischer. And after all, we guessed you'd be back, and he didn't want to miss seeing you again.'

'Fischer is a very rich man,' Ryker said. 'Is Hastings really the best you could find to protect the boss?'

A look of offence in Hastings's eyes though he clearly had strong willpower as he remained rooted to the spot.

Chester sighed. 'Let's go back to your previous question. I'm intrigued. What do you think is happening here?'

'Okay. Glad you asked,' Ryker said, acting deliberately nonchalantly. 'See, I found the people who kidnapped Parker, before he was murdered. A collection of young guys, mostly German and Turkish, working for a local gangster in London called Yunus Akkan.'

'I heard about him too,' Chester said. 'Dead, right? You have quite the storm cloud hanging over you. Everywhere you go–'

'Akkan was low level. There's no reason why he would have been involved in the ring Parker and Yedlin had going.'

'The ring?'

'Big money corruption. Funding for extreme politics. That wasn't Akkan. So someone paid him. A simple deal. Money upfront in order to pull Parker out from under our noses.'

'Because?'

'Because we were about to expose everything they were up to.'

'By *everything*, you mean exactly what has just come out in the British press this morning? Hardly earth-shattering now is it, if *The Telegraph* and *Guardian* were able to figure it out. What does that say about the aptitude of MI5?'

Ryker held his tongue for a moment. It was a fair point, in a way. Except the press only had the inside information because of a mole. So who exactly was the source?

'The point is,' Ryker said, 'someone paid Akkan. I think that someone was Fischer.'

That shake of the head again.

'I could always pass what I already have to the UK press to help them on their way,' Ryker added.

Chester actually rolled her eyes, as if she was in the midst of a conversation with a petulant child. 'If there was any real evidence that linked Mr Fischer to these people, I'm sure you wouldn't be skulking around a pine forest like you were just now. You have no evidence, because there is none.'

Ryker laughed. Deliberately mocking. 'Wishful thinking. Come on, we all know the truth here. Well, perhaps bozo over there doesn't. But you and me.' Ryker held Chester's gaze. 'Fischer was behind Parker and Yedlin getting taken out. And I'm pretty damn sure he, and you, were also behind the press leak. Money and power can buy you a lot of things, can bury a lot of things too, but it can't change simple facts.'

'Actually, over the years I've found facts to be quite fluid.'

A curious response.

'And then, of course, there's Sam Moreno,' Ryker said.

That stone-cold expression once more.

'Sam Moreno,' Ryker said. 'Former SIS employee. She went missing last week.'

'Interesting story,' Chester remarked.

'The thing is, Parker and Yedlin? I really couldn't give a toss that they're dead, though I do care *why*. But the biggest pull for me is finding where Moreno is. And if she's been hurt...'

'I don't doubt your sense of vengeance,' Chester said. 'I've seen first-hand the type of man you are. But let me ask you this, if Mr Fischer, and by extension myself, are really so devious, cunning, and ruthless as you are insinuating, to be involved in the deaths of these men, the disappearance of your friend, why on earth have you walked right into our hands?'

Ryker smiled. 'Because I'm not in the least bit scared of any of you, or anything you could possibly do to me. I actually find the whole set-up here quite pathetic.'

A slight twitch on Chester's face. The first sign of agitation.

'You do realise your own government has abandoned you,' Chester pointed out. 'Your concocted identity is meaningless. If you disappeared today, the world wouldn't bat an eyelid. No one would come looking. No one would care.'

'Now come the threats,' Ryker said. 'Just as I thought.'

He got up from the sofa. Hastings flinched. On cue, a suited armed guard moved across the open doorway to the room.

'Tell me what happened to Moreno.' Ryker looked down to Chester.

She said nothing. The man at the door stepped forward, pulled the barrel of his handgun a little higher so it was pointed at Ryker's midriff. A second man came into the room behind him.

'Tell me what happened to Moreno,' Ryker insisted. 'Neither of us needs the bloodshed.'

Chester still said nothing. Ryker looked over to the armed men, then to Hastings, then back to Chester.

Okay. This was bad now.

'Timing delay,' he announced.

'I beg your pardon?'

'I'm sure the concept is familiar with you. A timer. A preset event scheduled to happen at the end of an allotted period.'

'You've lost me.'

Ryker tapped the third from top button on his shirt.

'Tiny, right?'

Chester's eyes narrowed slightly as she stared.

'Every part of this conversation has been recorded,' Ryker explained. 'Everything you've said. Everything I've seen, including the military-grade weapons of those men outside, and your threat to me just now. So this is what will happen. I'm going to walk out of here. Untouched. If I don't, not only does the video of whatever you do to me play out for the world to see, but every piece of evidence I have against Fischer gets uploaded too.'

Chester opened her mouth to say something but paused, as though thinking better of it. Then she tried again.

'I really have no idea why you went to all that trouble.' She sounded offended. 'You are, of course, free to leave whenever you like. Even if you were technically trespassing.'

Ryker looked over to the two guards who were now grumpily standing down. Chester's words and demeanour had thrown Ryker a little. He'd expected more fight. More intimidation and peril. Had he misread the situation? The passive-aggressive nature of Chester?

Had there ever really been a threat here?

Ryker turned for the door. The two guards stepped aside. Ryker headed on out, Chester now up on her feet and close behind him. By the time Ryker made it to the front doors, they'd already been opened by the guard standing there. Slick. Once again, Ryker hadn't even caught a glimpse of the operation of the security there.

Ryker glanced back to Chester. 'See you soon,' he said.

Chester stopped just before the door. 'Life is all about choices, Mr Ryker. But if you so wish, you'll know where to find me.'

Her oily tone wasn't lost on Ryker. No, he hadn't misread the situation. The underlying threat was all too clear, and Ryker's subterfuge was likely the only reason he was now walking out of the mansion so easily.

Next time, he was sure it wouldn't be so simple.

He headed out without saying another word.

43

Haan would be lying if she said she wasn't filled with dread on her first return to France since the day they'd nabbed Wheeler in Frichebois. She'd been so stiff her bones hurt as they drove toward the border, she in the driver's seat, Anderson – a curious newcomer to the team – her passenger. Even when it was clear there was no welcoming party at the border, and they were safely travelling northwards to their destination, Haan still found it hard to relax.

At least Anderson was talkative enough to keep her distracted some of the time. They'd only met the previous day but Haan had already decided he was different in almost every respect to the likes of Barton. Haan actually quite liked Anderson. He was from Denmark, and like her he'd originally been in the army, then special forces, before moving on to even more shady roles which he acknowledged with as few words as possible. He'd only come out the other side of that dark life in the last twelve months, to pursue a more sensible and potentially less fatal career in private security. Strangely, despite his past, he seemed upbeat about life. But perhaps that was just a facade.

Chester and Fischer demanded certain qualities, and one of those qualities was an unerring dark side.

'You haven't been before, then?' Anderson asked as Haan checked the satnav screen before making the left turn that would take them into the village.

'No,' she said. 'Never even heard of this place until two days ago.'

Which was true, even if much of the rest of the reason for coming here was bullshit.

'Yeah, well I heard about what happened last time you came over to France. We're sticking together today. In sight always.'

Haan looked over at him. Anderson had a resolute look on his face now, quite a contrast to his cheeriness from earlier in the journey. Obviously, he'd joined the team *after* everything had gone tits-up in Frichebois. It wouldn't surprise her if he'd been brought in specifically to spy on her.

'Frichebois only turned into a mess because Barton wouldn't listen to me. If you do what I tell you to today, we won't have any problems.'

He shrugged nonchalantly. 'You got it.'

They managed to park directly outside the three-storey building they were looking for. The twisting street was lined both sides with a variety of two- to five-storey buildings, most of them now broken up into multiple apartments, and most of them old and in some need of repair. The village was small, rural and not particularly affluent, though the old-world character of the buildings was evident with original features including wooden shutters and wrought-iron balconies dotted all over.

'Top floor?' Anderson said.

'From what I could figure out, yeah.'

Not all her own work, mainly because Chester seemed to be

doing her best to keep Haan away from the centre of the action now, but Haan had still managed to make a breakthrough. Using her own wits, and the crumbs she was given by Chester and the others, Haan's research had confirmed that Wheeler and crew had used this town as a stopover, not just in the days leading up to the heist, but in an initial recce performed several weeks previously. Using the identity of a French soldier missing in action, they'd managed to rent this apartment on a six-month contract. Not a bad idea really, as the rental looked innocuous and left virtually no paper trail compared to them paying for multiple rooms in hotels for example.

The hope was that the apartment, the heist team's main fall-back point, would still hold clues about the heist, in particular who really set it up and why.

'Any idea how long they were here for?' Anderson said as they stepped out of the car into the mid-afternoon drizzle.

'Other than the date of the rental contract, no idea.'

Both of them had coats on, zipped up. Both had handguns holstered inside. Yes, it was a risk to be carrying firearms, particularly after how Frichebois had ended, but having the protection had to be worth it. They expected to be walking into an empty apartment today, but why take chances – especially as Haan was still technically wanted by the Gendarmerie, even if they didn't know her identity.

They headed to the communal front door for number fifty-four, a tall oak fixture that looked like it had been standing for over 200 years, and last painted in its first century of life.

Twenty seconds later they'd picked the single lock and were inside the grimy and dusty interior, climbing the stairs to the top floor. Absolute silence as they moved on past the closed doors to the other apartments – two on each floor.

Permanently empty or were the residents just out?

The door to apartment five was a lot newer than the outer door downstairs, though not any more secure. Once they'd picked the lock, Anderson and Haan stepped through, both of them with a hand inside their now partly-open jackets, just in case.

No need. It soon became obvious that the pokey two-bedroom apartment was empty. Not just of people, but also pretty much of furniture. The two bedrooms had nothing but a single bed and a double mattress between them. The living area had a threadbare sofa and a dated TV in one corner, complete with antenna.

'Well I guess it's not going to take too long to check then, is it?' Haan said.

Anderson didn't say anything, though he didn't look impressed.

'Let's do what we can,' Haan suggested. 'Under floorboards, look for ceiling spaces, any wall cavities, whatever. Why don't we take a bedroom each to start with?'

Anderson frowned. 'We do this together.'

Of course. She wasn't to be let out of his sight. Whatever.

'Fine. Let's take the bigger of the bedrooms first.'

'Bigger' was technically correct, but the space was all of twelve feet by twelve feet. At the front of the property it had a set of French doors that opened inward to reveal a Juliet balcony. The room was actually quaint, and if someone had bothered to spend a bit of time caring for the apartment the place would have been charming. Rather than lifeless, and just a little bit eerie.

But was its eeriness more because of Haan's mood?

They'd been searching for less than five minutes, and found absolutely nothing, when Haan stopped pulling on the floor-board in the corner and froze.

'What?' Anderson said.

'Shh.'

Both of them went silent. Haan turned around and straightened up. Anderson was the other side of the room, standing and staring at her.

'What?' he repeated.

Haan moved over to the window and pulled the moth-eaten lace aside to peer out. She had a good view of the street from there, but couldn't see the front entrance of the building.

'I heard something,' Haan said.

'What? Police?'

No. Not exactly.

'I don't hear a siren,' Anderson said. 'In fact, I don't hear anything.'

'I don't like this,' Haan stated. She looked back to him. She could tell he was dubious. 'There's no back exit, is there?'

'No.'

The building had been built way before modern fire escapes were a requirement, and clearly the landlord had decided against attempting to bring the place up to standard. Which meant Haan and Anderson were sitting ducks up here if anything went wrong.

Haan headed for the bedroom door.

'Where are you going?' Anderson stepped over as if to stop her.

'I'm taking a look down the stairs. Then outside.'

'What are you expecting to see?' He moved over to the window himself now. 'There's no SWAT team out there.'

'Then, in five minutes we'll both be laughing about my nervousness.'

He held her eye. What was he thinking?

She turned and continued to the door.

'I'm going with you,' he said.

She rolled her eyes. He didn't see.

Haan cautiously stepped out of the room, then out of the apartment and moved to the bannister. She glanced over the top and down below. Nobody there, not even another resident coming or going.

'So?' Anderson said, coming to her side.

'So I'm going to check outside, like I said. You know it would be better if one of us kept watch by the car anyway.'

'Not going to happen. Sorry.'

Haan shook her head.

They headed down, Haan in the front. Still no sign – or sound – of anyone.

Haan pulled on the handle for the ageing front door and stepped out. Two steps. Then she stopped and turned to Anderson.

'And?' he said, as he, too, moved into the open.

He froze when his eyes fell upon the half dozen Gendarmes, full riot gear, weapons trained on Haan and him.

A flurry of angry French followed. 'Don't move', 'hands in the air', and the like.

Anderson glared at Haan. Did he know?

His eyes pinched slightly. What did that mean?

She saw his hand flinch. She nodded to him, then her hand whipped into her jacket and she grabbed the gun. She'd managed to pull it out before the gunfire started, though her thumb wasn't even on the trigger when the first bullet hit her in the shoulder.

The weapon was soon out of her grasp, and Haan's body was falling to the ground.

She landed on her side, her head smacked onto the concrete. She was only faintly aware of Anderson, lying prone a few yards away, as her eyes slowly closed.

When Haan's eyelids slid open again it took several seconds for her confused brain to process what she was seeing.

'Just take it easy,' said the fuzzy shape next to her.

She squinted and blinked her eyes a few times until finally the world around her made sense. A very small world, as it turned out. The back of an ambulance. Haan was lying down on a gurney. One of two in the vehicle. The other was on the opposite side to her. The body on that one was covered in a white sheet, head to toe, not even a glimpse of flesh. Not Anderson, she didn't think. The frame was too short and too thin.

Sitting next to Haan was a man. Not a paramedic. Schiffler.

'Just sit tight,' he said when Haan squirmed and tried to prop herself up. 'You've taken quite a few rubber bullets. Non-fatal doesn't mean non-injury.'

Haan closed her eyes and groaned.

'Anderson?'

Schiffler didn't answer. She opened her eyes again and looked up to him.

'It was his choice,' Schiffler said. 'He could have surrendered. He could have stayed at home today. He could have not bothered signing up to work for Fischer in the first place.'

Could have surrendered? No, that wouldn't have saved Anderson. Rubber bullets for her, but not for him. Anderson was collateral damage. Just as Haan had known he would be. There hadn't been another way. Not with Chester intent on having someone following Haan's every move.

'If it's any consolation, Anderson was no angel,' Schiffler told her. 'I did some digging and he–'

'Stop,' Haan said, finding the strength to shake her head. 'I really don't want to know.'

Just like she didn't want to know who the poor woman was lying on the gurney next to her. Of course, Haan had known the plan, had signed up for it, but she'd deliberately kept herself in denial about certain key elements. Like the identity of the woman who would be buried with the name Daisy Haan engraved on her tombstone. Not that this woman – unlike Anderson – had been killed just to help save Haan's backside. She'd already been dead, her body 'procured' by Schiffler. Haan had left all the murky dealings to him, from finding the body to setting up the fake sting, to making sure enough people in the French authorities played their part.

'You did it,' Schiffler said. He took hold of her hand. Even though she didn't appreciate the gesture, she didn't try to remove her fingers from his gentle grip. 'Daisy Haan is dead,' he proclaimed.

Haan didn't say anything as she tried to push back the emotion welling inside her. What was that emotion?

'Daisy Haan is dead,' Schiffler said again. 'She's dead, so now you can live.'

44

Ryker didn't bother with the walk through the woods as he left the mansion. At least not until he was back near the spot where he'd left his car. Traipsing along the road, he'd been aware of watchful eyes still on him, though it wasn't until he was in his car, and on the road, that he actually spotted them. Not the camouflaged soldiers in the woods anymore, but a car – a small dark-blue hatchback – following him away from Fischer's.

Just another tactic by Chester to heap pressure on Ryker, make him feel constrained, unable to operate in the ways he wanted to because he was always under watch.

Ryker didn't do being constrained. Didn't want to be under Chester's spotlight. Which was why, when he was still a couple of miles from the nearest town and he'd just taken a sharp bend putting him out of sight of the blue car, he slammed his foot onto the brake pedal and pulled the car to a rocking halt at the side of the road.

He turned off the engine, stepped out and moved around to the rear of the car. He could hear the engine of the blue car, fast approaching, the driver likely increasing his speed to catch up with Ryker.

Not for long. The blue car came into view. Ryker spotted the startled reaction of the driver. Then came the screech of brakes.

Interesting that he'd chosen that option, rather than simply driving on past.

The blue car came to a stop less than ten yards from where Ryker was standing.

He walked toward it.

The driver and his passenger – Ryker recognised neither – were hurriedly talking to each other. The passenger opened his door and stepped out.

'Can you help me?' Ryker shouted to him. 'My tyre's gone.'

A muffled exchange between passenger and driver. The passenger closed his door, his hand near his hip where Ryker could see the obvious bulge beneath his jacket. In his jeans waistband, with the jacket over the top, the weapon was well hidden but was hardly in the best position for a quick fire.

One very good reason why Ryker carried on moving toward him. A little more quickly now than before.

'Do you speak English?' Ryker said, then half turned and pointed back to his car. 'I need help fixing my tyre.'

The guy said nothing, but with Ryker all of three yards away he now reached for the gun.

Too late.

Ryker rushed forward. The guy managed to get the gun in his hand, and in the open air, but that was about it. As he went to lift the weapon, two-handed, Ryker reached out, grabbed his wrists and tugged forward while he swept his leg to take the guy's feet off the ground.

The man plummeted face first and his forehead smacked off the bonnet of the car as he went.

Ryker crouched down, prised the gun away, and then straightened up, holding the guy around his neck to keep him subdued.

He turned the gun to the windscreen where the driver was fumbling for his own weapon. Ryker fired. Once. Twice. The windscreen was obliterated and Ryker pointed the gun inside.

'Toss me the gun,' he said.

The driver froze. He had the gun in his hand, but wouldn't have a chance at firing it before Ryker put a bullet in his brain. He must have realised that as after a brief stand-off he pinged the gun over and it bounced off the bonnet onto the tarmac.

'Thanks,' Ryker said.

He emptied the rest of the gun's magazine into the bonnet and the two front tyres then hurled the empty gun into the woods. He threw the passenger to the ground, grabbed the other gun and tossed that also into the woods.

By the time he was walking back to his own car, smoke whooshed out from within the mangled engine.

Ryker jumped into his rental, turned on the engine and glanced in his rear-view mirror as he pulled back into the road. The passenger was groggily hauling himself to his feet. The driver, sullen-faced, remained in position.

Ryker smiled. Soon, he was far out of sight of the blue car.

It took Ryker two hours to collect his belongings before finding another basic hotel in another French border town he'd never heard of. Better safe than sorry.

A frustrating day, in one sense. He still had nothing new on Parker, Yedlin, or Moreno. Yet getting inside Fischer's ultra-secure home hadn't been a pointless exercise.

Fischer was part of the rich elite in the world, but not all of them had such heavily-fortified homes. The security tech was one thing, but Fischer had a mini army of security. Something akin to having his own intelligence agency with not just brute physical presence, but sophisticated snooping capabilities, given their ability to track Ryker in France and to find his identity so quickly. All of that wasn't just because Fischer was particular about his personal safety, or because he was trying to protect a few home valuables. It was because he was hiding something. Something big. Secrets that could ruin him.

Ryker would find them. Expose them.

Sitting on his hotel-room bed, Ryker finally put the pieces into place for a phone call. Winter wasn't responding to him, so Ryker had found an alternative solution: he'd remotely hacked into Winter's mother's mobile phone. Winter may have been a Commander for the JIA, and pretty damn clued-up on technology security, but unfortunately – or fortunately for Ryker – that knowledge didn't spread through the whole Winter family.

The call rang through on Ryker's tablet. All Winter would see on his phone screen was an incoming call from mum.

'Hey,' came the upbeat response when the call was finally answered.

Bingo.

'It's me,' Ryker said. 'Don't hang up.'

A sigh. Angry. If a sigh through a tinny tablet speaker could convey that.

'How the hell–'

'She's fine. It's just a hack.' Ryker paused, awaiting a response. None came. 'I'm sorry, I didn't know any other way.'

'You've got a bloody nerve–'

'Just give me two minutes.'

Another pause. Better than an empty line.

'I'm getting closer to Fischer,' Ryker said. 'I still don't know everything, but Fischer is bad news.'

Silence. That was strange. Ryker had expected a bite back. For Winter to tell him he was barking up the wrong tree, or had gone off on a wild tangent, or should just give up and go home.

'I saw the press reports,' Ryker went on.

Another sigh. 'Give me a second.'

The line stayed connected, Ryker heard nothing but breathing and bangs and knocks. After a while he could also hear the faint whistle of wind and the groan of inner-city traffic. Wherever Winter had been, he was now outside.

'I've never seen anything like this,' Winter said. 'It's no understatement to say the whole structure of the UK intelligence services is on the verge of implosion. It's not just what came out today, whoever is doing this has years' worth of dirt.'

Ryker closed his eyes. 'The JIA?'

'At this stage we're no more protected than MI6 or MI5.'

'I think Fischer has something to do with this.'

It was a leap. But it made sense, didn't it?

'He's trying to cover his tracks,' Ryker continued, 'because we were too close on Yedlin and Parker. This whitewash is nothing more than distraction.'

'Ryker, for god's sake, our involvement in the Yedlin and Parker sting is just the tip of the iceberg. You know damn well the things we've done over the years, the things we had *you* do. If it all goes public...'

'If it all goes public, what?'

Silence.

'I need to know, Winter. Whatever Fischer is doing, I can stop it, but I need to know everything you know. How is he linked to Parker and Yedlin? How is he linked to the UK government? JIA, MI6, MI5, whatever?'

Winter's continued silence suggested Ryker wasn't far off the mark.

'They found my identity,' Ryker said. 'In the space of twenty-four hours, from seeing my face in Paris, they'd figured who I am, and who I worked for. They've got teams of security guards, secret agent types, soldiers, whatever, they've got links to the Paris police, to the press, their reach is–'

'Daisy Haan,' Winter said.

'What?'

'I honestly don't know everything, and until recently I knew nothing at all, but that name is something I do know now. Daisy Haan.'

'Who–'

'I'm sorry. I've got to go.'

The call went dead.

Ryker didn't bother calling back. It was clear Winter had told him all he would, or could. His tone during the conversation... the Commander had sounded genuinely rattled. He wasn't being evasive with Ryker because he no longer trusted or saw Ryker as an ally, he was being evasive because of the pressure on his own back.

Yet he'd still given Ryker something. Daisy Haan. A name Ryker had not come across before.

He got straight onto the internet to search for leads. Daisy Haan wasn't exactly a common name, it turned out, but it also wasn't a one-off. None of the social media profiles in the search results were of interest, but then a news story caught his eye. Dated nearly three years ago, and published by the small local paper of a town on the outskirts of Essen in the industrial Ruhr district of northern Germany. A thirty-five-year-old woman had been shot dead by the French Gendarmerie in...

Shit.

That was enough of a connection for Ryker. The town Haan had been killed in was one that Ryker had passed the previous day on his way from Paris to the Black Forest, one of numerous small towns lining the vast French-German border.

Ryker carried on searching, moving into French now to try to figure out what had happened to Haan.

Finally, he found a more detailed article from a publication that had carried the story the day Haan had been killed. Not just Haan, in fact, but Haan and a Danish man named Anderson, both of whom were wanted individuals. The two had got into a gunfight with the Gendarmerie. Both had been killed before they could be arrested. The press had likened their demise to Bonnie and Clyde, though it seemed to be pretty much a non-story that hadn't had any legs after the event.

Which itself was odd, given the circumstances.

But odder by far was the picture of the two victims that accompanied the article.

Ryker had never seen the man, Anderson, before.

But Daisy Haan... Ryker stared open-mouthed at the tablet screen.

At a woman he knew not as Daisy Haan, but as Sam Moreno.

45

Ryker was soon back in his car, his head a mess of unanswered questions. Why had Winter given him this lead? And why now? Perhaps most importantly, how had Winter himself known, and for how long?

No, that wasn't most important. Figuring out what linked Haan, aka Moreno, to everything else was, because that had to be the case, otherwise Winter wouldn't have mentioned the name at all.

Ryker's starting point in finding some of those answers was the town of Velbert, just south of Essen. Ryker had been to the Ruhr district of Germany before, but was unfamiliar with this particular town. The wider area was heavily industrialised, and had been since the early twentieth century when the Ruhr had a huge part to play in the infrastructure of the German armed forces in both world wars. Modern-day Ruhr was far more technologically advanced, though heavy industry remained, spread through a collection of large cities all intermingled into one huge metropolitan area. Velbert, though, despite its proximity to those industrial monoliths, had a small-town quaintness to it. At least the parts Ryker saw.

He'd found out what he could about Daisy Haan in the brief time before he'd set off for Velbert. She'd been thirty-five when she was shot dead. A German national who'd been born and raised in Velbert. An only child, both her parents had died before her. Ryker fully believed that Haan's entire existence was a carefully concocted legend for Moreno. But that didn't explain the whole story, or how the lives of two people had allegedly been taken by the French authorities.

He hoped to find some answers in Velbert. Such a tightly crafted legend as Haan's meant accomplices, but also people who Haan – aka Moreno – had interacted with. People who knew Haan only as Haan, but also people who knew the real story – that Haan was really Sam Moreno.

The main point was that by digging into Haan and her past, Ryker hoped he would unearth a clue as to where Moreno now was.

The heavens had opened by the time Ryker made it to the cemetery on the outskirts of the town. Flanked by a gothic, grey stone church, the cemetery took up a sweeping hill with views over the leafy town below. Ryker didn't have an appropriate coat, or an umbrella, and he was already soaked by the time he was slowly walking among the tombstones.

Five minutes later he was standing in front of the heavily weathered stone he'd been looking for. Nothing elaborate here. Just a simple black marble-effect stone with gold engraving bearing Haan's name, date of birth, and date of death. No flowers adorned the grass in front of it, and it didn't look like there ever had been anything here. Clearly Haan didn't receive many visitors.

But Haan had still received a burial. So what on earth, or who on earth, was really in the casket six feet under?

Ryker took out his phone and shielded the lens from the rain as he snapped a picture of the headstone. He opened up a text and sent the picture to Moreno's email.

I know.

He stood staring at the screen for a few moments, as if expecting an instant response, even though he'd heard nothing from Moreno for several days, and all attempts to contact her had proved fruitless.

Once again he received nothing in response.

Disgruntled, Ryker stuffed the phone back in his pocket. The long silence led to a grim conclusion: she wasn't ignoring him, but unable to get in touch.

Was she already dead, just like her alter ego, Daisy Haan?

Ryker thought he now had a fairly good idea of the person responsible for kidnapping Moreno.

He turned around to head back to his car. There were two more places in the town that he wanted to visit this afternoon.

He made it back to the car, but didn't get in. Instead, he stood by the driver's door, hand on the handle, as he stared across the small parking area to the side of the church. A hooded man was casually standing there, hands in pockets, under a small canopy that protected him from the now driving rain.

One of Fischer's guys?

No. For some reason Ryker didn't think so. Though he still readied himself for action as he slowly walked toward the figure. Eyes looking around him, Ryker spotted no one else. This man was alone.

When he was a few yards from him, the man took his hands from his pockets. Empty. A good sign. He pulled back the hood to reveal a somewhat youthful face in contrast to his mussy grey-brown hair. Ryker had seen this man twice before. Once outside the South Greenwich Hospital. Once on a CCTV screen.

'I wondered how long it'd take you,' the man said. His voice was friendly yet formal. His accent gave just the tiniest hint that perhaps English wasn't his native tongue. 'She insisted that once you knew, you'd turn up here.'

Ryker's eyes narrowed. The word *she* sent two very conflicting images through his mind. Moreno, and Chester.

Ryker tensed a bit at that thought.

'She?' he said.

'Moreno. My name's Schiffler. Kyle Schiffler.'

He held out his hand for Ryker to shake. Ryker didn't take it.

'You know where Moreno is?'

Schiffler smiled. 'More than that. If you want, I can take you to her.'

46

The chapel attached to the church in the cemetery was quiet, warm and dry. As good a place as any for the conversation that Ryker wanted, and needed, with the man calling himself Schiffler.

Did he trust him? Not really. But Ryker would go along with it and find out more, even if he wasn't about to jump into a car with the guy and head off into the unknown on the promise of reconnecting with Moreno.

'Talk to me,' Ryker urged.

They were seated on adjacent wooden benches, the central walkway to the small stone altar between them, two walls of the chapel dominated by tall stained-glass depictions of various aspects of Jesus's life. Birth, the last supper, the crucifixion.

There wasn't a single other soul inside the chapel. The main door, off to Ryker's left, was still open, and he could make out his car plus a good chunk of the cemetery. No one in sight except for an old lady, carrying a bedraggled bunch of flowers through the rain.

'Moreno worked for me–'

'No. Tell me where she is. Prove to me that she's okay.'

Schiffler thought for a few moments. 'I can't do that here. I can arrange for it, but it's not as straightforward as that.'

'Why?'

'Why do you think?'

'You're protecting her?'

'She's protecting herself.'

'From who?'

'That's what I was coming to.'

A short pause as Ryker mulled that over. 'Go on then.'

'Moreno worked for me for the best part of five years.'

'MI6?' Ryker asked.

'Close enough.'

No point in asking any more questions about that. He wouldn't get a straight answer. He'd found Schiffler – nameless to Ryker at that point – in the MI6 system with the picture from the CCTV, but his profile was only accessible to top-level access. A step up even from Winter's pay grade. That said a lot.

'For the first two years we steadily built, and she gradually lived, the identity of Daisy Haan,' Schiffler explained. 'Right here, in Velbert, for some of that time.'

Which was what Ryker had suspected, and why he'd chosen to come here. Though he hadn't quite expected to be accosted by Schiffler – a man with all the answers, it seemed.

Was it all too easy?

'You've worked deep undercover, right,' said Schiffler. More of a statement than a question.

Ryker nodded. How much did Schiffler know about Ryker's past? Strangely he saw a lot of Winter in this man he'd known for all of five minutes, though he wasn't sure if that made him trust Schiffler more or less.

'You probably know what it's like in those early stages,' Schiffler continued. 'Creating a new life, living it, breathing it, putting all the pieces together before you can even think about approaching the targets.'

Ryker knew it. Did Schiffler?

'Two years. And then she was on the inside. Daisy Haan. Recruited by Bastian Fischer as part of his core personal protection team.'

Ryker grit his teeth. There it was: the link between Moreno and Fischer. 'Why? Why Fischer?'

A stifled laugh from Schiffler. 'How long have you got?' he said. 'Let's start with corruption. Corruption on a scale you wouldn't even believe.'

'Doesn't surprise me in the least,' Ryker responded.

'It should, when you hear the details. We're not talking about a few million here. If we were, MI6 and the like wouldn't be anywhere near it. We're talking about billions and billions spread across people all over the world. Fischer has influential connections everywhere. Bankers on every continent, market traders, hedge-fund managers on the financial side. Intelligence agents, judges, police, politicians on the other side. Fischer's businesses make money, but he's one of the richest people in the world for one very simple reason.'

'Basically he steals it.'

'In a roundabout way, yes. It's a whole dirty network of corruption where everyone involved gets rich off lies.'

'So if you've known this for... what? Eight, ten years? Why are we still here?'

'Seriously? Didn't you listen to what I said? Judges, intelligence agents, police, politicians. Fischer doesn't just line his own pockets, he lines everyone else's too. To put it simply, his network is more powerful than we are. More powerful than any one government. Doesn't that say it all?'

'So what happened to Moreno?'

A big sigh now. 'The Haan identity was working as well as we could have hoped. She was even promoted to head of house security, and she was steadily building a huge picture of the inner workings of Fischer's kingdom. Right up until the shit hit the fan.'

Ryker raised an eyebrow. 'They rumbled her?'

'Perhaps they'd known all along, and were playing her, to see for themselves where her connections within the UK government led. Not a bad tactic really. But the turning point was the heist.'

'What heist?'

'Four men. Highly skilled. They broke into Fischer's mansion. And, if you've seen that place yourself, you'll know that's no mean feat.'

'How?'

'Two expert hackers, two experienced and highly intelligent bank robbers. They made it inside, but only one of them made it out alive.'

'And that was bad for Haan how?'

'We never did get to the bottom of who set those four up. My suspicion was always that it was another government agency. The Germans perhaps, trying to find dirt on Fischer. Perhaps even a rival of his. Of course the break-in was never reported as a crime. Fischer and his crew, under Kathy Chester, ran amok rounding up anyone involved, and making them disappear. Permanently.'

'And the one that got away?'

'The biggest problem of them all.' Schiffler sounded resentful at that. 'Adam Wheeler.'

He said it as though the name should mean something to Ryker. It didn't.

'Ex-malicious hacker. Ex-GCHQ whizz. Ex-con. The problem was, he was also Moreno's ex. Dating back to a sting the two of them ran while he was with GCHQ and she was in hiatus after leaving the army, though I never did understand how that all came about, or how it fell apart.'

Ryker tensed up. At the mention of Wheeler being Moreno's ex? Did that actually bother him?

'The heist team never made it into Fischer's vault, where he's got god knows how many millions stashed away in gold, hard cash, jewellery, art.'

'Did they intend to?'

'I think so, given one of them was captured in the anteroom. But they did make off with the digital wallets to over two hundred million dollars' worth of cryptocurrency.'

Ryker whistled as he shook his head.

'Which only added to my suspicion that these guys had inside information, and were looking for a haul that could cause big problems for Fischer. The theory was that Fisher himself had amassed all that crypto through having a controlling hand in the global market price. Regulation in the crypto arena is essentially non-existent even today, yet it's a market worth billions. Through his own network, Fischer could manipulate the price up or down at whim, setting the whole thing off on massive bull or bear runs, always betting the right way, and making a fortune in the process. I think Wheeler and his gang somehow knew all this, or at least whoever sent them in did.'

'But Wheeler was caught?'

'Haan tracked him. A little reluctantly,' Schiffler told him. 'And her indecision with how to deal with Wheeler was ultimately the final nail in the coffin for her. Chester and Fischer had identified Wheeler, and through his past we were sure they'd figured out who Haan really was.'

'So you killed her.'

'In a sense.'

'So who's buried out there?'

Ryker glanced outside.

'Doesn't matter. The point was, we got Moreno out. And after twelve fraught months off the grid, we got her back working again.'

'And then last week she disappears.'

'Which I'm afraid is down to you.'

The scathing comment elicited a glare from Ryker.

'I don't know the full details of how, but we knew people close to Fischer were tracking you, and the risk was too big that Moreno would be rumbled,' Schiffler pointed out.

Ryker clenched his fists. Was it all his fault? 'Because we were investigating Parker and Yedlin? So Fischer was involved with those two?'

'Most likely, wouldn't you say? People connected to Fischer had you in their sights because you were too close. The risk was that you would take them right back to Moreno, and Fischer and Chester would realise they'd been duped with Haan.'

A knot tightened in Ryker's stomach at the thought that he'd inadvertently put Moreno in such danger. He thought back to those few days after the Parker kidnapping. The eyes on him all the time.

MI5, MI6. Fischer's people. Perhaps they were all one and the same.

The knot soon turned to anger. Schiffler seemed to gauge this.

'I know the type of man you are, Ryker. I know you're not interested in doing this by the book.'

'There is no book for what I do.'

'My point exactly. Moreno won't be safe until–'

'Don't you worry. I know exactly how to finish this.'

'I'm sure you do. But first I need you to do something for me.'

Ryker's eyes narrowed.

'What?'

'I need you to–'

The sound of a car engine outside. Low revs. The rumble of slow-moving tyres. No, not one car. Two.

Schiffler glanced over to the open door. When he turned back to Ryker he was taken aback by the force of Ryker's glare.

'I'm alone,' Schiffler said. 'That's the truth.'

'Yeah,' Ryker said. 'Except we're not now, are we?'

47

'You're armed,' Ryker said to Schiffler, who tapped the bulge on his side in response.

'You're not?'

'No.'

Both men got to their feet and cautiously moved for the exit, Ryker in front. He hadn't made it the whole way when he spotted the nose of one of the cars, black paint glistening as the rain pelted off its bonnet. No one in the driver's seat, but Ryker caught a brief glimpse of a figure darting out of view.

They were being surrounded.

'They weren't tracking me,' Schiffler fumed. 'It's you they've followed.'

'Back door,' Ryker said.

He turned, rushed along between the pews and took a left at the altar to where there was a narrow arched doorway. Ryker pulled the antiquated handle on the battered wooden door. The latch released. He inched the door open. No sign of anyone. He slipped out, keeping his body pressed up against the stone wall on the outside where water cascaded off the eaves in thick drops.

Schiffler was soon by his side, gun in hand. Ryker stared

across the grass. A pedestrian exit was a hundred yards away. Two men stood in wait there. Judging by their body language, they'd just spotted Ryker and Schiffler. Yet perhaps heading that way was still the best option for escape.

Slow, cautious footsteps off to Ryker's left.

He looked to Schiffler and nodded.

Then Ryker burst out around the corner. Two men there. Both armed. Ryker flung his fist into the gut of the first man. The guy's body folded over from the blow and Ryker went to wrestle the gun from his grip.

Then came a clank behind Ryker.

Metallic on the rain-sodden tarmac.

He had just enough time to cower and close his eyes before the grenade exploded.

Ryker was on the ground. Bulbous droplets of rain pelted down on him. His head was swimming. His body distant and leaden. He squeezed his eyes shut and growled as he tried to move.

He knew what had happened. Why he was still breathing. A flashbang grenade. Designed to incapacitate rather than seriously injure. This wasn't a hit squad.

Ryker heard voices. Muffled. Though was that just because of the ringing in his ears and the tumbling in his brain?

'Both of them,' he thought he heard a gruff voice say.

Hands on his shoulders now. Trying to haul him up. Probably just what Ryker needed to get back to his feet.

He tensed. Summoned an inner strength that took every bit of concentration he could muster.

When he was finally upright he planted his feet and sprang into action. At least he tried to, yet his body wasn't responding. Ryker bucked and span, trying to arc a punch at the heavyset man holding him, but instead he was caught out by a fist to the back of his head, and a stinging blow to the kidney. He found himself heading face first for the tarmac once more.

Ryker stuck his elbow out to save his face. He rolled, the after-effects from the grenade slowly diminishing with each beat of his heart, even despite those two hits.

He saw the boot heading for his head. Grabbed it. Shot to his feet and yanked upward in swift motion. The guy who'd been holding him tumbled backward and Ryker jumped down on top of him, knocking the wind from his lungs.

Actually, from the crack he heard he thought he'd probably broken a rib too. The look of searing pain on the man's face confirmed this, and the rasp in his next breath suggested the broken bone had perhaps even punctured a lung.

This man was out of the fight.

Ryker reached down the man's body, looking for a weapon. Found nothing. He jumped back to his feet. Spun around. No one in sight now.

What the hell?

Where was Schiffler?

A car engine fired up. Then another.

Ryker growled in anger. He tried to race into action, but he ended up in a quick shuffle-cum-hobble, his legs still heavy and bursting with pain. He got to the corner of the church. One car was already speeding for the gates. The other was just turning. Ryker carried on, heading right for it. Intending... what?

He never got there. The car didn't stop. No one got out to attempt to tackle him. They weren't interested.

Moments later the second car was heading out too, and with it Schiffler: Fischer's means to finally get his dirty grip on Moreno.

48

Ryker didn't know who he was more angry with: Schiffler, Fischer, or himself. Moreno even.

He was bombing along the Autobahn, heading away from the Ruhr. A new rental car now. The last one he'd left in Velbert. Why? Because after he'd watched Fischer's crew – with Schiffler as their captive – heading away from the cemetery, it had taken Ryker all of five minutes to find the tiny tracking device stuck under the front wheel arch of his last car.

Why the hell hadn't he checked before leaving the forest earlier?

He'd let them set the trap. Let them snare Schiffler. A man who knew so many secrets. A man who knew where to find Moreno.

What would it take to get Schiffler to spill all?

Best not to think about that. Ryker just hoped he could get to them in time.

Darkness had fallen by the time Ryker was back on the twisting road that led through the pine forest to Fischer's home. Even having driven at speed from the Ruhr he thought he was nearly two hours behind Fischer's men, because he'd had to do some basic preparation before coming here, the new car included.

Would those two hours prove fatal?

There was nothing he could do about that now.

Having spent a little time perusing satellite footage of the area before he'd set off from Velbert, Ryker's plan was to park in a similar position to the last time, but to then move around and approach the mansion from the opposite side. A slightly longer route, but given there was no direct road leading to the property in that direction, Ryker hoped his approach from that side would give him the element of surprise. Unless the house was already on full lockdown. What would that mean for his plan?

He hadn't quite made it back to his previous parking spot, however, when he rounded a corner and saw flashing blue lights up ahead. A police patrol car, parked to straddle the narrow road. Ryker slowed. His headlights lit up the scene. One officer, a female, was in the driver's seat of the police car. Or rather police pick-up truck, as it sat high on thick off-road tyres and had a sturdy-looking bull bar on its front end. As Ryker approached, a second officer stepped out of the passenger seat of the pick-up and came around to the front.

Ryker already had a pretty clear idea why these two were here. This road went nowhere but to Fischer's home. Whether these officers were on Fischer's payroll or had simply been told to come out here by a corrupt boss, Ryker didn't know, but their being here was a ruse, no doubt about it.

He pulled to a stop a few yards from the pick-up truck and the male officer, one hand now on the gun on his hip, walked forward.

Ryker opened his door to step out. Much better to have the room to manoeuvre than to be stuck in the cabin if events went awry.

Which they most likely would.

'*Guten Abend,*' Ryker said, before switching to English. 'Is there a problem?'

'I need to see some ID,' the officer declared, moving more cautiously now that Ryker was out in the open and almost within touching distance.

Ryker glanced over to the female officer, still behind the wheel. She was looking a little more confident than her colleague. After all, she was safely inside the car. She also had easy access to her radio.

Not good. The worst possible scenario here was for her to call backup – whether genuine police backup, or Fischer's team.

'Your ID, please?' the officer repeated, a little more nervous now.

'Sure,' Ryker said. He moved forward with purpose. 'My wallet's right here in my pocket.'

His hand went down. Except he didn't reach for his wallet at all, but instead for the sheathed hunting knife strapped to his side, one of his new purchases for tonight's action.

The officer realised this too, but by then Ryker was already lunging forward. The policeman drew his weapon. Ryker slashed across his wrist with the knife. The gun fell from his grasp.

Ryker grabbed the policeman's other arm. He twisted against the joints, kicked at the back of the man's ankles to unbalance him and then used the pressure on the arm to fold him down onto the ground. He pushed his knee into the side of the policeman's head, pinning him to the tarmac.

'Get out of the car,' Ryker shouted to the policewoman, who was reaching for the radio.

She hesitated for a second. Ryker held the knife to the man's throat and pulled his arm to bursting point, just a simple twist and push needed to dislocate both elbow and shoulder. The policewoman soon stepped out of the car.

'Hands where I can see them,' Ryker commanded.

She tentatively lifted her empty hands above her head.

'Slowly, take out your gun. Finger and thumb only. Anything stupid and I'll damn near take his head off with this knife.'

Ryker prodded forward with the knife. The razor-sharp blade nicked the policeman's skin and he squirmed and moaned as blood dribbled down.

The policewoman got it. They weren't prepared for this. She nodded and shakily moved a hand down to her side, finger and thumb like pincers as she picked out her handgun.

'Throw it this way.'

She did so, and the gun clattered a few feet from Ryker. He'd pocket both of the guns soon enough. Although he'd had time to equip himself before coming here, the only real weapon he had was the knife.

Not anymore.

'Now take out your cuffs and come over here.'

Five minutes later and the policewoman – Officer Berg – was driving Ryker the rest of the way to Fischer's house. They'd left her colleague, Hauser, in a ditch by the side of the road, both his wrists and ankles cuffed. Even shackled like that, maybe he'd try to get somewhere to raise the alarm. He wouldn't succeed before Ryker got to where he needed to be.

The cabin was silent. Now at least. To start with it hadn't been. When Berg had explained to Ryker that she and Hauser had been sent specifically to wait for a certain James Ryker to turn up. And that when he did, they were to take him into custody and deliver him not to the local police station but to Fischer's home.

She didn't seem to think this was in the least bit unusual.

Ryker still wasn't sure if she was a fully-fledged bent cop or if this was simply the way people around here operated, with Fischer as some sort of demigod way above the law.

Well, Berg was sticking to her instructions. And in doing so she was delivering Ryker right where he wanted.

They arrived at the gate to Fischer's home. No sign of an armed militia here. A good start. Were there still men in combat gear wielding assault rifles in the woods, Ryker wondered? If not, why not?

'Do anything stupid, and you know how it ends,' Ryker warned, tapping the barrel of the handgun he was holding on the central divider for effect.

Berg nodded.

She wound down her window and pressed on the intercom.

'We have James Ryker,' she said. Nothing more. Ryker knew whoever was on the other end would be able to see her face, too, and he pushed his head back, out of view.

'We'll come and meet you at the front,' was the response from a male voice Ryker didn't recognise. Not Hastings.

The gate began to slide open. Berg's window glided back up.

'Get out,' Ryker said to her.

She looked over to him quizzically.

'Get out, now,' Ryker ordered.

She seemed hesitant, as though she wasn't quite sure of the implication of the instruction. He wasn't about to shoot her in the back, if that was her worry. Ryker was giving her a chance to get away before the carnage started. She should take it.

Of course, she could run off to sound the alarm and get backup, but other than through Fischer's men she had no means of communication with the world around her apart from her voice, and she was over four miles from the nearest town.

She opened her door. Ryker was already jumping over the central divider into the driver's seat as she pulled her trailing leg out. Ryker grabbed the door handle and slammed it shut. Berg turned and looked at him with something between concern and bewilderment. Ryker released the parking brake. Slammed the accelerator to the floor.

The gate had opened just enough. Almost enough anyway, as the left-hand wing mirror snapped off as the truck passed through. Whatever. He didn't need that.

Beyond the gate, the inside of Fischer's compound was lit up by a series of bright security lights. Was that for Ryker's arrival, or had the occupants been on high alert all evening?

Up ahead, three men holding some big old weaponry, were stationed at the front entrance to the mansion. Then the doors opened. Two more armed men stepped out. Still no Hastings. No Chester. No Fischer.

Ryker pushed his foot harder to the floor, trying to eke out every bit of power and pace from the pick-up truck. It wasn't long before the waiting army realised something was wrong. Was it the sound of the churning diesel engine, or could they see Ryker, and only Ryker, behind the windscreen?

Ryker smiled. The needle on the pick-up truck swept toward fifty. He reckoned he'd make it to sixty at least.

The doors to the mansion were closing again. Like everything in this place, they were top grade security doors with cutting edge technology – PIN codes, fingerprint scanners, cameras everywhere. Ryker could have broken through the multiple layers bit by bit, with time and effort. But soon he'd put the house's security to the ultimate test. A two-and-a-half ton beast complete with galvanised bull bar travelling at over sixty miles an hour.

One hell of a battering ram.

Impact was seconds away. The men had figured out what was going on. Ryker ducked his head down to avoid the inevitable rounds of gunfire. And braced himself for the pounding head-on smash that was now unavoidable.

Ryker could see only his own legs as gunfire filled his ears.

Bullets clanked and ricocheted.

A thud. The car rocked. Another thud. Guards too slow to get out of the way?

Ryker tried to relax his body as best he could...

BLAM... belt digging in... airbag... pain...

Lights out.

49

Rough hands on his beleaguered body. Nerve synapses fired. Electrical impulses shot up through the network of fibres to his spine, onward and upward. His brain boosted, his heart thudded deep and hard with a surge of adrenaline.

Ryker's eyes sprang open.

Two men on him. Pulling him from the wreckage. Steam and smoke billowed around them in the dark, stained red from the blood dripping into Ryker's eyes. A siren swirled in his ears. From where? The house? The mangled police car?

Ryker's leg was caught in the crumpled footwell. He grimaced in pain.

'Get him out of there!' came an angry shout. Not one of the two men tugging on Ryker.

He craned his neck. Couldn't see where the voice had come from. Too much smoke. Too much blood in his eyes.

The two men yanked hard. Ryker's ankle came free but not before the skin and flesh tore across a jagged piece of something.

He was dragged out and thrown to the ground. He remained limp. Not least because although his brain was steadily recovering, he needed time to get his body in working order again.

'Get him inside with the other one.' That same angry voice. 'Then figure out what the hell we do with this mess.'

They should have just shot him. They should have done something to ensure that Ryker had no chance whatsoever of fighting back.

Now out of the car and on the ground, Ryker waited for his moment. One man went to take his legs. The other went to grab him under the arms.

He was the one. His assault rifle was dangling off a strap on his shoulder, right in front of Ryker's eyes. Perhaps they thought he was still too out of it. After all, he'd very deliberately acted that way.

Ryker summoned everything he had. He kicked out, fending off the hands trying to grab him, and reached up. He snatched for the assault rifle, wormed his finger onto the trigger. Held down.

A burst of fire. One, two, three bullets sped from the barrel, heading upward. One, two, three direct hits. Chest, neck, chin of the man above Ryker.

Blood spurted, his body crumpled.

Ryker snapped the gun from the strap as the man fell. He swung the weapon forward. Another three shots. Not all direct hits this time as the second man had already had a moment's longer reaction time. Still, the third bullet tore into the side of his neck leaving a gouge from which thick blood pulsed out as he collapsed to the ground.

At least one more to go, the man Ryker had heard – but were there more?

The problem was Ryker had only heard but not seen that man, only had a vague sense of the direction he was in. In a split second he took in the gaping hole in the front of the mansion. The glorious front facade, its extra-tall windows, the sliding security doors, were obliterated with the police pick-up truck wedged several feet inside. A mound of rubble and mess lay strewn over the previously pristine slabbed floor.

No sign of the man. Defence first. Ryker dragged himself to his feet and, crouched down, scuttled toward the back end of the pick-up truck, away from the house. A gun fired and bullets raked the ground around him. Ryker didn't look back. He threw himself forward and rolled to cover behind the police car.

No hits. And the shots had given away where the man was.

Up against the back of the pick-up truck, Ryker sniffed. Diesel. Not good.

Or was it?

He sped out from behind the car, heading further away from the entrance, toward the side of the house. He'd moved five yards when he glanced back. Sure enough, there was the man, pulling out into the open by the back end of the pick-up truck. Aiming to take out Ryker.

Ryker aimed the rifle behind him as he kept running. He opened fire. Kept his finger depressed. Four, five six... nine bullets blasted out.

Toward the end of the flurry he finally got the result he'd hoped. A spark of metal flitted to the diesel-soaked ground. Fire leaped around the edges of the truck. All of two seconds later, with Ryker diving for the ground, the fire had backtracked far enough, and built up enough pressure within the engine for the explosion.

The pressure wave lifted Ryker off his feet and tossed him forward. He smacked into the ground as a blast of superheated air cascaded over him. He hunkered down until the initial wave had receded, then quickly swivelled, back flat on the grass, so he was facing the now raging fireball.

The charred body of the gunman lay several feet away from the truck, unmoving.

By his own reckoning that was five men Ryker had felled. As he looked around there was no one else in sight now.

Time to find out who remained on the inside.

50

Ryker's body was bruised, battered and bleeding, but he did his best to ignore the pain as he edged toward the inferno. He held the assault rifle, a modified Austrian Steyr AUG, at the ready, wiping blood from his eyes every couple of steps, the liquid pouring from a wound on his forehead.

The heat from the flames was immense, and the roar of the fire drowned out everything else. For the first time, Ryker could properly take in the carnage as he approached. Bodies – and body parts – were spread across the front of the mansion from a combination of the crash, the gunfight and the explosion. But surely more than five people were here. So where was everyone else? Where was Chester? Hastings?

Schiffler?

Discomfort wormed through Ryker's gut. Was he too late?

There was a seven-foot gap leading into the mansion entrance, next to the burning pick-up truck, and Ryker shielded his face from the heat with his arm as he quickly moved through and into the destroyed entrance foyer of Fischer's home.

Rubble and debris was scattered across the usually pristine

space. Water cascaded from sprinklers in the ceiling, creating a mucky sludge on the marble floor.

Across the way a guard was propped up against the wall. Staring at Ryker.

Ryker pointed the barrel of the rifle at the man's centre mass then stepped toward him.

'Where's Schiffler?' Ryker said, his voice commanding.

The man didn't say a word. One of his bloodied hands was resting on the floor. The other clamped against his belly where his black jacket glistened with blood.

'Chester? Is she here?'

The man slowly and painfully shook his head.

Ryker reached him and crouched down. He was in a bad way. Barely breathing. His eyes big and black.

This man wasn't a threat.

'Let me see,' Ryker said.

He reached forward and pulled the man's hand away. He didn't resist. Shrapnel. A shard of metal, three inches poking out, who knew how much more buried inside the man. Given the amount of blood oozing, the metal had most likely severed a major blood vessel. The man was dying.

'Chester's not here?' Ryker said, talking calmly.

Another shake of the head. Helpful. Did this man see Ryker as his one chance of being saved?

'Schiffler?'

A nod. 'K... k... keller.'

Basement. The man's eyes flicked to the left, as if indicating the doorway that side of him. Ryker hadn't been that way before.

'How do I get in? Is there a code. A scanner?'

No answer now.

'How do I get in the basement?' Ryker demanded.

The man's eyes were still staring right at him, but his face

ROB SINCLAIR

was frozen. Then his hand flopped from the wound on his belly
to the floor with a soft thud.

He was dead.

Ryker straightened up. Looked around him. Then made his
way through the doorway. It led into a corridor. He carried on
down, moving cautiously but not too slowly. He passed several
rooms of various sizes and uses until he came to a gargantuan
kitchen. Beyond the kitchen was a pantry. A utility room. Two
closed doors here. One which Ryker guessed led outside,
judging by the array of locks on the inside.

He moved to the other one. A keypad sat on the wall next to
it. Ryker tried the handle. Unlocked. Curious. As if the house's
security system, rather than being on lockdown, had given up.
Had a combination of the carnage at the entrance, and the fire,
disabled the internal locks? Good for Ryker.

He opened the door. Then ducked when he spotted the gun
barrel poking out from around the corner at the bottom of the
concrete stairs.

A single gunshot. The bullet blasted into the wall next to
Ryker's head sending plaster dust into his face.

Ryker could have backtracked to safety. Instead he did the
opposite. He reached forward and returned fire, bounding down
the stairs at the same time.

He was three steps from the bottom when the magazine
attached to the rifle was spent. He didn't have another.

He was two steps from the bottom when the gun barrel of
the man who'd shot at him moments before emerged again.

Ryker dived forward, arms out in front of him as though
diving into a pool. He hurtled toward the concrete floor.

Thankfully he was saved from a horrific impact when the
man came into view. Ryker clattered into him and they thudded
down onto the floor. Ryker grabbed the man's head and
smashed it onto the concrete. His eyes rolled after the first

smack. His body shuddered after the third. Ryker was ready for a fourth...

No need. The man was out for the count.

Ryker disarmed him, and looked across the space he'd landed in. Brightly lit but bland and sparse. Industrial in its look and feel, with plain walls and plain concrete floor. Three doors off here. Two were closed. One was open. Not fully. But just enough for Ryker to make out a little of the room that lay beyond.

'Shit.'

He jumped to his feet and raced forward. Pushed open the door to the room.

Schiffler was there. Laid out on a metal gurney. The type used in a morgue for carrying out post-mortems, bevelled for blood to flow away from the corpse as it was cut apart.

Except this was no corpse.

Bloodied tools lay on a bench by the side. Schiffler was naked and unmoving, except for the faintest rise and fall in his chest, making a sad and desperate whistle as he tried to breath. Tried to stay alive.

'Schiffler.'

Ryker moved up to him, trying to hold back nausea at what he saw. What he could *feel*. He'd been tortured before. He'd seen others tortured horrifically. He wasn't sure he'd ever seen anything quite so brutal as this.

And it had all taken place in what? One, two hours?

To Schiffler it must have felt like a lifetime.

Whole sections of Schiffler's skin had been cut or peeled away leaving clean-looking squares and rectangles of gaping deep-red flesh. Horrific burns covered other parts of him. Fingers were missing. Toes. An ear.

A tear formed in Ryker's eye. His body was shaking.

'Schiffler?'

He looked down at the sorrowful pile of mangled flesh.

Schiffler's panicked eyes were open. He was staring straight above him at the ceiling. A drip hung over his head. Feeding who knew what directly into his veins. Most likely a heavy drug concoction designed to keep him lucid and alive through his ordeal.

'I'm... sorry,' he uttered, the words barely audible.

He didn't need to say anything more. Ryker got it. Chester wasn't here. Fischer wasn't here. Nothing more than a skeleton crew now. There was one very obvious reason why that was the case.

They already knew where Moreno was.

'Just tell me where she is,' Ryker said. 'You have to tell me everything.'

51

Of all the places in the world that Moreno could have gone in her time of need, it felt to Ryker like fate – luck? – that her likely very deliberate planning had seen her end up on the same continent. Not so close as to be in the Black Forest, or Germany even, but the city of Trieste in northeastern Italy was only an eight-hour drive from where Ryker had started. A long, gruelling drive. A spectacular drive, Ryker was sure, if it had been daylight, with the roads he took traversing forests and mountains and valleys and plains.

Sunrise was still nearly an hour away when Ryker arrived outside the city. He'd been here twice before, long before he'd met Moreno. He was unsure what link she had to this place that had made her choose it as a refuge.

Or was that the point? There was no link.

Nestled at the far edge of Italy, on a narrow strip of land between the glistening Adriatic Sea and Slovenia, Trieste was a city with a rich multicultural past, but it also had a history of bloody warfare and violence from the constant push and pull of surrounding civilisations. In that sense, Ryker felt an affinity with the city, and given Moreno's own troubled past, he could understand why she, too, would feel at ease here.

Not that Ryker would be seeing the best that the city had to offer tonight. He was only edging along the outskirts. The city's waterways and seaport and promenades all lay a couple of miles further to the east. The roads at the periphery of the city remained quiet, as they had been for the entire journey here. Ryker had needed to stop only once in the Range Rover he'd stolen from Fischer's home, in order to refuel for the 500-mile journey, and he was now nearing empty again.

Unless he hit a problem, he'd make it. Just.

The intervening eight hours since he'd left Schiffler to die in that putrid basement had been long and fraught. Ryker had tried to call Winter, hoping his old ally could provide some sort of assistance, but all his attempts had failed. And Ryker really had no one else he could call upon, especially at such short notice.

Finally, the chequered flag came into view on the map on the Range Rover's high-definition screen. He was only a mile away. That mile seemed to take as long as the entire rest of the drive as Ryker snaked slowly left and right through the mainly residential streets.

He took a left turn. The final turn. His destination was a plain-looking apartment block 200 yards in front of him. A hodgepodge of three- to six-storey buildings lay to his right. A dark and seemingly empty space off to his left. A small park or green square, judging by what he could see on the map, though there was no sense of its layout in the darkness of the night.

What Ryker could see, however, about halfway between him and his destination, was a row of three parked cars. Big, dark, expensive. At least compared to the other vehicles parked on the street, which were mainly banged-up smaller cars.

Ryker pulled over, convinced the cars in front were part of

the posse sent to retrieve – kill? – Moreno. But was there anyone still inside? He was sure Chester wouldn't be part of the initial assault team. Was Fischer also here?

Ryker switched off the engine, and without his headlights on the poorly lit street was plunged into near darkness. He remained in position for a few seconds, barely moving, his eyes flitting between the three cars and the third and top floor of the building further ahead. No sign of anyone outside at all. No sign that his arrival had alerted anyone in the cars either.

Ryker looked over to the seat next to him, to the two hand-guns he'd brought with him. Plus the assault rifle for which he'd obtained four additional magazines from the various downed guards at Fischer's home.

He grabbed a handgun and stuffed it in the waistband of his jeans. Filled his pockets with the magazines then picked up the rifle and opened his car door.

He only had one foot out when the huge explosion erupted.

52

Ryker threw himself down behind his open car door. In the space of a couple of seconds a thousand thoughts went through his mind. The first was that he had been the target of the explosion. A hand grenade? An RPG? He quickly figured that wasn't the case when he realised he was still alive and in one piece, and so was the car he was standing next to. So, too, were the three cars further ahead.

Beyond them, however, the apartment building where Moreno had been hiding out was now a monstrous fireball with huge yellow-and-orange flames leaping and spiralling out of what used to be its top floor. Smoke billowed all around.

Ryker stared aghast. He heard screams, shouts. Then a flaming body cascaded out of the mess and tumbled to the ground with a thud. Ryker's heart pounded his chest.

He looked over to the three cars. A door opened. Then another. Then another. Two men stepped out. Both armed. Then a woman. Chester.

Ryker's eyes narrowed. He clenched the rifle a little more tightly.

All three of them were staring ahead at the burning building. Then one of the men turned around. Shouted out to Chester, a look of confusion on his face. Ryker was too far away to hear what he said, or what the response was, but they didn't look happy.

He got it. Moreno. Not a damsel in distress. Far from it. Yes, she'd left London in fear of her life. She'd travelled here to hide. But she'd also planned for the worst. Had planned for this very event.

Moreno was not the type to go quietly into the night.

Ryker jumped when there was a flurry of rat-a-tat gunfire from his right. He hunkered down and pointed the gun in the direction of the sound, almost immediately adjacent to him.

Out of the shadows came a darkened figure. Ryker was about to open fire...

'James.'

She let off another round and Ryker heard a groan in the distance.

'Sam.' Ryker wasn't sure whether to smile or not. In an instant it was like they were back in Africa. A deadly duo. Even if events there hadn't panned out well for her.

Would they this time?

She darted as quickly as she could on her prosthetic from behind a van and over to Ryker's Range Rover, two bullets smacking into the tarmac just inches from her toes. She slid down, pressed herself up against the metal, her face a painful grimace and her breathing laboured. She wasn't hurt as far as Ryker could see, just unused to this kind of physical exertion.

'They're right over there,' Moreno said. 'Fischer and that bitch. In the same fucking car.'

Ryker wasn't sure he liked the bloodthirsty look in her eyes.

'I'm going to finish this,' she said. 'You with me?'

'Wh... Sam?'

'Are you with me or not?'

Both of them squirmed when another round of gunfire blasted into the front of the Range Rover, though they were both too far in cover for the shots to trouble them. For now.

'They're trying to surround us,' Ryker said.

'Only two shooters left,' Moreno replied. 'But I'm not waiting around here for the police or the cavalry to arrive. Cover me?'

Ryker nodded.

Moreno jumped to her feet and darted from around the car. Ryker bobbed up over the car door. Spotted one of the men out in the open, attempting to circle around to the rear of the Range Rover. Moreno had seen him too. She squeezed the trigger of her rifle – an ageing AK47 – as she ran. Perfect shot. The man went down.

Then the last man standing peeked from behind a parked car the other side.

'Sam!' Ryker shouted.

She ducked, changed her course. Enough distraction as Ryker darted right to get a better view and then pulled hard on the trigger of the Steyr. A flurry of bullets. Another direct hit.

Moreno was almost at the cars. Chester – what was she doing? – jumped back out of the middle car, unarmed, as if she could talk Moreno down now. Moreno didn't give her the chance to say a single word. She swiped the rifle against Chester's face, then grabbed her and threw her into the back of the car.

Moreno looked back to Ryker. A questioning look on her face.

At least that was what Ryker thought he saw.

No. Not a questioning look. One of concern. And she wasn't looking at Ryker, but beyond him. To the cascade of police cars that were now racing along the road.

Moreno mouthed something to Ryker. Then jumped into the driver's seat of the car. The rear lights flicked on and the car jerked out into the road.

'No!'

Ryker darted back into the Range Rover. Fired up the engine. Before he'd even swung out into the road, the fuel indicator warning blinked angrily. Five miles to empty.

He growled in frustration. The car Moreno was in, a gleaming BMW M5, was already nearly out of sight. Ryker floored it. The Range Rover lunged forward. He took the hard left to follow, and the tall SUV rocked on its heightened suspension, the damn thing near toppling over. Ryker shook his head in frustration. On twisting urban streets he had no chance of keeping up with Moreno in the far superior M5.

But did he need to keep up with her, or just lose the police?

It took him less than two minutes before he realised there was no police to lose. Had they stayed at the site of the carnage and not realised that Moreno and Ryker had scarpered?

The problem for Ryker, though, was that Moreno had pulled even further ahead, and when the fuel indicator on the Range Rover hit zero, she was nowhere to be seen.

'Come on!'

Ryker banged on the steering wheel in frustration. He turned into a narrow alley. Kept his eyes on the rear-view for several seconds. No. Definitely no police on his tail.

But where the hell was Moreno?

He looked at the map on the Range Rover screen. He was only one street away from the seafront now, right alongside the city's sprawling seaport. An area filled with all manner of warehouses and storage yards.

That had to be why Moreno had come here. She'd planned this. Planned to steal Chester and Fischer – her nemeses – away from the clutches of the police, away from their own crew, away from everyone.

Ryker put the Range Rover into reverse, then carried on. Low revs, low speed now. Because he was desperately looking all around for any sign of the BMW, but also because the engine was running on fumes.

Ryker turned right and was soon on a long straight road that trailed into the distance. Warehouses loomed high on both sides, but to his right the scene was also dominated by hulking industrial cranes and storage yards with sea containers stacked high. In the night the road was quiet of traffic, but areas of the seaport, where some of the businesses worked around the clock, were bathed in bright white light.

For the first half a mile, all of the premises Ryker passed looked to be in use, even if they were locked up for the night, but after that the buildings and the grounds became more and more unkempt.

This had to be the spot. Somewhere near here.

Ryker glanced at the satnav screen. It wouldn't be long before the seaport ended altogether and he was on a barren road heading out of the city and out of the country.

So perhaps Ryker's instinct was wrong. Moreno had already scarpered. If she had, Ryker really had no way of tracking her, particularly with his transport about to give up on him at any moment.

Then Ryker spotted it. A warehouse off to his right. No sign of the BMW, but the security fence for the abandoned unit was hanging open, and although the forecourt beyond appeared empty, there was the faintest orange glow emanating from a slit up in the corrugated steel roof of the windowless building.

Ryker pulled into the forecourt. Headed slowly around the side, toward the water, so his vehicle would be out of sight from the road.

No sign of the M5. He parked the car and got out, grabbing the Steyr as he did. A chilling wind blasted off the Adriatic and Ryker shivered as he looked across at the warehouse. Even with morning approaching the night was as silent as it was bleak.

Then a noise cut through. A shout. Of pain, or fear?

Not from the warehouse after all, but from beyond the security fence at the other side of the grounds.

Ryker held the rifle at the ready and moved for the fence. He found another break in the clumsily erected criss-cross metal. Beyond was a railway track, and a mishmash of decrepit industrial railway engines and carriages.

And there was the BMW.

Not far away were three figures. Two of them on their knees, facing away from him. The third was Moreno. On her feet, standing over her captives, gun in hand.

'Sam!'

She jumped at his voice and looked around. Agitation clear on her face even in the thinnest of pre-dawn light.

'You can't stop me,' she shouted. 'Please don't try.'

Did he want to? He really couldn't be sure. Whatever wrongs Chester and Fischer were responsible for, and Ryker was positive there were many, was it sufficient and acceptable to simply execute them?

No. That was the clear answer in Ryker's mind. Not because they didn't deserve to be punished, but because there was far too much he still didn't know about Fischer's corrupt life. Secrets that Ryker wanted exposed. Accomplices that Ryker wanted exposed.

Would the truth be buried with Fischer?

And yet if he'd been in Moreno's shoes...

'Sam, please.'

Ryker went to take a step forward, onto the railway line. Then jumped back when out of the dark a bulbous shadow loomed. Ryker stumbled and fell back as the clattering diesel engine of the train rattled past.

He bounced back to his feet. Looked to his right. He was perched, ready to dash forward across the line, but the train's multitude of carriages kept coming and coming as it came to a stop at the edge of the seaport further ahead.

'Sam!'

Ryker balled his fists as frustration gripped him. He stooped down and glimpsed flashes of Moreno through the gaps between the passing carriages; it felt like he was watching the action unfold in strobe lighting.

'No!'

He couldn't hear the shots. But he could see the flashes of light.

Chester crumpled.

Then Fischer.

Then Moreno hunched over and heaved Chester's limp body which toppled over the edge of the dock, out of sight.

Next was Fischer.

The last carriage had already swept past as Moreno completed the task.

'Sam!' Ryker shouted again as he raced forward.

Moreno turned to him. A look of anguish on her face. Ryker knew from experience there was never any satisfaction in taking the life of another, however much it was deserved.

Ryker darted to the edge. Looked down. He could see nothing of Fischer or Chester, just ripples on the black water.

He looked at Moreno. She was staring at him, the anguish on her face growing with each second that passed.

'It's done,' she said. 'They're both exactly where they belong.'

Her voice quavered. Her body was shaking.

Ryker said nothing. Moreno moved toward him. She was only inches away. Ryker still held on to his rifle. He stared deeply into her eyes, trying to read her thoughts.

Then he let go of the rifle, opened his arms and pulled her close.

53

For two weeks, Ryker had watched the scandal unfolding on the TV, had read about the fallout online and in the newspapers. Winter couldn't have been more right. The intelligence services landscape was changing forever. For the better? Ryker didn't know. Nor was he sure where the media's attention was likely to stay focused – on the UK's intelligence community, or on the widespread wrongdoing and corruption of Bastian Fischer that was only now coming to light following his death.

Perhaps the problem was that those two areas of focus were inextricably linked, as a result of the reach of Fischer's prickly tentacles.

Ryker still feared that the full truth, the full list of corrupt conspirators working with Fischer, would never be known. He could at least hold out hope.

Two weeks. It had felt far longer to Ryker, even if he had spent the majority of that time on the move. Today he was walking through Burneside in the UK's Lake District, a village nestled in a valley among the jagged and spectacular Cumbrian hills. Ryker wasn't staying in Burneside, but it was a good enough and quiet enough place to meet. Since leaving Trieste,

Ryker had only been back to London once – to collect his belongings – and he wasn't planning on going back again. Not if he could avoid it.

He arrived at the small café with an outer terrace above the trickling River Kent. The sky was blue, the sun was shining. Walkers in their muddy boots and colourful jackets roamed free.

Peter Winter in his smart loafers and dark jeans and designer jacket looked seriously out of place. He was sitting at one of the café's tables, two take-out cups in front of him.

He spotted Ryker approaching, got to his feet and grabbed the coffees. He looked pissed off. Ryker was vaguely amused by that as he was sure the bad mood was due to Ryker's choice of location.

'Seriously?' Winter sounded disgusted. He handed Ryker one of the cups.

'Seriously what?'

'Don't tell me you've taken up hiking or something. What on earth are you doing all the way up here?'

'Living,' Ryker said.

Winter looked around him as though none of it made sense. Could a man who ran agents working in all manner of places across the globe – from the exotic to the downright awful – really be unnerved by such a quiet and quaint place? Perhaps it was the smell of manure drifting across from the nearby fields which he couldn't hack.

'Why don't we take a walk,' Winter suggested.

Ryker nodded and the two of them set off along the far from bustling streets.

'So this is a stop-off?' Winter asked.

'Just passing through,' Ryker said.

Winter raised an eyebrow.

'On your way where?'

Ryker shrugged. Winter waited, as though expecting something more.

'I'm guessing you've been keeping up to date with the shitshow?'

'Hard to miss it. Even out here.'

'What you might not have heard is that Chester's body finally turned up. At least we believe it's her. Off the coast of Croatia. It's under wraps until we–'

'Under wraps? Come on, I thought the whole issue here was too many secrets. Isn't that what started this mess?'

Winter sighed. 'We held the last ever committee meeting last night.'

'No more JIA.'

'No more JIA. And even if MI5 and MI6 survive this, nothing will ever be the same.'

'You'll want a new job then,' Ryker said. 'I hear the pub down the road is looking for a barman.'

'Ha-bloody-ha. Actually, I'll be fine.'

Ryker glanced over but the stern look on Winter's face told him he wasn't going to get any more information on that. Ryker was a little surprised. The very public furore into the Parker/Yedlin investigation had only been exacerbated by the deaths of Kathy Chester and Bastian Fischer at the hands of an active MI6 agent. Moreno hadn't been named in the press, but the fact the press were carrying the story showed that the problem of inside information leaking out was still real and present even after Fischer's death, and only created more barriers to MI5 and MI6 operating effectively in the future.

The revelations had led to heads rolling all over – MI5, MI6, GCHQ, Westminster. The JIA had essentially imploded. Then came the allegations of corruption. Moles. Fischer's dirty hands all over the UK government's most secret of corners. Ryker hoped that there was more still to come. That just because

Fischer was now dead, it wouldn't mean everyone else would get away with it.

Perhaps that was what Winter was referring to. Had he been asked to lead the ongoing investigation into Fischer?

Whatever the case, the fact the JIA had been dismantled and MI6 and MI5 would never be able to operate so brazenly as before, didn't mean all the spies, all of the handlers, would just disappear and start new lives. Perhaps Ryker was overly cynical, but he was sure that once the dust had settled, a new form of the JIA would take over. Smarter and bolder than before, to ensure they didn't make the same mistakes. Intelligence gathering would always be there; it had been since the beginning of civilisation.

'How's Kaspovich in all this?'

Winter looked a little surprised. 'How do you mean?'

'I think you know.'

Ryker had never gotten along with Kaspovich. Had frequently considered whether he was one of the moles within MI5. Not that he'd ever openly said that.

'As far as I know he's still in position. I've had no contact with him.'

Ryker said nothing to that.

'How's Moreno?' Winter asked.

'I haven't spoken to her.'

The truth.

'You haven't spoken to her?'

'Not since Trieste.'

Winter looked confused.

'Do you know where she is?' he asked.

'No idea.'

A lie. Ryker did know where she was – or at least where she'd last been. And he had a means to contact her. But he hadn't done so. He wouldn't, however sad the prospect of not seeing her again made him. Whatever bond there was between the two of them, as much as it pained him to not see her, they both needed to start new lives now. Not because they didn't need each other, in so many different ways, but because them being together would only ever put them in danger. After all, it was Ryker's actions which had inadvertently brought Moreno's painful past to the fore. If they were together, it was only a matter of time before she reciprocated in kind.

So why the lie to Winter?

To protect Moreno and Ryker – and Winter himself. After all, look at what had happened to Schiffler because he'd known where Moreno was.

Ryker shivered at the thought.

He finished his coffee and put it into a bin by the side of the pavement. He stopped walking.

'So this is it?' Winter said, coming to a stop, too.

'This time, I really think it is.'

Both men went silent. Ryker felt there was still so much that could be said.

'Whatever happens from here,' Winter said. 'Know that you did make a difference. A positive difference. To so many lives.'

Ryker said nothing.

'And if you ever–'

'Thanks for coming.' Ryker reached out and put his hand on Winter's shoulder. 'Thanks for everything.'

Then he turned and walked away.

An hour later, Ryker was packing his things into his rucksack. He'd been in this hotel for four nights already, and was due a change. He'd thought he would have felt better having met with Winter. Had hoped the conversation – the final conversation –

would lay demons to rest, would be cathartic. So why did he feel much worse now? More pensive and glum? Mournful even.

It didn't matter. He'd made his decision. Both in relation to Winter, and Moreno. This was a step he had to make. For their safety. For his own sake and sanity.

He left the room, headed down the stairs, handed in his key to the receptionist, then stepped onto the pavement outside. He looked left and right, paranoia still ever present. But there was no one here watching him.

Was there anyone out there who even cared?

Ryker didn't know. Which was why he'd always have to live like this, forever on the lookout.

He slipped the rucksack over his shoulders, then turned and headed off toward the sunset. No final destination in mind, there was only one thing clear to him: wherever he was going, he was going alone.

THE END

ABOUT THE AUTHOR

Rob specialised in forensic fraud investigations at a global accounting firm for thirteen years. He began writing in 2009 following a promise to his wife, an avid reader, that he could pen an 'unputdownable' thriller. Since then, Rob has sold over a million copies of his critically acclaimed and bestselling thrillers in the Enemy, James Ryker and Sleeper series. His work has received widespread critical acclaim, with many reviewers and readers likening Rob's work to authors at the very top of the genre, including Lee Child and Vince Flynn.

Originally from the North East of England, Rob has lived and worked in a number of fast-paced cities, including New York, and is now settled in the West Midlands with his wife and young sons.

Rob's website is www.robsinclairauthor.com and he can be followed on twitter at @rsinclairauthor and facebook at www.facebook.com/robsinclairauthor

A NOTE FROM THE PUBLISHER

Thank you for reading this book. If you enjoyed it please do consider leaving a review on Amazon to help others find it too.

We hate typos. All of our books have been rigorously edited and proofread, but sometimes mistakes do slip through. If you have spotted a typo, please do let us know and we can get it amended.

info@bloodhoundbooks.com

Printed in Great Britain
by Amazon